When Boomers GO Bad

The Ladies' Killing Circle

When Boomers GO Bad

A Crime and Mystery Collection by the Ladies' Killing Circle

edited by
Joan Boswell
Sue Pike
and Linda Wiken

RENDEZVOUS PRESS

Cover art: Christopher Chuckry

Le Conseil des Arts | The Canada Council
du Canada | for the arts
depuis 1957 | since 1957

We acknowledge the support of the
Canada Council for the Arts
for our publishing program.

RendezVous Press
Toronto, Ontario, Canada
www.rendezvouspress.com

Printed in Canada.

09 08 07 06 05   5 4 3 2 1

Library and Archives Canada Cataloguing in Publication

        When boomers go bad / by the Ladies' Killing Circle ; edited by Joan
Boswell, Sue Pike and Linda Wiken.

ISBN 1-894917-31-6

1. Detective and mystery stories, Canadian (English) 2. Canadian
fiction (English)—Women authors. 3. Canadian fiction (English)—21st
century. 4. Baby boom generation—Fiction. I. Boswell, Joan II. Pike, Sue,
1939- III. Wiken, Linda IV. Ladies' Killing Circle

PS8323.D4W48 2005   C813'.0872089287
C2005-903467-X

Table of Contents

Where Were You Then?

I know where I was
When Buddy Holly died.
I was swinging on my swing.
And when I heard
That JFK was shot,
I was in the high school gym.
When Martin Luther King
Dreamed his last dream,
I was yelling at my spouse,
And when the King
Lost his crown
I was knocking off the louse.
But when the cops
Questioned me
Where the hell was I?
My short-term memory loss
Kicked in…

I forgot my alibi!

Despite her penchant for murderous poems, **Joy Hewitt Mann***'s primary writing is in the literary field. A short story collection,* Clinging to Water, *was published by Boheme Press, Toronto, in 2000, and she recently finished another collection, a full-length book of poetry, and a novel, all seeking publication. With the help of a Canada Council grant, she has just finished the first draft of the first book in a trilogy.*

Spoils of War

Barbara Fradkin

Mila's dog started acting peculiar long before she caught the first whiff of rot. They had been walking for an hour down the old logging road behind her cottage. Around them, the June afternoon hung soggy and hot, redolent with the scent of pine loam, and nothing stirred but the deer flies buzzing around their heads.

Pavlov began to zigzag along the road, swinging his shaggy head in restless, searching arcs. Suddenly he picked up speed, and just as Mila dived for his collar, he vaulted over the ditch and bolted into the trees. It was then, watching him disappear, that she finally caught the smell. The unmistakable, rancid stench of dead flesh.

"Goddamn stupid dog!" Cursing at the prospect of his swaggering back in half an hour reeking of dead animal, she took up pursuit. Shoving aside branches and swatting mosquitoes, she fought her way deeper into the forest. Suddenly the brush opened up into a small clearing protected in the lee of a rocky outcrop, overgrown with daisies and interwoven with a network of paths. The stink hung like a pall in the radiant heat.

Mila stopped, her gaze settling in surprise on an ancient picnic table in the middle of the clearing. Nearby sat the rusty shell of an automobile. Curiosity drew her closer. For years, the local farmers had been warning her about a squatter on her land, but she'd never run across him, and with hundreds more acres than she could possibly use, she'd never begrudged him a few.

Pulling the weeds away from the car, she was able to make out the round roof of a Volkswagen beetle with patches of yellow and purple paint still defying the rust. Shock bolted through her, for she'd once owned a beetle painted purple with a yellow sunflower on its roof. After university, she'd driven it across the country with Dean the draft dodger during a year-long odyssey of self-discovery. When she finally left him, she'd given him the car as a consolation prize, for he had no home to return to and little energy left after years of LSD and Moroccan gold. That she had ended up in suburbia with a dermatologist instead, raising two children and working for the government, still gave her a twinge of shame from time to time.

Her shock gave way to reason. She'd left Dean over thirty-five years ago, three thousand miles away. Although he'd made noises about coming for her, he'd never shown up. It was ridiculous to think this was the same car. She peered through the broken windshield, but the fabric seats had long rotted away, leaving only blackened springs.

Wrinkling her nose against the smell, Mila squatted in front of the fender, pawed aside the weeds, and uncovered a licence plate lacy with rust. Oklahoma 1971. She sat back with relief. The car she'd left Dean had an Ontario licence plate.

Puzzled, she looked around the clearing for other clues. Along one side stretched three orderly rows of vegetable garden, and near the picnic table was a blackened iron grate propped over a circle of stones. The fire pit was cold but free of weeds, which meant someone had been here until recently.

In the distance she heard a single bark, more a question mark than a threat. She called out, but there was no sign of Pavlov. The idiot dog would only return when he'd had his fill of adventure, so she continued exploring. Tucked into the bush, an old river dock had been sawed into four pieces propped on their sides to form walls and topped by branches and moss. Probably little defence against a Northern Ontario winter, but a paradise if you were down and out.

She tugged at the slab of plywood that served as a door, and it broke off its hinges. Dank, mouldy air rushed out. As her eyes adjusted to the gloom, she made out a sleeping bag neatly stretched out on a pad of straw and two wooden planks propped on cinder blocks, which served as shelves for dishes, clothing, and dozens of books. The earthen floor was swept and the clothes folded. This hermit had obviously settled in for the long haul.

Bending to clear the low ceiling, she crossed the room to study the books. She'd always thought you could tell a lot about a person from their books. In keeping with his armchair rebel's identity, Dean had devoured conspiracy thrillers and protest literature, all of which solidified his choice not to follow Uncle Sam into an immoral war.

The hermit's paperbacks reflected a soul far more preoccupied with the brutal side of life. *In Cold Blood, Helter Skelter, Confessions of Son of Sam, Hunting Humans...* All tales of lives gone horribly wrong and violence unleashed.

Disquiet piqued her. What kind of man was this beneath his Spartan precision? What would he do if he found her in here? She scrambled back outside, her gaze raking the surroundings. The tall weeds in one corner caught her eye, and she stared in disbelief, followed by anger. Christ, the guy's been using my land for his goddamn grow-op. Some nerve!

In disgust, she turned to leave, when in the distance Pavlov gave a sharp bark, as if he were calling for her. A moment later, he came bounding back through the trees, but her relief was short-lived when she saw he had something in his jaws. Something bleached and rotting. He dropped it at her feet and backed up, his bright eyes fixed on her expectantly. When she looked down, her stomach lurched. A long bone, picked white in places. Flies covered the bits of flesh still clinging to the ends. A deer, she thought, but dead at least a week and no doubt the source of the stink.

"Thanks a lot, Pav," she muttered, sidestepping the gruesome gift and reaching to snap on the dog's leash. But Pavlov danced away, barking as he tried to lure her towards the woods.

"Come here, you idiot," she snapped. "No more smelly bodies."

The dog circled the bone, more agitated than she'd ever seen him. Reluctantly, she bent down to peer at the bone.

"What is it, Pav? What did you find?"

The bone was about eighteen inches long. One end bore the unmistakable marks of teeth, as if it had been gnawed from the carcass. The other end had two smaller bones, not a hoof as she'd expected, but something more delicate. Something almost...

She felt a rush of horror. Glanced around the campsite, which showed signs of recent neglect. Was it possible the hermit was dead? She backed away, trying to gather her sickened thoughts. Should she call the police? Raise the alarm over a single bone and, if she was wrong, expose this harmless recluse to the heavy hand of the law?

Swallowing her revulsion, she turned to Pavlov and gestured towards the woods. "Okay, go find. Show me where this came from."

The border collie set off at a trot down a well-worn footpath leading deeper into the woods. She struggled to keep pace. As the stench grew stronger, her resolve faltered and she cursed her idiocy for not calling the police.

Squinting through the sweat in her eyes, she barely noticed Pavlov until she nearly fell over him. He was standing over a large, amorphous mass at the base of the tree. Flies and maggots covered nearly every inch of visible surface, but even so, one glance was enough.

*   *   *

"Be awhile before the coroner and the crime scene boys get out here, ma'am," said Constable Leblanc of the Ontario Provincial Police. "My partner will drive you back home, so you can get cleaned up."

Mila nodded gratefully. She'd been trying to answer his questions intelligently, but suspected she looked as sickly green as she felt. She'd been forced to lead the police back to the grisly scene, and she was covered in dirt, insect bites and the stench of death.

"Any idea who he is?" she asked.

"Never seen his camp before, but I heard it was back in here someplace."

"Who?"

"Dan. That's the only name he ever gave when he came to town. Which wasn't often, mind you. Kept to himself, obviously had some kind of survival training. Dead-eyed Dan, people called him."

Dan, Dean... She felt a twinge of worry. "How long has he been around?"

"Since I can remember. I was raised in Iroquois Falls, and

the rumours about Dead-eyed Dan eating kids were around when I was knee-high."

Which wasn't all that long ago, Mila thought. He'd tilted his peeked cap low over his brow to add menace, but the baby blue of his eyes ruined the effect.

"Eating kids?" she echoed dubiously.

He chuckled. "Dan was harmless. Had this thing about non-violence, wouldn't kill so much as a mouse if he was starving to death. But he had this mass of shaggy hair and these coal black eyes that sent a chill right through you."

Mila thought about Dean's dark eyes and shaggy hair, about his abhorrence of killing. Then about the violent books in the dead man's library. Something didn't fit. "Where did he come from?"

"Never knew. He just shows up in Iroquois Falls two or three times a year to buy supplies."

"What happens now?"

"Depends on what the autopsy shows. Most likely it was misadventure, maybe a bear. Big problem will be locating next of kin. I don't imagine anybody will be missing him after all these years."

"There's a car back in the bush with an American licence plate."

The constable shrugged. "Yeah, but that could have come from anywhere. I'd say he's been squatting on your land for over thirty years. Just your luck, I guess."

A fresh queasiness washed over her as she thought of the shaggy-haired, down-and-out recluse with the purple VW. Luck, or something else?

*   *   *

One of the perks of working for the Immigration Department was that Mila had connections all over, and even from her cottage, she knew how to ferret out obscure information about foreign nationals in the country. A quick call to a friend in Security netted her a contact in Oklahoma State who could help her track down the licence plate.

Roy had a deep gravel voice, as if he'd smoked three packs a day for a hundred years. "Nineteen seventy-one?" he wheezed, sounding both dubious and intrigued. "Tricky. When do you want this for?"

Yesterday, she thought. "No hurry. When you can get to it."

She supplied no explanation for the request, and he didn't ask for any. Both were good public servants who knew the value of hiding behind ignorance. Roy took her phone number and promised to get back to her. To quell her impatience, she fed the name Dean Fellows into a variety of databases. Dean had known about their family cottage up north, for they had spent one glorious, back-to-the-earth summer there in 1970, before Nixon began napalming the hell out of villages and before body bags began arriving back in the U.S. by the planeload. Dean had felt safe at the cottage, far from the scrutiny of the law.

Once they'd re-entered civilization, he retreated behind a wall of fear, picking fights in bars and impugning the motives of innocent passersby. And increasingly as they drove west, he coped through a haze of drugs. She suspected that, for all his lofty ideals about non-violence, he was struggling with a deep shame about abandoning the country he loved. And about his childhood friends who had gone off to war, some not to return. It was a gut-level guilt, below the reach of reason, but it wore down the edges of his soul. He saw it reflected in the eyes of strangers and even in the cheery embrace of this wide-open land. It drove him in on himself until she could stand it no more.

He'd been such a hopeful young playwright when she'd met him at McGill. He had spectacular, long-lashed dark eyes and lithe, sensual hands that still set her body on fire when she thought of him. When no one wanted his plays, when critics scoffed at their adolescent tone, she watched the hope slowly fade from his eyes and the doubts crowd in. Had the past thirty-five years destroyed him entirely?

The first database she searched was Immigration, which had no record of a Dean Fellows applying for status of any kind. Next she tried the provincial departments of transportation and finally a simple Google search. Nothing. As if he'd fallen into a black hole.

Discouraged, she logged off and headed outside, just as a white Malibu pulled into the cottage drive. A burly man with grizzled hair and florid cheeks emerged, waving a police badge. "Mrs. Hendricks? Detective Watts of the Ontario Provincial Police. I have a few questions."

A detective. Had something suspicious come out of the autopsy? She gestured him inside briskly. "Have you identified the man yet?"

She held her breath, but instead of answering, the detective poised his pen over his notebook. "Who else besides you comes up to this property?"

"All of us occasionally. My three children, my two brothers and their families. But so far this season only me."

"Mr. Hendricks?"

She tensed. "Divorced. Long ago."

He raised his eyes from his notebook to study her. Purple bags under his eyes made him look like a prize fighter with too many bouts under his belt. "When was the last time you visited that section of your property?"

"Years, actually. I don't usually go back there because it's too buggy."

He kept his voice deadpan. "And why did you do so this time?"

You should know damn well why, she thought, because Constable Leblanc took a detailed statement. But she suppressed her impatience and repeated her runaway dog story. Watts didn't take a note.

"Does anyone besides your family use that road? As a right of way, perhaps?"

"No."

"Have you seen anyone in the vicinity in the past month or so? Anyone come to call, anything happen out of the ordinary?"

She'd been shaking her head in answer to all his questions, but by the end, her thoughts were on full alert. She tried again, more sharply. "Have you identified him?"

"The investigation is ongoing," he replied, which she took to mean no. "Had you seen the man before?"

"I have no idea. I couldn't tell from the..." Her voice faltered at the memory of the faceless flesh.

His sharp, pig-like eyes met hers. "Then do you have any idea how your name came to be inscribed inside one of his books?"

She gaped. "What book?"

He didn't reply, merely waited. She groped through her surprise for a benign explanation. "I have no idea. Maybe he bought it at a local used book store. MacIsaacs donate books all the time."

"Not MacIsaac, just Mila. With an affectionate inscription."

Her thoughts began a free fall. God, could it be true? How? Why! Why would he hide out under her nose for thirty-five years without so much as a hello? "How...how old was the book?"

His lips parted slightly in a smile. "Curious you should ask that. The inscription was 1971."

Anger flared inside her, one strong emotion sparking another. "Look, you obviously think there is something suspicious about his death. I'd appreciate knowing what, since he died on my land, and I discovered him."

"The autopsy has raised certain questions. We are tying up loose ends, that's all. He obviously knew you."

She hesitated. She had no wish to tell this hardass about an old love affair gone wrong, at least until she knew what was going on. But a man had died, and she needed answers more than she needed her pride.

"You might check into the name Dean Fellows," she muttered. "He's a man I knew years ago."

Watts scribbled down the name, fired a few more questions, and hustled back to his car. Before the Malibu had even disappeared from sight, she was trying to get Roy from Oklahoma on the line. He was gone for the day.

"What happened to no rush?" he asked when she reached him the next morning.

"I got impatient."

He grunted. She could tell he wasn't fooled. No doubt a police query on the licence plate had already reached him through official channels. "Lucky for you I got curious," he said. "Your licence plate was registered to a Barry Mathers of Driftwood, Oklahoma. Beige '67 Caprice."

Mila's relief was so great that she barely noticed the last part. Belatedly she snatched at the shred of information. "Not a Volkswagen beetle?"

"About twice the size, honey. They made them BIG in 1967. Your man never registered it again, by the way. Never registered anything else in the State of Oklahoma either."

She cast about for her next move. How the hell had the licence plate ended up on a purple VW? "Do you have any photo of him on file?"

"I located one for you, but it's way out of date. 1970. Shows some scrawny kid of eighteen, all teeth and Adam's apple."

"Fax it to me anyway."

Roy agreed, no questions asked. What a sweetheart, she thought. Too bad he's smoking his way to an early grave. While she waited for the fax, she puzzled over the two cars. Had Dean stolen the plates from Barry Mathers, or had the two of them done a swap? Why? And who the hell was Barry Mathers anyway? Where would their paths have crossed? On a whim, she keyed his name into the Immigration database. Nothing. She tapped her desk in frustration. Maybe the database didn't go back far enough. Or maybe there was nothing there.

As her fax machine began to hum, she phoned Roy back. "I know I've used more than my quota of diplomatic goodwill, but I wonder if you can check one last thing."

He chuckled that ominous, phlegmatic rumble. "Always happy to keep you one step ahead of your police."

"Was Barry Mathers a draft dodger?"

"Draft resistor, honey. We like that better."

She paused to absorb this new aspect of kindly, helpful Roy. "Sorry, resistor. Do you have access to those records?"

"Don't ask," he replied, and the next instant he was gone.

It took him less than an hour to get back to her, and his voice seemed to have gained an octave. "I don't know what you've all stumbled onto up there, honey, but this Barry Mathers dude was no draft resistor. He was a deserter. Did one tour in Vietnam in '71, came home on medical leave, and went AWOL from the psych ward the very first night."

Afterwards, she picked up the photo Roy had faxed her and stared at it. The face rang a very faint bell. She scrabbled through her distant memory for a connection. Somewhere. Something. Out of the mists it emerged. July 1st weekend. Fireworks on a beach, a campfire, guitars, the ocean hissing over the sand. A kid talking to Dean, so young he barely had a beard. The kid had been standing in the surf, staring out over the Pacific. Breakers crumbled and swept over his feet, but he didn't move.

"That bozo's too wasted for his own good," Dean had said, and he got up from the circle and crossed the beach to talk to him. They'd walked along the shoreline a long time. Dean tried to draw him towards the fire, but the kid shook his head. He kept flinching and looking around, as if he saw things no one else did. Must be one hell of a trip, she'd thought at the time.

Dean had stayed out all night, and in the morning she found him sprawled on the beach, fast asleep. Two empty bottles of rum and the crumpled remains of foil wrap—the last of their hash—lay beside him. When she'd shaken him awake, he'd looked around in bewilderment for the boy.

"Man, that is one fucked-up kid," he said.

"What was he on?"

"Nothing." He snorted. "Just tripping on flashbacks. Seeing firebombs and Viet Cong ambushes all over the place."

His disdain shocked her. The old Dean would never have said that, in the days before booze, drugs and self-pity had eaten away at his core. As she contemplated him, slack-jawed and filthy amid the remains of his binge, she realized she'd reached the end.

Leaving him there to sober up, she went in search of the boy. She found him huddled in the hollow in the rocks nearby, shivering against the wind from the Juan de Fuca Strait. He was rocking fitfully, his eyes pressed shut and his lips moving as if in silent prayer.

She wrapped her jacket around his shoulders and gave him a hunk of bread. As he ate, he began to weep, the tears running down his cheeks onto her jacket. She reached for him and he snuggled in the crook of her arm like a small child. They didn't speak, and gradually his tears stopped. But still he held on tight.

"Are you Dean's girl?" he asked.

"Yes."

"I never even kissed a girl. Never had a date, never even had a job. Then I went to Nam."

She hugged him, searching in vain for words strong enough to comfort him. A sudden shadow fell over them. "What the hell's going on?"

Dean was scowling down at them. They jumped apart, and Mila's jacket slipped from his thin shoulders. The boy scrambled to his feet and backed away, scrubbing the last traces of tears from his cheeks.

"Nothing. She brought me some food is all."

Dean stood in silence a moment, his hands on his hips. His glare gradually softened. "You should have gone to the camp, Barry. There's plenty of food there. You'll catch your death here."

"I already have," Barry said in a small voice as he turned to clamber over the rocks, not towards the camp but away towards the empty highway.

Dean didn't speak to her, merely snatched up her jacket and strode away towards the campsite. It was that silence, that unspoken condemnation more than anything else, that made her decide to leave him. If it wasn't about his needs and his suffering, then it wasn't worth talking about.

When she caught up with him at camp, he was rolling a

joint. Not even down yet, and he was toking up again. "Dean, I can't do this any more. I'm going home."

He paused only long enough to flick a glance in the direction Barry had disappeared. Fury boiled through her. She shoved her clothes into her knapsack, threw the keys to the Beetle at him, and stomped off towards the highway. When she risked a glance behind her, Dean was standing by the fire watching her. He didn't even wave goodbye.

That was the last time she saw either one of them. But Dean did write her once, sounding closer to the Dean she'd once loved. He apologized for failing her, then thanked her for forcing him to confront the pointless life he'd chosen. He'd also said something about coming for her someday. She tried to remember his exact words, but years of disappointment had blurred the memory.

*   *   *

It took her two hours of rummaging through musty attic boxes to find her mementos of those hippie years. Packets of yellowed photos and notebooks held together with elastic bands—herself in fringed smocks and bell bottoms, Dean peeking out from behind his full beard and shoulder-length black hair. Snippets of poems and songs, all horribly bad and poignantly naïve. And beneath all the photos and notebooks, at the very bottom of the box, as if she'd wanted to put it furthest from her sight, was Dean's letter.

She sat down on the bottom stair and unfolded the neatly written page. Dean had been educated in philosophy and the classics, both of which proved utterly useless in procuring a job, but had made for breath-taking prose. His words brought a rush of emotion. Nothing was as magic or as visceral as first love.

July 10 1971.

Dear Mila,

The world is a master of disguise, donning cloaks of black, brilliant red, and shimmering, celestial white. I learned, too late, that love is the only lens that sees beyond the black. People hate each other in the abstract, but we can only love one on one. The statistic of six million boggles the mind, but Anne Frank makes us cry.

So I have found a new path. To reach out wherever I find a single soul floundering. I'm a draft resistor. Let that resistance to slaughter stand for something more. Let it stand for peace and healing. I have already started, with the spirit of that lost soldier boy. Our country destroyed him, made him terrified of the killer within himself. That morning on the beach, you showed him a glimpse of light through his visions of death, and he has never forgotten you. Neither have I. And when I feel I have earned the right, I will come east for you.

Forever yours,

Dean

Mila reread the words carefully. Beneath the overblown prose and the metaphysics, Dean was referring to Barry. He had been helping Barry overcome the nightmare of his wartime experiences.

As she thought about the obsession with violence in the hermit's lair, a chill began to slither down her spine. Which man had been camping in her back woods? Was it Dean, who'd come back east as he'd promised but in the end lacked the courage to face her? Or could it have been Barry Mathers, a destroyed soul drawn to the only woman who'd ever held him in her arms?

There was no police tape around the compound, so after tying Pavlov firmly to the picnic table, she headed straight for the hut.

The police had left it in disarray; the fastidiously smooth sleeping bag was rumpled, and the books were scattered on the bed. She picked up the nearest and flipped to the front page. No inscription. The second and third, nothing. Then she spotted *Dr. Zhivago*, a book whose theme of love stood in stark contrast to the others. Tragic love, to be sure, but still a voice of hope amid the devastation of war. She opened the cover and there it was: *June 20 1971. Happy quarter century, and may love bind us for eternity. Forever yours, Mila.*

She stared at the words. At the book, as memories flooded in. She had given it to Dean as an inspiration on this milestone in his life. He would have reached another milestone, sixty, last week. Had he celebrated it all alone, out here in his chosen home?

She looked around the room for other evidence that the hermit was Dean. The pots and pans were probably salvaged from the dump, and the clothing was too filthy to be recognizable. But wedged deep into the dirt in the corner under the straw mattress, she found a small cookie tin which rattled when she picked it up. Inside she found the peace medallion Dean always wore, his Quebec driver's licence, and a folded square of paper containing a hand-drawn map of Ontario. Her cottage was marked "target".

But beneath the map was a small note in a scrawl nothing like Dean's elegant hand. "Thank you, Dean, for making the ultimate sacrifice to the cause of love".

Panic drove her outside into the afternoon sun. She sucked

in the fresh air, trying to slow her pounding heart. Whose handwriting was that note? Barry's? Had he stolen Dean's ID, his medallion and his car? Why? And where was Dean? What was the ultimate sacrifice?

So many questions, the answers unthinkable. She phoned Detective Watts the instant she got back to the cottage. Her mind clamoured with the enormity of her discoveries, but before she could even begin, he interrupted her.

"Relax, Mrs. Hendricks," he said in a surprisingly gentle tone. "We have established cause of death, and we are close to an ID."

"Who...? Is it...?"

"We're waiting on DNA, but we believe it's Barry Mathers, a U.S. army deserter who fled the States during the Vietnam War. The crazy fuck still had his dogtags on."

She allowed herself a faint hope. "Not Dean Fellows then?"

There was a pause on the phone, and Watts cleared his throat. "That's what I wanted to tell you. Dean Fellows died in Esquimalt on July 15, 1971."

Tears burned her eyes. Her throat closed and she sucked in a breath, unable to get the question out. The detective seemed to anticipate it. "Shot in the head. Case never solved."

Till now, she thought numbly. She groped to put the pieces together. "And this Barry Mathers...?"

"His head wounds were consistent with a bullet fired at close range, and we found his gun in the brush three feet away. The coroner's ruled it self-inflicted. Judging from insect activity, he'd been dead about a week."

She sank down into a chair as understanding began to dawn. She thought of the terrified young soldier she'd held in her arms. Of harmless Dead-eyed Dan who couldn't kill a mouse if he was starving to death, but who had shot Dean in the grip of his private nightmare war.

And who, on what would have been Dean's sixtieth birthday, had splattered his own brains all over the leafy forest floor.

Barbara Fradkin *is a child psychologist with a fascination for how we turn out bad. Her gritty short stories haunt numerous magazines and anthologies, including the previous Ladies Killing Circle books. She is also the author of four detective novels featuring the quixotic Ottawa Police Inspector Michael Green, published by RendezVous Press, and is a four-time nominee for the Arthur Ellis Award.* Fifth Son *won the 2005 Arthur Ellis Award for Best Novel.*

Plenty of Time

Melanie Fogel

She sneezes, and now the pouches under her eyes are polka-dotted with mascara.

She reaches for a piece of toilet paper to dab off the polka-dots, but her hand lands on a cardboard spool. She opens the cabinet under the bathroom sink for a new roll and finds only rumpled shrink wrap. Does she have any toilet paper?

Never mind. She can use a Kleenex. She heads for the box on her night table, thinking she'll have to pee before she leaves. She doesn't like using Kleenex to wipe herself; it always itches afterwards. So where's the toilet paper she bought on sale, not two or was it six weeks ago?

AAADD. That's what Stephen calls it. Age Activated Attention Deficit Disorder. Some joke he read on the internet. How you know you're middle-aged. Start to do one thing, and that task splits you off onto something else, and those two split and you end up getting nothing done. "Except with her it's not age," she can hear Stephen saying, laughing, to a customer. "She was born with it. That's why she needs me to run the business."

Not any more, Stephen dear.

Kleenex in hand, Donna tunes her clock-radio to the news station. She may not be able to fake shock when the police call or arrive at her door. This way, she can say she heard it on the radio when she woke up. She sets the alarm for half an hour earlier than usual, giving herself plenty of time to hear the news, to prepare herself for the police.

Take no chances whatsoever, she thinks, before blowing her nose and tossing the Kleenex into the wastebasket.

Nearly an hour to go. She wishes the phone would ring. Even a telemarketer would divert her mind for a few minutes. Even Heather, who always calls when it's inconvenient to ask where her "soon-to-be ex-" husband's sleeping nowadays, and to bitch about what a bastard he is.

Still, if Heather hadn't thrown him out, Donna wouldn't have this opportunity. She'd been warned, when she told people she was going into business with her best friend's husband, that business was like a marriage, that she'd learn things about Stephen she didn't want to know. But even Heather had thought it a good idea at the time. Neither of them thought him a bastard back then. Now they both hate his guts. Donna stares at the phone, willing it to ring.

What if it rings when she's out? But who would call after eleven? Unless it's an emergency... I was in the shower, she could say. I was really tired and shut the ringer off before going to bed. But should she set the answering machine?

Donna flicks the switch to on. Then off. Then on again. Then off, because she's still home and will be for another hour. How to fill the time?

She spreads the contents of her shoulder bag on the bed, to check it against her list which she will have to burn before she leaves: pepper spray, in case Stephen wakes up violent; gloves, hammer, keys, money but no wallet—no ID in case the cab gets into an accident and she wakes up in a hospital; toque, wig, wire cutters; gun. She marvels again at how easy it was to get the gun. Easier and scarier than imagining herself crushing

Stephen's skull with the hammer. The wig and makeup came in handy; even if they find the gun she'll ditch in the shopping centre dumpster, even if they trace it back to the druggie who sold it to her, he'll never connect the stylish, middle-aged, brunette boutique owner with the sleazy blonde tart.

She cradles the gun in her right palm, savouring its weight, slides her index finger along the trigger she's never pulled. Shall she tell Stephen why she's killing him? That the keyman insurance is the least of it? She pictures him sitting on the cot he's set up in the cramped stockroom, hair tousled from sleep, eyes bugging at the gun. I don't need you, Stephen. I can hire an accountant to do your work. A hired accountant with no delusions, he has the flair to manage a business like This 'n' That. You're an okay bean-counter, but nothing more. A better bean-counter than you are in bed, according to Heather, but she's biased.

This 'n' That is my business, Stephen. My idea, my talent for choosing the knickknacks and gewgaws fashionable people like to decorate their homes with. Your bean-counter brain is killing it. Buying low and selling high only works when what you buy is what people want to spend money on. That's why I'm killing you, Stephen. The insurance and your mockery have nothing to do with it.

Then she'll pull the trigger.

She replaces all the items in the shoulder bag. As she lifts the gun to place it in the zippered side pocket, she realizes her fingerprints are all over it. Halfway to the kitchen to fetch a J-cloth, she stops to contemplate the preferability of using a Kleenex. She might get gun-oil or something on the J-cloth, and then she'd have to dispose of it. Kleenex she can burn along with the list.

Kleenex reminds her. She turns, heading for the broom

closet, where she's sure she placed the toilet paper. Two eight-roll packages. Why can't she see them?

She fetches a kitchen chair to stand on, so she can see the top shelf. She finds a box of steel wool she'd forgotten about, as well as a cellophaned trio of hand soaps she'd put there in the hope their sickly-sweet smell would fade. She sniffs. It has. She steps down from the chair to place the steel wool in the cabinet under the kitchen sink, and the soap in the bathroom. She glances at the unfamiliar blonde in the mirror. Oh yes. The polka dots. She reaches for a piece of toilet paper and remembers.

She ransacks the cubby hole the condo saleswoman called the laundry room. Not there. Two eight-roll packs! How can anything that big hide?

She's tempted to forget the search, but she hears Stephen's mocking laughter: So disorganized, she couldn't find a refrigerator in a kitchen.

The top shelf of the coat closet. No. The back of the bedroom closet. No. The bottom drawer of her filing cabinet. No. The spare-bedroom closet. No.

Her search turns up a balaclava that could work better than the toque. Except what would it do to her makeup? Where did she put all those cheap cosmetics? Because she'll have to toss them down the garbage chute before the police find them.

She murmurs a prayer of thanks to God as she envisions the white plastic trash bag atop her dresser, left out in the open so she wouldn't forget. That's organization. But she can't throw it out now. It's still too early; a neighbour might see her. She'll take it with her on her way out. And drop it in the dumpster along with the gun? No. If the police should find the gun, they'd wonder why someone threw away all those almost new cosmetics, and perhaps make a connection.

Take no chances whatsoever.

She enters the bedroom to reassure herself the bag is indeed there and finds one more place to search. On hands and knees, she peers under the bed. Yes! Just out of reach. Flat on her belly, she snatches a slippery edge, but as she backs out from under the bed, the wig catches on a spring.

She freezes. Inches forward. The wig tugs. Creeps to her right—no, not a good idea. Nor to her left. She tries forward again. She rocks her aching neck. Finally, she slides out from under the bed, wigless.

In the bathroom, the mirror shows her where the foundation has rubbed off her chin, and how negligent the cleaning lady has been about vacuuming unseen places. And the polka-dots are still there.

"Get organized," she commands the gorgon in the mirror.

She plans. First, wash off the makeup. Then remove the black T-shirt. In that order, she runs no risk of staining the shirt. Then shake out the shirt over the bathtub, rinse the dust from the tub, reapply makeup—no!—shirt back on, reapply makeup... It's only 11:05. That's all right, she really did want to leave at midnight. Plenty of time.

Donna contemplates her clean, slightly damp, reflection. Without cosmetics, hers is the face of a sufferer from AAADD. Not the face of a killer. She must remember not to wear any makeup when speaking to the police.

She puts on the T-shirt, returns to the mirror, sees she's forgotten to shake it out, takes off the T-shirt, shakes it over the bathtub, accomplishes little by way of removing the dust. Cursing the cleaning lady, she mentally scans her wardrobe for anything else suitable. But it's all suits and dresses, a wardrobe for a successful business owner selling unique home accents for discriminating tastes. Doesn't she have a lint-remover someplace?

Eleven-fifteen. No more time to hunt. Stacy's and every

other bar closes by two, and there are no sidewalk phone booths in the area. Stephen must be dead by 1:50. In her office, winding Scotch tape around her hand, she curses Stephen's last-minute announcement that tomorrow he moves into his own condo. If Donna is disorganized, it's because Stephen never tells her anything until the last minute. She's coped, she reminds herself as the Scotch tape makes tread marks in the dusty T-shirt. She's coped beautifully. Here she was, thinking she had weeks yet to rehearse her plan, and now she has to kill him tonight. She'll cope with this, too. She'll cope.

She can wear the T-shirt inside out. In the dim cab, and dimmer Stacy's, who'll notice? It's only a bit of the neckline that shows under the trench coat. Eleven twenty. Still plenty of time. She puts on the T-shirt, reaches for the bottle of foundation, drops it in the sink.

It doesn't break, but it does remind her she's nervous, must take care. She should use a towel as a make-up cape. Towels she has handy, but can't manage to tie a knot in one behind her neck.

Safety pin. She knows where she keeps them.

Except there's only three little ones, all pinned together like a paper-clip chain. Too small to fit through the thick towel, although she tries. Where are all her bigger ones?

There's the skirt that popped a button she didn't have time to sew on. Which skirt? One by one, she removes each skirt hanger from the closet, examines it and puts it back. Could it be at the cleaner's? She's positive not; the cleaner would have asked if she wanted the button replaced. She inspects each skirt again, this time removing the jacket, if there is one, rather than just raising it to inspect the waistband. She did, she did, she did pin a skirt.

No, she didn't. It was her grey flannel slacks, as she discovers fifteen minutes later. But now the towel is around her neck and she can plaster on the orangy foundation, turquoise her eyes and be very, very careful not to sneeze when she applies the mascara.

The wig needs brushing. She's read about finding hairs in hairbrushes, or saw it on TV. She plans. Brush the wig, clean the brush, flush the hairs down the toilet. Flush the toilet again, and again. Take no chances whatsoever. Wig on fist, she kicks up dust as she brushes. She sneezes.

A careful check in the mirror puts her mind at rest. The mascara has dried, her pouches are polka-dotless. She flushes, flushes again, and the running water makes her want to pee. She hauls up the mini-skirt, hauls down the black pantyhose, catches a glimpse of the empty toilet-paper holder as she lowers herself.

But her urge is too great. Now what does she do? Drip-dry?

Men shake themselves. She tries it, doubts it's effective.

She wants to cry, but knows that will destroy the makeup, and she hasn't time to begin all over again.

Staring at the grey-brown spool gives her an idea. How absorbent is cardboard?

The sensation of blotting herself with the cardboard tube is not unpleasant. She's lived alone too long. Once Stephen is dead and she's running the store by herself, she'll have even less time to meet men. But she'll have more confidence with the ones she does meet—perhaps a recent divorcé furnishing his new apartment?—without the fear of Stephen muscling in and mocking. Heartened, she places the tube end up on the floor, since she can't reach the wastebasket. She doesn't like the idea of urine-splotched cardboard remaining in her apartment; she'll put the tube in the bag with the cosmetics.

The slight tear in the wig doesn't show at all, except for the cowlick on top there and to the left. A little gel—a lot of gel—takes care of it. Now to repack the shoulder bag, get on the boots and boogie on out to kill Stephen. She feels invigorated.

Where is the gun? Pepper spray, gloves, hammer, keys, money, toque, wig on her head, wire cutters—but no gun. She scans the floral bedspread once more. The bedside light isn't very bright, but she should be able to see a gun.

She runs a flat palm over the bedspread. Runs it again. Gets on the bed and slowly moves her body across it, careful not to upset the wig. If it fell on the floor, would she have heard it land on the thick carpet? She takes a deep breath, holds it, pictures herself the last time she had the gun.

She turns her head hopefully to the night table, and there it lies, beside the box of Kleenex. She sits up, pretending she isn't as relieved as she is, and wipes her fingerprints away.

Now the spread is rumpled, but she'll go right to bed when she comes home, so no point in straightening it.

She's forgotten something. What? She runs through the list in her mind. Empties the bag once again, careful this time to place everything close together. Pepper spray, gloves, hammer, keys, two twenty-dollar bills for the cabs, toque, wig on her head, wire cutters, gun—what?

She envisions herself getting out of the cab—yes, she has the money. Walking along Graham—yes, she has the toque. Letting herself into the store—yes, she has the keys. Confronting Stephen—yes, she has the pepper spray (please, God, let me not have to use it!) and the gun. Bullets? She checks the clip as the druggie had showed her. She should really fire a test shot, but where? Wire cutters, hammer, she's out of the store.

The paper list. She upends the shoulder bag, shakes it out on the bed. The slip of paper flutters out. She checks the items spread out on the bed against it, then double-checks as she puts each item back. Now to burn the list. She has matches, and she knows where they are.

Opening night jitters, that's all it is. Now for the fuck-me boots and she's out of here.

As she stuffs her right leg down the imitation patent-leather sheath, she feels her big toe pop through the pantyhose. Damn! She'd meant to buy a spare pair, because the same thing happened when she tried them on in the Sally Ann. Should she switch to miel-doré?

She checks her wrist. Five to twelve. No more time, not unless she's willing to risk hailing a cab after the bars close, and the store's alarm is screaming. She pulls the toe of the pantyhose up and away from her foot and wraps the stretched nylon underneath it. Then, clutching the nylon with her toes, she eases her foot into the boot. The hose slips only a little.

She is very, very careful with the left boot.

Donna peeks into the corridor, silent as death at midnight. She quietly closes her front door, then snicks the key in the lock. It's so late, she's tempted to take the elevator, but she can't risk recognition by a neighbour. She'll use the stairs. It's only eight flights.

The metal stairs clang softly as she steps down them. Clang, clang, cloing as her ankle twists, but she catches herself on the railing. The boots, half-impossible in her carpeted apartment, are hard against her soles and weak around her ankles stepping down stairs. One foot in front of the other, and concentrate. It's not like she's trying to chew gum at the same time, as Stephen would tease.

Chewing gum would make her look even more tarty, but it's a habit she never formed. Just something to think about as she wobbles down yet another flight. Better to think about than how hot it is here in the stairwell, and how much her ankles ache. How much her scalp itches. How much the cheap, sweaty makeup is stinging her eyes.

She almost opens the door to the lobby, but it's only another half-flight to reach an exit that will take her outside. Emergency exit only, the sign on that door says, but she's tested it, no alarms ring when you open it.

The cool air washes her with relief. She's on her way, now. Really on her way. She steps—clump, clump—along the asphalt lane to the front sidewalk. Her left boot cuts in a bit on the left side, but her ankles feel much better. She daren't rush, too noisy and too risky; she might fall on her face. Slow and steady, clump, clump like an old horse, but even if someone hears, they wouldn't get out of bed to look.

On the concrete sidewalk, the clump becomes a clop. A few curtained windows glow with light, but what could anyone see other than some blonde woman dressed in black? They'd never recognize her as Donna.

She's in a rhythm now, clop, clop and on her way, only twenty minutes to the phone booth at the shopping centre. How long did the stairs take her? It seemed forever, but...

At the streetlight, she checks her watch. Damn dainty watch-face. If the light were brighter, or she had her reading glasses... She's walking slower than she had in flats, but she's still on schedule, once she changed her departure from eleven to midnight. Her elation eases the pain in her left foot. It's really not that bad, she can make it to the shopping centre and rest the foot in the cab.

Clop, clop, clop, and something's cutting into her right toe. The torn pantyhose has slipped. It hurts, but not that much. She can always take them off in the cab. It will make her a more memorable fare, but also give her the opportunity to keep her head down, so that's okay. Clop, clop, clop.

Her left foot is another matter.

Maybe she can cut the pantyhose with the wire cutters, use

a scrap as a pad to protect her foot. She imagines herself doing it in the fifteen or so minutes of the cab ride; concentrating takes her mind off the pain.

She concentrates on killing Stephen. She pictures his bewildered face. Will he plead for mercy? Did you ever show me any, Stephen? When you printed off that joke about AAADD and framed it and hung it on the wall behind the cash, was that merciful?

Clop, clop, clop. She ignores that nagging little voice telling her she's forgotten something. Opening night jitters.

Her lower back, protesting its unaccustomed angle, nags her, too. But if she'd driven her own car, someone might have spotted her empty parking space in the condo's garage. Or some drunk might back-end her, or sideswipe the Volvo once she'd parked it. And she'd have had to park it blocks and blocks away, and still have this pain getting to and from the store. Stop second-guessing yourself! It's a good plan, it's working, you're even ahead of schedule. If the cab comes right away...

The shoulder bag slips. She catches it deftly in the crook of her arm, tilting her already contorted spine. It doesn't hurt that much. No, not that much. Not as much as the pain in her toe from having the circulation cut off.

The traffic light at the shopping centre intersection is red. There are just enough cars about not to risk jaywalking. It's a long light. Donna uses the time to contemplate the pair of phone booths shining softly just across the street. The light at the end of the tunnel. She repeats the cab company's number in her head; she chose the firm with the easiest number to remember. She repeats it again. Back breaking, feet aching, face itchy, scalp prickly, she envisions herself making the call.

And remembers what she forgot.

Slowly, Donna turns to regard the long, long stretch of

sidewalk she has trod. She might be able to hail a cab, get change from the driver to make the call for the trip home. Or she could die from a gangrenous big toe right in the taxi. She turns again. It's possible, if luck is with her, that someone left a quarter in one of the phone booths. About as possible as her managing to clop, clop all the way to This 'n' That from Stacy's. Maybe if she got off at the corner of Acacia...

Miracle of miracles, she spots a glowing white triangle in the traffic. The cab is heading away from the Heights, but she flags it anyway. The driver halts on the other side of the street; he won't U-turn. She hobbles across the road, wrenches open the rear door and as she bends to step inside the shoulder bag slips once again, to the sidewalk this time, and she doesn't know if she'll be able to pick it up.

The cabbie gallantly gets out to help her, no doubt thinking she's either lame or drunk. She sinks into the upholstery, excruciatingly aware of every bone and muscle, and gives him the address of her condo.

It was a good plan; she just didn't have enough time to perfect it. She'll have to perfect another. She can find some way to persuade Stephen to work late. She still has the gun, after all, and they're both of them far from retirement age. There's plenty of time.

Melanie Fogel *is the editor of* Storyteller, *Canada's Short Story Magazine and a creative writing teacher. Over the years she has authored two books on writing* (The Storyteller Fiction Writer's Workbook *is still in print), as well as humour, essays, editorials and short fiction, for publications as diverse as* The Canadian Journal of Contemporary Literary Stuff, The Ottawa Citizen *and* The Mammoth Book of Future Cops.

My Sister Caroline

Brenda Chapman

I always felt like I was on the outside looking in, for I was the last of the baby boomers—too young to be an active participant in the free love, psychedelic generation, but old enough to remember it clearly with unabashed longing. My sister, Caroline, seven years older than me, was a child born under the sign of Pisces. In keeping with the water sign, her life has flowed and woven effortlessly. In the late sixties and early seventies, she was the quintessential flower child in smock tops, jeans and leather sandals, her body slender and melon breasted. With her Peggy Lipton hair and dreamy blue eyes, Caroline never had to try to be popular. She just was. I was the intense one—a Scorpio to the tips of my toes—secretive, jealous and brooding—never quite fitting with the "in" crowd. Entering the teen years, I grew to envy my sister's free spirit and her ability to slide from one situation, one relationship, to another without a backward glance. By the time I entered university, my envy had metamorphosed into a fierce desire to be different from Caroline, to prove myself better than her in work and in love. I would feel worthy, but it meant treating my sister and all she stood for with complete disdain.

Looking at Caroline that mellow spring afternoon, the sun spilling across her hair and face from the coffee shop window, I noticed the spidery lines around her eyes and mouth that hadn't been there on our last meeting the summer before, for even though we lived at opposite ends of the city, we met infrequently. Caroline spent a great deal of time travelling, especially during the winter months, and we'd fallen into the habit of corresponding by e-mail, even when she was home. I preferred it that way, since I was able to control how much I revealed to her about my life. I'd been somewhat surprised, therefore, to get her message the day before asking me to meet her.

"I thought you'd given up smoking," I said, watching her shake a cigarette from a packet that she threw back into her purse. Head bent, she jerkily rummaged around in her bag until she pulled out a silver lighter with her initials engraved in flowery script. She lit her cigarette and sucked in a deep draught, sitting back as the tension left her shoulders and smoke spewed from her nostrils.

"God knows, I've tried." She shrugged and turned up her palms on the table. "Phil had a real thing about my smoking, if you remember, so I pretended I'd quit. Maybe, that's what you remember."

Phil. Husband number three. Caroline had met him on a Club Med holiday and married him a month later. He'd been a lean, loud man with a receding hairline, if memory served. Caroline was currently working on number five.

"How's Gerry?"

"Oh, all right. We haven't been getting along so well lately. I'm considering my options."

That could only mean she'd spoken with her lawyer. Caroline never came out of her marriages without a chunk of money. She was amazingly mercenary for a product of the hippie generation.

"Will he go quietly? As I recall, the others weren't too happy about getting the boot."

Caroline tilted her head and squinted at me through a veil

of cigarette smoke. "He's lucky I've given him this long."

"You must be seeing someone else. Anybody I know?" Caroline hadn't lived alone since turning seventeen. Collecting men was her hobby.

She laughed, low and throaty. "I didn't call you to discuss my love life, although it's a subject of endless fascination, I know. I actually wanted to talk something over with you."

"Oh? Should I be bracing myself?"

"That depends."

I was tired of the evasive word games that she'd always used to make herself appear mysterious, and I irritably changed the subject. "Mom asked about you the night before she died. Why couldn't you make it to see her again?"

Caroline raised her hand and signalled to the waitress for more coffee. A silver ring encircled her thumb, while emeralds and diamonds sparkled on her middle finger. "My stars weren't lined up. It was a bad karma time, and I didn't want to bring my bad energy into mother's sphere."

I looked across at her, my mouth gaping. "My God, Carol —she was dying. Your bad karma wasn't going to make matters any worse."

"How was I to know she was going to die? She always pulled through before."

"Because I phoned you and said, 'Mother's dying.' How much plainer did I have to make it?"

"Let's not quibble about what you may or may not have said. Anyway, you're so much better at handling tragedy. I'd just have fallen apart."

The helpless card—it always exasperated the hell out of me when Caroline played it, even while I marvelled at her ability to get people to do what she wanted. I'd been more like a bulldozer, demanding my place and pushing forward until I'd become a successful executive in a high tech company. I was the only woman to make vice president, and I could hold my own in any boardroom. The real pain had been in my personal life. Caroline seemed to read the direction of my thoughts.

"Any word from Rick? He's been gone, what? Two months now?"

"We're talking about a vacation in Mexico to see if we can patch it up." I tried to sound offhand. I wouldn't let her know that Rick's departure had me sleepless and distracted. Too many times, I found myself sitting in my car outside his new residence, sobbing into the steering wheel.

Caroline's eyebrows rose in surprise. "I thought you were happy it was over? That's what one of your e-mails said."

I shrugged. It wasn't in me to expose my underbelly, especially to Caroline. "So what did you want to talk about? I really have to head back to work in a few minutes. I have a big presentation tomorrow and need to finalize the handouts."

Caroline pulled her streaked blonde hair away from her face and let it ripple over her shoulders. She leaned closer. I smelled her familiar musky scent. "I think I'm being followed, Lucy. I have this feeling... I'm scared to go out alone any more. I don't know what I should do."

I searched her face. "Who would be following you?" I was highly skeptical of Caroline's words. She'd never been all that grounded in reality.

"I don't know. It's just so spooky. Every time I talk on the phone, I hear clicks, and I could swear someone follows my car whenever I go out. You know how you feel when someone's watching you? Like creeped out?"

"Surely, you're imagining things? It's not like you're involved in anything illegal." I tried to laugh. It came out a sharp bark of disbelief.

Caroline pushed back against her chair. "I knew you'd think it was ridiculous. I can always count on you to be practical and...clear-sighted." She closed her eyes, and when she opened them and looked at me, she had put away whatever else she was going to say. "It would be nice to see you again soon, Lucy. Don't be a stranger."

I was happy not to have to dig any deeper into Caroline's psyche. I swallowed the dregs of my cold coffee and stood to leave. "Sure thing. Next time, I suggest we go for something stronger than coffee." I looked down at her bowed head and hesitated. She was my only sister, after all. I couldn't deny that we shared a long history. "If this...feeling of being followed doesn't go away, you should call the police."

Caroline raised her sky blue eyes to mine, managing to look martyred and brave at the same time. "Thanks, Lucy. I'm sure it's just my imagination, like you said. I won't give it another thought."

I inwardly cursed her ability to manipulate me. "Just call if you need anything, okay? I'm a phone call away."

April and May were busy months for me, and I didn't think about Caroline and her imaginary stalker at all. Rick and I spent our holiday together in Puerto Vallarta, and while we wandered its cobblestone streets and sunbathed next to the jewelled water of the Pacific, we somehow reached a marital truce. When we returned home, Rick moved back into our house, and I made every effort to keep regular working hours. He would have preferred that I give up my career to have a family, but I wasn't wired for motherhood. My biological clock had all but expired, and therein lay the biggest rift in our marriage.

One afternoon, I received a call from Caroline as I was packing up my briefcase to go home. I'd found that I could secretly work an hour or so in the evening when Rick went out for his after-supper jog. At first, I didn't recognize her voice.

"Caroline? Is that you?" I had to strain to hear her words.

"It's me. I wonder if you and Rick would like to come over Saturday for a party I'm throwing to celebrate Gerry's fifty-fifth. It won't be anything elaborate, but I'd like if you both could come." She sounded down—her voice shaky.

"We'll be there. Can I bring anything?"

"No, I've hired a caterer. Come around six, and we'll have a drink before dinner."

"Is everything okay, Caroline?"

"Of course. I just haven't been sleeping well, and the sleeping pills make me a bit groggy. See you Saturday."

"See you then."

It wasn't until I was home leaning against the fridge while I waited for a packet of chicken to defrost in the microwave that it occurred to me that Caroline's sleeping pills should have worn off long before her late afternoon call to me. Was she adding sleeping pills to her repertoire of soft drugs? My flower-child sister was never far from her stash of weed, but as far as I knew, she'd outgrown the stronger drugs that she'd experimented with in the seventies.

Saturday night arrived all too soon. I would have preferred to skip Gerry's party and spend the evening at home with Rick. He'd been working out a lot at the gym and seemed to be avoiding alone time with me. The week before, he'd said I'd become more possessive since he'd moved back in. I knew it was true, but I couldn't seem to stop myself. I hadn't liked living without him for the few months when he'd gone to stay with his brother. His departure had been a wake-up call—he wouldn't wait forever while I built my career. Rick looked over at me as he turned off the car. His jaw was set, and his black eyes were unsmiling.

"Who would have thought Gerry'd be turning fifty-five? Time sure flies," I said, reaching over to touch his cheek.

"We're all getting older, Lucy."

I dropped my hand. "I hope this party goes okay. Caroline's awfully stressed lately."

"Are you crazy? She's one of the happiest people I know. She takes life in stride and never seems to have any regrets. We could all take a page from her book."

"Maybe." I was already pushing myself from the car seat. Rick's defence of my sister had me shaken. He'd always talked like she was from another planet, yet he seemed to be aligning himself with her against me. Tingles of jealousy began to snake upwards from my belly, and I turned my face from Rick to hide the hurt he'd see in my eyes.

Caroline was beautiful that evening. A black silk blouse and leather pants showed off her figure, while her hair hung loose and shimmery. Next to her, I felt frumpy. Without much forethought, I'd put on a conservative navy pantsuit that I usually wore to work. I was trying to grow my own blonde hair longer, and it was at that unattractive in-between stage.

Gerry stood beside Caroline, holding a glass of red wine. He looked completely at ease, his stocky body dressed in a white madras shirt and black corduroy jeans. "How are you, darling?" he asked, and I leaned into him to receive a kiss on my cheek. His beard scratched my face.

"Oh, can't complain," I said. "You're looking gorgeous at fifty-five."

Gerry chuckled. "Your sister keeps me young. She wouldn't stand being married to an old bugger."

I looked over his shoulder and saw Rick giving Caroline a long hug. He was whispering something into her ear. I strained forward, trying not to look obvious. Gerry turned his body sideways and followed my line of vision.

"How're you and Rick doing?"

"Pretty good." I forced a smile. "And Caroline? Has she been depressed lately?"

"I wouldn't say depressed exactly. More like preoccupied. She's out a lot. Tells me she's joined a gym or something. Maybe I should join too." He patted his belly that hung over his belt and chuckled.

"Working out's for sissies," I joked, while my chest tightened. Had Caroline joined the same gym as Rick?

"I'm with you, kid. I've lasted this long without it. Let me get you a drink. White wine?"

"Lovely, yes," I said, moving with him toward a bar set up in the dining room, trying to shake my unease. A smorgasbord of hot and cold food lay spread before us on the table surrounding a vase of red roses. On the hutch sat a large chocolate iced cake, crowned with blue candles. I accepted the cold wine glass while Gerry looked over my head.

"Hi, love. The food looks wonderful," he said.

Caroline stepped past me and kissed Gerry on the cheek. "I'm glad you're pleased."

Gerry grinned at me and said, "I'll go mingle and leave you two to do some catching up." He tenderly squeezed Caroline's shoulder before leaving us. I could hear his booming voice greeting guests in the living room.

Caroline turned to face me. "So?" she asked. "How've you been?"

I stubbornly marked my territory. "Rick and I are working on our marriage, and we're doing better."

Caroline glanced at my face then looked down at the floor. "I'm asking Gerry for a divorce," she said, finally raising her eyes to mine. "I'm waiting for a good time. The days leading up to his birthday party didn't seem appropriate. Telling him would have been a damper." She laughed and reached for a shrimp, dipping it in seafood sauce before popping it into her mouth, running her tongue around her red glossed lips.

"Does he have any idea?"

"I don't think so. He's amazingly thick sometimes."

"Like all men," I said. Was I amazingly thick too? I felt a pang for Gerry. I wanted to probe Caroline's reasons for leaving, but others joined us, and I never had another chance to get her alone. I spent most of the party hovering near Rick, attentive to his food and drink needs and making certain that I was part of his conversations. If he was annoyed by my ministrations, he never let on, and to everyone at the party, we appeared the perfect couple.

During the drive home, Rick drove without speaking, his black eyes unreadable. As soon as we got inside the front door, he disappeared into the basement to play a video game. The effects of too much wine were starting to wear off, and I dragged my exhausted self off to bed. Still, it took a few hours before I could relax enough to fall asleep. I didn't hear Rick come to bed.

It was a week after the party when I began waking in the middle of the night, the sheets wrapped around my legs in a sticky, damp shroud and my nightgown soaked through. Mornings, I was so tired that I had trouble concentrating at work, and I was often overcome by moments of flu-like heat that flushed up from my spine and covered my head like a skull cap.

"Hot flashes," my doctor informed me. "You're about the right age—maybe a bit young. Welcome to the beginning of the change of life."

More like welcome to the end of Rick's fatherhood dreams. I didn't dare tell Rick, and for days, I moped around, thinking what it meant to be getting old.

One hot June day after work, Rick arranged to meet me at Chez Moi—a neighbourhood bistro that we'd frequented when we were dating. I got caught in a meeting and had to rush to make our rendezvous.

"Sorry I'm late," I said, trying to gauge his mood as I slid into the booth next to him. He looked cool in a white T-shirt with his sunglasses tucked into the collar. The black stubble on his cheeks made him attractively rugged. I slipped one foot out of my high heel and rubbed my foot up his calf.

"We should meet like this more often," I said. I felt Rick shift slightly so that his leg moved out of reach.

"This isn't working, Lucy," he said. "I moved my stuff this afternoon while you were at work to make it as easy as possible. I haven't been happy for some time, and..."

A throbbing began in my right temple. "It's Caroline, isn't it?" I couldn't get the image of the two of them hugging at Gerry's party out of my mind, and a red haze clouded my vision.

"Caroline?" he seemed surprised, but I knew he was a consummate actor. Hadn't he hidden their affair from me all this time without any slip-ups?

"I can't believe this is happening." I shook my head, trying to shake out my panic. "How could you do this to me?"

"I'm not doing anything to you. You can't tell me that you've been happy either. Let's just end this like two mature people. We want different things out of life, and we both deserve to at least have the opportunity to make our own dreams come true. I'm sorry, Luce." His voice softened, and I thought maybe he'd change his mind if I could just convince him of my love. I grabbed his hand.

"Please Rick. I'll make it better," I begged, but he stood and looked down at me, a flicker of pity playing across his face.

"I've taken care of the bill. Stay and eat if you like, but I've got to go. Don't follow me this time, Lucy," he said and left so quickly that I didn't have time to react.

I sat for a long time afterwards, drinking Scotch and running images of Rick and my life through my memory bank. We'd loved each other once; I still loved him. It couldn't be over. I'd win him back from Caroline if it was the last thing I ever did.

A cruel epilogue to Rick's announcement arrived without premonition, the way evil has a way of sneaking into your world unannounced. This time, it came disguised as a Manila envelope in our mail box. I tore open the flap without hesitation and stood wide-eyed as the pictures spilled onto the counter—photos of Rick and Caroline together in a bar, holding hands, talking with their heads close together, holding each other. Their betrayal lay spread before me, blown up in black and white. I felt like I was looking at their faces from far away, my heart a jackhammer in my chest, all that made my life worth living slipping away, for I had never given up the foolish hope that Rick and Caroline weren't together. I was back on the outside, looking in on my sister and my husband mocking me with their smiles. My pain was too great to care about who'd sent me this evidence of their betrayal. I did the only thing one can possibly do when faced with the end of sanity—I cut the photos into a million pieces with the kitchen scissors before drinking a bottle of Glenfiddich and mercifully passing out.

If I'd been a workaholic before, now I was twice as obsessed. I put in fourteen-hour days, seven days a week. Those who expressed concern soon stopped bothering me with their invitations and offers of shoulders to cry on. I did no crying. Instead, I left conciliatory, then long, pleading messages for Rick on his cellphone and waited for him to come to his senses.

One day, I found a message from Gerry on my home voice

mail, reporting that Caroline had left him. His normally jocular voice sounded small and sad. He said that I wouldn't believe who she'd moved in with and to give him a call when I had a minute. I erased the message without calling him back. I didn't want to share Gerry's pain or to let him into mine.

The weeks tumbled by and before I knew it, summer was over and the trees were wearing their autumn colours. I awoke to frost on the ground that gave way to brilliant afternoons and shorter evenings. It was a week before Thanksgiving that Caroline finally called.

"I need to see you, Lucy," she said. "I know I've been out of touch, but we need to talk."

"I can't think what we have to say to each other." I closed my eyes and tried not to picture her with Rick. I willed myself to feel nothing.

"I'm in trouble, Luce. You have to meet me. I'm being...that is, I can't talk over the phone. Remember where we used to walk when we lived on Clayton?"

"Yes." I pictured the trail up to Gussy"s Peak. We'd found the path quite by accident, snaking into the woods behind the Starlight Theatre.

"Meet me there at noon tomorrow. I'll explain everything. Please, Luce."

Maybe seeing her would put to rest the hatred that had been building in my heart. I'd tell her how angry and hurt she'd made me, and that would be a catharsis. I'd be able to sleep through the night.

"Okay. I'll be there."

The next day was one of the last jewels of autumn before the trees lose their leaves and their branches rest black and spindly against the sky. I wore a white fleece and blue jogging pants, grabbing a pair of gloves as I left the house. I arrived at our appointed meeting place first, parking behind the theatre near the garbage bins. Caroline's green Volvo arrived a few minutes later. She stepped out of the car, wearing red runners and a grey track suit. Somehow, she made the outfit look sexy—her hair pulled back in a braid and dark sunglasses hiding her eyes from mine. We nodded hello before searching for the entrance to the path, which had become grown over by bushes since our last visit. The path was still there, but we had to trample the grass and push past branches the first while. The soil higher up didn't support the same vegetation, and soon it was easier going. As if by mutual agreement, we hardly spoke until we broke into a clearing near the top of the hill. We were both breathing heavily when we finally stopped. The view spread out before us, evergreen trees clinging to the side of the cliff and lower down a canopy of reds and yellows. Caroline stepped off the path and moved closer to the edge. I knew the ledge dropped off suddenly to a forty-foot drop and called to her to be careful.

"I could just end it here and now," I remember her saying. "It would be so easy."

"Don't talk nonsense," I snapped. "Why did you bring me up here, Caroline?"

She spoke with her back to me. "I wanted to talk to you in a place where we couldn't be overheard. Someone is still following me...do you remember when I told you in the coffee shop?" She continued as if I had responded. "It's worse now. I think sometimes that I'm going crazy." She raised her arms to the sky and turned her face toward the sun.

Anger wormed up from my stomach. She was on display even here, even with just me for an audience. I realized I'd always been her audience. "I'm sure Rick has been a help, getting you through this tough time." I couldn't hide my bitterness.

"Sweet Rick," she said. "We have talked, yes. I think you

44

were a fool to let him go, by the way."

"Me a fool?" My voice rose to a shriek, "I had no choice, unlike you."

Caroline seemed in some sort of reverie. She stepped sideways along the edge until she was a few feet from me. She turned and looked at me, my reflection distorted in her sunglasses.

"You always have a choice with men," she said. "They do all their thinking with what's between their legs." She laughed at their weakness and at my inadequacy.

My vision clouded over in a film of red. Rick, the man I loved with my whole heart, the man she'd stolen from me, was nothing more than a sex object to her. She'd destroyed my life without batting one selfish eyelash, and for what? To mock me? To feed her inflated ego? I felt the heat rise up my back and radiate across the nape of my neck. I stood outside my body and watched a woman in a white fleece and blue track pants barrel at Caroline and shove her over the side of the cliff with the force of a woman scorned. Above the woman's frenzied panting, I listened to the cracks and thuds as Caroline's body loosened rocks and tumbled hard down the precipice. Someone, who wasn't me, who couldn't be me, put gloved hands over her ears and crouched into a ball waiting for the end of her sister's long scream and the crash and thump of her body striking the rock cut with the scramble of rocks following in her wake. Only then, did the woman raise her head and look over the side to see her sister twisted and unmoving far below, her head angled on a jagged rock, dark blood already seeping from her head and pooling in the crevices. That was when I let out a scream, twisted by agony and hatred, before I ran back down the path as if pursued by a host of demons.

I feigned surprise when they recovered my sister's broken body on the rock crevice partway down Gussy's Peak. I didn't have to pretend my grief. All that kept me going was my self-righteous anger at Caroline and my unspoken hope that Rick would come home to me. The police had questions, but in the end, they ruled her death a suicide. Gerry told them that Caroline had talked about killing herself, and I repeated her words about ending it all. Of course, I didn't put myself anywhere near Gussy's Peak.

A week after the funeral, I heard a knock at my front door. My heart quickened. If I knew Rick, he couldn't ignore my pain forever, but my hope plummeted cruelly when instead of Rick, I found Gerry standing on the other side of the door, a bottle of single malt Scotch in his hand. His eyes glowed strangely, and I wondered at what I saw in his face.

"We'll be needing a drink," he said, stepping inside and closing the door.

"A drink. Yes, I could do with a drink."

We settled at the kitchen table, and I poured thirsty tumblers of Scotch neat.

"Cheers, love," he smiled and we clinked glasses.

I studied him over the rim of my glass. "You look like you're recovering nicely."

"And I have you to thank," he said. "Killing your sister saved me untold trouble."

My thoughts stumbled over each other. "How did you know...?"

"That you killed Caroline? Who do you think was tapping the phone line and following her? The tooth fairy?"

"But you let Caroline go with Rick." My head felt stuffed with wool. I tried to keep Gerry in focus.

"There never was a Caroline and Rick," he said, laughing. "She met him a few times to try to convince him to go back with you. Those pictures you got in the mail were innocent enough. You just saw what you wanted to see."

"You mean, I saw what you knew I'd see." Black dots began

swimming in my line of vision. "My God...why?"

Gerry shrugged. "I get to keep all the money, and you can't say a word. Nobody even knew she was leaving me, except you and the bloody lawyer. Caroline had her faults, but she tried to look out for you in her way." He chuckled. "You should have seen your face when you screeched out of that parking lot."

It was then that I felt the red heat rising along my spine and up the back of my neck. Caroline's face flashed before me, and I cried out.

Gerry pushed himself out of the chair, still laughing as he said, "You always lorded it over Caroline. Telling you this is my parting gift from your sister."

He was turning for the door when I watched, as if in slow motion, a woman pick up the Scotch bottle by the neck and raise it over her head. From a distance, I saw the woman lunge forward and heard Gerry grunt heavily as his body crashed to the floor in a shower of glass and liquid amber. The woman dropped into a fetal crouch and rocked herself like a wounded child, a soft moan humming in her throat. The woman, who wasn't me, who couldn't be me, covered her eyes with both hands to hide what she'd done.

This time, I did not scream.

Brenda Chapman *grew up in Terrace Bay, Ontario. She graduated from Lakehead University with an English degree and Queen's University with a Bachelor of Education degree. She taught special education for many years before working for the federal government. Brenda has had several magazine articles published, including in* Canadian Living. *In 2004, Napoleon Publishing published her first young adult novel,* Running Scared. *Brenda lives in Ottawa with her husband and two daughters.*

Booming

In the U.K. the boomers are known as the bulge
And hopefully not 'cause they like to indulge
And I'm told that in these parts we're known as boomies
So I'm guessing that's meant to rhyme with loonies.

But in my house I'm neither bulging nor loonie
Though I'm caught in that spread twixt forty and sixty.
So I'm telling you sister, Yes, you Generation X,
Lay your hands off my mister or you won't like what's next.

Sure, he's middle-aged crazy with you whispering in his ear,
While I'm waiting at our table gripping my beer.
You may think that I'm standing three steps from my tomb
But this boomer is itching to lower the boom.

Joy Hewitt Mann

Slow Burning Fire

Bev Panasky

I can't believe it." I flipped through the papers again. "The will leaves it all—the house, the business, everything—to the both of us."

Eddie Henrickson's broad shoulders filled the doorway to the shop's back office, his brow furrowed. "But Cheryl, I thought your dad disowned your brother years ago."

Armstrong's Nursery, the business my father had spent his whole life building, was quiet, as though mourning him. Only the fitful clanking of the air conditioner and the soft, steady tick of the wall clock dared to break the silence. Until two weeks earlier, when he'd fallen and fractured his hip, my father had been a fixture in the store. On good days, he was happy to stock the seed racks and chat with old friends; on bad days, when Alzheimer's took him to a far-off place, I stayed behind the cash and kept him in sight. On those days, Eddie did the watering, helped customers and loaded vehicles. Even so, I never had the heart to hire someone and leave Dad at home. Then, in the hospital, his hip filled with infection, and without warning he was gone.

I slumped into my chair. Scorching late July pressed against the window glass, competing with the air-conditioning. The heat threatened to win the battle. I pushed aside a stack of seed catalogues and a sickly geranium, resting my elbows on the desk, my aching head cradled in my hands. "He talked about changing the will so often over the years, I thought he had." I sighed. "But, you know what a softy he was." Tears welled up in my eyes. "He probably just couldn't do it."

Eddie's ruddy face shone behind a light layer of sweat. "He always scared me, your brother."

Vincent scared me too.

*   *   *

Vincent was two years younger than me and had used that position to his advantage every chance he got. More than once, I'd been set up to take the fall for some petty offense he'd committed. Broken vases were always traced back to me, and it wasn't unusual for a small, precious item of mine to be found at the scene of his crimes. My parents followed the adage "boys will be boys but girls will be perfect" and were blind to his actions, at least until the night of my twelfth birthday.

The party had been a great success, netting me some funky jewellery, a Neil Sedaka album, a new Monopoly board, the book *To Kill a Mockingbird* and from my grandparents, who still seemed to think I was seven, the newest Barbie—dressed all in red. I would have loved to look that good, though in truth, my not-quite-teen body wasn't up to Barbie's standards.

So there we were, six girls on a sugar rush swaying around the living room to my favourite song, "Johnny Angel", when the night was shattered by the wail of the fire siren.

My dad, a volunteer firefighter, banged through the door and sprinted towards the fire station two blocks away. We rushed to the window. The night was lit by a bright orange glow reaching into the sky from the middle of town.

We piled out onto the street in a flurry of arms slipping into coat-sleeves and feet into runners. My mother warned us to stay well back and out of the way.

The night crackled with the sharp smell of smoke as we thundered up Main Street, past the shops with their black and orange Halloween decorations. Huddling with our schoolmates, we watched with a mixture of fear and excitement as the Calvary Baptist Church burned. In the end, the fire didn't actually amount to much—some damage to the back rooms, no one hurt. What it did result in was a police car showing up at our door with my sooty, glazed-eyed brother in the back seat.

That had been the start. Things had just got worse from there.

* * *

"Have you made all the arrangements?" Eddie's voice brought me back to the present.

"Arrangements?"

"For your dad. You know, the funeral."

My dad had made his arrangements years ago, right after my mother's death. After the fire, he and my mom had felt compelled to join the Baptist Church—an ongoing penance perhaps—and assuming there wasn't a sudden rash of deaths in our little town, he'd likely be one of the last people sent off from the church's original site. It had taken thirty-five years, but the church's Building Committee had finally put together enough money to construct a new church about six miles out of town. Surrounded by trees, it offered a tranquil setting and room to grow. At the time, I'd thought it was a bit morbid for my dad to set up his own affairs, but I was grateful now. "Yes, everything's arranged."

Eddie turned to leave, then paused in the doorway. He

looked at me, his gaze soft and concerned. Not the kind of look you'd expect from an ex-construction foreman. "You know, I can take care of stuff here if you want to go home."

I nodded, blinking back tears. "What am I going to do at home?"

*   *   *

It had been a long day. More people stopped by the shop to pay their respects than to buy gardening supplies, and by the time I put out the CLOSED sign, I was ready to crawl into my bed and sleep for a week. No such luck.

I made the familiar trek up the Main Street hill and turned onto Anson Street. My family home, at the far end of the block, was part of a collection of deep-set older houses with wide lots and mature trees. My stomach dropped, and my mouth went dry at the sight of a battered tan Buick dripping oil onto the pavement and obliterating the usual calming view of lavender and black-Eyed Susans bordering my driveway. A tall, sandy-haired man sat on the front step. I knew who he was, even though I hadn't seen him in a decade or more. Like a moth drawn to a flame, the gleam of money had landed Vince on my doorstep.

"Hey, Sis." He was thin and pale, as though he hadn't seen the sun in a few months. Throwing a cigarette butt into the flowerbed, he leaned in to kiss me, but I twisted away.

"Hey," I said.

"So." He gave me an open-handed shrug. "The old man's gone, huh?"

I ignored him and pushed past, fumbling with the door lock.

Inside the cool, dark house, the only sound was the grandfather clock marking time. Kicking off my shoes, I padded down the hall into the kitchen and pulled a carton of orange juice out of the fridge. I finished my second glass just as Vince entered the kitchen.

"Nothing's changed," he said. He looked around, pausing to run his hand over the old scarred table. "Lots of antiques in here."

"Yeah, Vince, I'm sure the house is pretty much as you remember it." Catching a glimpse of myself in the kitchen window, however, revealed that some things had changed. Grey streaks shot through my dark hair, and lines fanned out from the corners of my mouth and eyes. I tore my gaze away from the reflection. "With Dad's mind so stuck in the past these last few years, it didn't seem fair to make any big changes." I thought of my dad, happily settling into his recliner to watch *Judge Judy* as I got supper ready. Tears burned in my eyes. "When he couldn't remember where he was, or who I was any more, sometimes one of his trinkets would bring a flood of memories and stories."

Vince didn't say anything.

"But I don't suppose you want to hear about that. Seeing as you couldn't find time in your busy schedule to come and visit him. How long has it been, Vince? Ten years?"

He shrugged.

The small hairs on the back of my neck stood up. His silence was ominous. It brought back bad memories. By the time I was seventeen, Vince had been three inches taller and thirty pounds heavier than me. One day, when I'd refused to lend him any more money, since he had a habit of not paying me back, he grabbed me from behind and pushed me to the floor. Smiling and silent, he'd sat on my chest while pinning my arms down with his knees. He held up a book of matches and proceeded to light them one by one. Each match burned down almost to his fingers before he flicked it at me. I blew frantically at the falling matches, trying to extinguish them before they landed on my face. All the while, he silently smiled at me. I was left with a small teardrop-shaped burn scar on my throat to remind me of that day. When he'd run out of matches and let me up, he'd told me if I ever squealed, he'd sneak into my room one night and set my bed on fire. I lent him the money, and I never told.

"I've got plans for this place now, though," I babbled. I ran my fingers over the faded yellow and blue flowered wallpaper of the kitchen. "New paint, updated furniture." I needed a balance between making it my own place and still retaining some memories. I didn't want to constantly turn the corner or come down the stairs, expecting to see one of my parents.

"We're not keeping it," Vince said.

"What do you mean?"

"Well," he gestured to the room, "the house, the nursery and all the contents are half mine. I say we sell it all and split the dough."

My heart thudded wildly in my chest. "You've got to be kidding. I didn't think you'd want anything to do with this place."

His face creased in something approximating a smile. "I don't. All I want is the money."

"No way. We're not selling. This is my home. My life."

"You want to stay in this dump? In Deadendsville? If you have half a brain, you'll sell up and move to the city."

"There's nothing for me in the city."

"This is a wasteland." His gaze fluttered over me, cold and appraising. "You're what, forty-six, forty-seven? That's not quite geriatric yet. You could still have a life."

Like acid, anger welled up and engulfed my fear. "Oh, yeah, you're a big expert on having a life. You've spent half of yours behind bars. What do you know about having a life?"

He sighed, pulled a cigarette and box of matches from his breast pocket. He scraped the match across the kitchen table, touched it to the cigarette and inhaled. "Yeah, you're right." His cold blue stare brought a metallic taste to my mouth. "I learned a lot in jail, though. You don't want to cross me."

I swallowed hard and unclenched my hands. It was true, I didn't want to make things worse than they already were. "Look, Vince, I really don't want to sell the house and the business." A million thoughts churned in my head. "Maybe we can work out some kind of deal. I could pay you a salary as a partner in the nursery."

A cruel smile twisted his mouth. "Why would I take some little pittance on what, a yearly basis? I'll tell you what—if you have the money, buy me out. Otherwise we sell."

Vince turned and headed for the front door. "Don't think I'm leaving," he said over his shoulder. "I'm just getting my bag to take up to my room, in my house."

Late into the night, I lay in bed as caustic anger ate away at me—my head throbbing and my throat raw with trapped screams. Every creak and groan the old house made zeroed my gaze onto the flimsy hook and eye lock on the door, being used for the first time in a decade. Heart drumming, I strained my ears, waiting for any sound from Vince's room. The soft clang of the grandfather clock striking one hour after another was my only comfort.

How could Vince just walk back in like he'd never left? Where did that leave me? If I sold the house to pay him off, could I keep the business? Could I contest the will—say my dad wasn't in his right mind? What would Vince do to me if I tried? Just before sleep finally descended, I resolved to go to the bank the following day and see where I stood financially. Maybe I could buy him out. I needed to get rid of him.

* * *

The next day, shortly after lunch, I left Eddie to handle the shop and trudged the three blocks to my local branch of the Bank of Montreal.

The news was good or bad, depending how you looked at it.

"Are you serious?" I asked.

Brian Guthrie was built like a whippet and had a persistent nervousness about him. It was not the most comforting trait in a loan manager. He ran his fingers through his receding blond hair before responding. "This is good news, Cheryl. You'll have to get a professional assessment, of course, but houses in your neighbourhood are going for around three hundred."

"Thousand?" I asked, my voice an octave or two higher than normal. Call me naïve, but I'd never really thought about the value of my parents' house. It had always just been there. I knew from old stories that they'd only paid $24,000 for it when they bought it in the early sixties. Who'd have thought its value would increase more than tenfold in forty years.

"Lots of people are looking for those big, old houses, especially if they're in great shape. You shouldn't have any problem selling."

I stared at the diploma on his wall and tried to calm my breathing.

He continued, "There's no telling how much the business is worth. All the merchandise would have to be itemized and valued. It would be a big job."

I felt sick. Swallowing with an audible click, I asked, "Assuming your figures are right, would it be possible for me to borrow half the value?"

Brian studied me for a moment before leafing though the file folder on his desk. "The store hasn't been doing very well this year, has it?" he asked.

"It's been too hot. People are tired of replacing their scorched plants."

He nodded. "The mortgage your father took out against the house in order to build the new greenhouses isn't paid off yet, so I'm afraid your credit is already at its limit."

Flames of fear licked at me. "You know I'm good for it. This has just been an abnormal year."

He had the self-satisfied look of a small man who thought he looked big. "I'm sorry." He shrugged, a half smirk playing at his lips. "You realize, if your brother wants his money, you'll have to sell the house at the very least."

My head spun, nausea gripping me with cold, clammy fingers. "So that's it? What am I supposed to do now?"

Brian stared at his hands, fingers splayed like large bleached spiders against the dark wood of his desk. "Why don't you put it up for sale? What do you need that big of a place for anyway?"

* * *

Indeed, what did I need that big old house for anyway? It's not like there was a family to fill it up. Fate and time had seen to that. My high school sweetheart had waited for me as long as he could, but I'd dropped out of university in my second year to take care of my dying mother, and eventually he met someone he had more in common with. My mother had fought hard for three years before slipping away, and after her death I spent a few years not really wanting to do anything. Then my father had started showing the first signs of Alzheimer's, and I'd found myself in charge of running the shop. I'd had a few relationships over the years, but they seemed to sputter out before they ever got established. Eddie was the only one who ever looked at me with affection any more. I wanted to feel the same way about him, but when I looked at him, all I saw was the pimply, knock-kneed boy from high school, not the man who'd spent close to twenty years on construction sites, only to be forced off the job by a back injury.

What did I need the big house for? Because it was my home, dammit!

I stuck my head in at the shop to see if the place was overflowing with customers. Not bloody likely. "Eddie, I'm kind of tired. I'm going home for the rest of the day. If it gets real busy or you need anything, just call."

He gave me a sad smile. "Okay."

*　　*　　*

As I stepped through the door, I could feel Vincent's presence polluting my home. I found him sitting on the floor in my parents' room, sifting through my father's personal belongings.

Heat crept up my neck and into my face. "What do you think you're doing?" I grabbed the dark wood jewellery box from him. "Can't you even wait until he's in the ground?"

"What?" He held a pair of cufflinks to his sleeve. "It's not like you're going to use this stuff."

"I can't believe you."

He smiled and blinked his hard blue eyes at me. "Believe it, baby. Did you figure out how you're going to get the money yet?"

I didn't answer, just spun on my heel and headed out of the room. I closed the door to my room and stood, looking around for somewhere to hide the jewellery box. I tucked it into my gym bag, figuring Vince would never think to check in there.

Seeking therapy, I headed out into the garden. Weeds were few and far between—even they suffered from the heat—but I attacked a thriving patch of crabgrass. Using the hoe, I hacked the clumps to pieces, all the while wishing it were Vince under the blade. Like a tongue worrying a loose tooth, my thoughts kept creeping back to the idea of selling the house. *Selling my home. Selling my home.* How could this have happened? How could I be on the verge of losing my home to someone who had no respect for it?

Trading the hoe for a spade, I worked my way around the edge of the flowerbed. My beautiful garden. Tears trickled down my face and plopped on the greedy dirt. Tears for my father, tears for myself.

I finished edging the beds just as the sun began to descend behind the trees on the west side of the yard. Sitting on the step, sweating and exhausted, I stared into the gathering twilight.

Vince banged open the screen door and came out onto the porch. He yawned loudly and clomped down the stairs. "You and dad always were the gardeners in the family." The stub of a cigarette bobbed in the corner of his mouth as he spoke. He dropped the butt into the flowerbed, where it glowed briefly. Taking a book of matches out of his pocket, he walked it backward and forward through his knuckles as he stared at the house. "How much insurance have you got on this place anyway?"

Something tight and hot lodged in my throat, choking me. The sweat on my body alternated between hot and cold.

He smiled in the gathering evening, a flash of white. Letting the threat hang heavy between us, he turned to survey the backyard. The ornamental belt buckle my father had received when he retired from the fire department glinted at Vince's waist in the last rays of daylight.

Reaching down to ruffle the leaves of the dwarf burning bush next to the step, Vince said, "I don't think it'll come to that. This garden is going to be an excellent selling feature."

I don't remember standing up. One second I was sitting on the top step, the next I towered over him with the spade in my hand like an axe. Without thinking, I swung.

"We should get a good price for—" Vince never finished his sentence. The spade caught him on the side of the head with a resounding thwack, and he went down as if someone had cut off his legs.

Pitching forward, Vince landed in the midst of a stand of Miss Pepper Phlox. Only his feet protruded from the patch of spiky flowers. The blood-covered spade dropped into the dirt with a thump, and I started to shake. I wasn't sure if I was more scared I had killed him, or that I hadn't. A little voice inside my head whispered hit him again, just to be sure.

A second blow wasn't necessary. Pushing aside spikes of pink phlox, I leaned down and touched his neck with my fingertips. Shaking, I had a hard time deciding if there was the throb of a pulse or not. As I leaned closer, the answer was obvious—there was a deep, crescent-shaped dent where I'd hit him. I started to giggle, "Who's got the edge now, Vince?"

The giggling transformed into gagging, I turned away and threw up amongst the crimson impatiens. On my knees in the dirt, I realized I needed help, and there was only one person I could call.

*   *   *

One of the things Eddie was renowned for in high school was his knack for solving the unsolvable problem.

I sat on the top step, clutching my arms across my chest, cold despite the heat, as Eddie surveyed the situation. Without a word, he went back into the house and started banging around. When he came out, he was armed with my rubber gloves, duct tape and a box of garbage bags.

He placed the supplies on the top step, sat close to me and leaned over so his lips just brushed my ear. "Now, we just wait for full dark," he said.

Bagging Vince in the dark amongst the plants took the two of us. He had started to stiffen up, and with one arm thrown forward to break his fall, our finished product resembled a large, plastic-wrapped swordfish.

We pulled the Buick into the backyard and dragged Vince into the back seat—it was the only car big enough to carry him in his stretched out state. I covered him in old blankets and newspapers while keeping an eye on the nearest neighbour's house. I wasn't too concerned though, since the old codger was pretty much deaf and couldn't see more then three feet beyond the end of his nose.

Pulling out of the driveway without turning on the headlights, Eddie headed for the construction site where the foundation of the new church had recently been dug.

With only a Coleman flashlight and the moon to light our way, we climbed down into the unfinished foundation and began to dig. It was hot, sweaty work, and I wished we'd thought to bring some water, but the long hours spent in the garden and hauling flats of plants at the nursery had prepared me well for the task at hand. We took turns, and before long we had a hole big enough to dispose of our problem.

"They're going to pour the cement tomorrow," Eddie said.

I nodded. In the moonlight, his face had a chiselled strength I'd never noticed.

He put his arm around me. "It'll be okay," he said. "We'll get through this."

Back at the house, Eddie changed into a pair of my dad's old overalls, loaded up Vince's belongings and drove away in the Buick. I took the clothes we'd been wearing out to the fire pit. A squirt of barbecue starter, the rasp of one of Vince's matches and fire consumed them.

It rained the day of my father's funeral. It was the first rain in thirty-three days. Falling as a fine drizzle, it muted the pastor's voice and turned the world a soft gray. Eddie held an umbrella over us, and I leaned against him slightly, gathering strength as I said goodbye to my father.

As we walked toward the car to head off to the reception put on by the ladies of the church, Brian Guthrie approached.

"I really am sorry about your father," he said.

"Thank you."

"I didn't see your brother here."

"He took off. Decided he didn't like small town living."

Brian's brows furrowed. "Before the funeral? Without his part of the money?"

I took Eddie's hand. "No one has ever been able to figure Vince out."

Brian's mouth puckered as he mulled over my answer. Then he smiled. "Just as well. If he'd have stuck around, he probably would have tried to burn down the new church when it's built."

I looked up at Eddie and smiled. "Oh, Vince has changed in that respect. Nowadays he's very involved in supporting the church."

Bev Panasky *is an award-winning mystery writer from the hotbed of crime writers in Canada's capital city, Ottawa. She's a member of Capital Crime Writers and the critiquing group CrimeStarters. "Slow Burning Fire" is the second of Bev's stories to be included in a Ladies' Killing Circle anthology. When not plotting nefarious crimes, Bev can be found in her tiny garden oasis entertaining the squirrels.*

Call him Ishmael

Janice MacDonald

I wish a whale would come and swallow him whole. Then I would be rid of him once and for all. My friend Margie disagrees.

"Too many people survive being eaten by whales."

"What? What do you mean? I can only think of Jonah and Gepetto."

"Right. And how many people can you name who have been swallowed in the first place?"

I see her point. I do not want a survival rate of 100%. I want him gone. I don't want him to suffer the pain of shark bites or barracuda mastication, just to be swallowed and to sink without a trace would satisfy me. I think this is rather benign of me, and I pat myself on the back for thinking of something so painless in terms of removal from this sphere.

"It'll never happen." Margie reads the swirls of creamer in her coffee as if she were divining the future. "You think this is bad, it's just going to get worse."

She is likely right. She is very often right. I used to be right quite a bit of the time. I wonder when I got so stupid, when I became a victim rather than a conquistador.

"You're not a victim. You were just sort of stupid about men when you married him. You were on the rebound, your biological clock was ticking, and he said he loved his mother. Three strikes, anyone would be out. Sheesh, it's not as if you hit a school bus full of retards or anything. Let up on yourself a bit." Margie reaches for the sugar.

I am not sure what shocks me more, Margie's political incorrectness or her insight. I think a killer whale might bite. A blue whale would just open its vast jaws and take him in, like baleen, and small appliances. I am the good one, after all.

What I wonder is whether the kids will ever be able to distinguish this, if they will ever look back over this time in our lives and remark on how wonderful I was not to rant about their father's perfidy; how magnanimous I was to allow them the pretense of having more than one parental unit who cared whether they had new shoes for school. Or will they go on adoring him, in the blissful ignorance they do now, without the evidence that mounts in the metaphorical closet I stand against, in case the door swings wide and all the shit falls out onto the shiny, worn kitchen floor.

Part of me longs to tell them about the mistresses, and the lies and the bills unpaid because he was spending money on phone sex lines. Part of me wants to explain to them the reason we ate spaghetti so often wasn't because mommy loved it so much, but because he was balking at paying the requisite amount of child support. Part of me wants to tell them that our new car was almost repossessed because their father had used the old car we'd traded in as collateral on a loan, even though it wasn't registered to him. Part of me wants to tell them of his furor whenever he was questioned about his tremendously questionable spending practices. Part of me wants to cry.

Part of me wonders where one can find a blue whale in a landlocked province.

Margie is working her way through the yeast-laden

cinnamon bun we had ordered to share. I don't feel hungry. I haven't felt hungry in two years. This is just as well.

"So, if you can't have him disappear off the face of the earth, what else would you want?"

I look into Margie's bland face. I am slightly annoyed that she has thrown my blue whale back out of the boat so flippantly. I had thought I was being deliciously wicked in having this thought at all. Now Margie wants more?

I think about what I really want. I want my children to be well-adjusted and happy. I want not to have to monitor my words, my thoughts, my bankbook quite so rigorously. I want him branded, so that everyone he meets will know right off he is a jerk and a liar. Most of all I want to be free.

An older woman I know told me about hearing about the death of her ex-husband. They had been divorced for years, the children grown, lives disentangled, and yet she had found herself pouring a glass of cooking wine and dancing about the kitchen at the news. She'd told me that she'd felt as if she'd been paroled all those years ago, and suddenly she was truly free.

I want that feeling.

I don't want my children ever thinking they are the product of bad genes. This is what all the divorce books warn against. Telling the truth about your former mate within earshot of the kids will make them wonder if you hate the part of him that is in them. I don't want that to happen. Anyway, I believe more in nurture than nature. They will turn out fine, as long as I can find the money for the orthodontia.

Margie and I leave the café and wander down the street, pausing to window-shop. We pause at the consignment clothing shop. The prices are too steep in there; I go to the Goodwill these days. We keep walking. Margie remembers she has to buy a card, so we duck into one of the trendy gift shops.

I automatically adjust my purse so that it is firmly under my elbow. I don't need to break things at these prices.

We laugh at a few cards, but the overtly sexual ones begin to depress me, so I wander over to the knickknacks and gifts. Maybe I can find something for the girls. Fat chance, things are really too pricey here, and I am trying to wean them from always expecting gifts.

Margie is still deciding on a card.

I let my hand wander through the bin of plastic animals. Amid the dinosaurs and the tigers and what seems to be a warthog, I find myself holding a whale. I laugh to myself at the silly synchronicity, but I don't toss it back into the bin. I look over the aisles to see Margie looking at candles. I head to the cashier, who takes my money without looking me in the face. Maybe she is embarrassed at the prices. More likely, she just hates people. I put the small white plastic bag in my purse. Margie joins me at the till. She hasn't noticed my purchase, and I say nothing. We head back to my car. I drop her off and head home to the empty house. The house always seems so much bigger on the weekends that the children are away.

I busy myself with laundry, with chores for work next week, with scrubbing the kitchen floor. I look at the chairs lined up in the hall and regret that I didn't leave this job until the kids were back. They like to play train when I wash the floor. I make a pot of tea and take it into the living room, a mug dangling from my fingers, the almost empty carton of milk in the other hand.

I have rented a movie, but it doesn't grab me, and I don't turn it back on after I've taken a bathroom break. I wander down the hallway, bemused at the sight of myself walking towards me in the mirror at the end of the hall. I am always surprised to see myself in the mirror, and I wonder why I cannot retain an image of myself away from reflective surfaces.

The whale is sitting on my desk. Four ninety-five is too much for a molded piece of plastic. I am still not sure why I bought it, I am telling myself, even as my hands are wrapping it in used tissue paper left over from the toes of a new pair of shoes for my eldest. I place it in a small mailer box and type a label, although I don't kid myself that he will have ever bothered to notice any identifiable characteristics of my handwriting. I wear kitchen gloves to affix the label, and I wet down a line of five stamps, which should be enough to transport it across town. I pop it into a plastic grocery bag and hang it on the back doorknob, to drop in a mailbox on my way to pick up the children tomorrow.

It is several days later that I see an advertisement for a collector's plate featuring killer whales in one of the safe, family magazines at the grocery line up. Once upon a time I would have been too "sophisticated" to put one of these magazines on top of my boxes of frozen waffles. Now, though, I cannot bring myself to buy other magazines, the sexy ones that scream "Tell him what you really want in bed" from their covers. It would be too embarrassing to let the check-out clerk think I would read those. However, there is no shame in reading "How to organize your kitchen" and "When your child is bullied". I watch carefully as the bagger slides the magazine between the boxes of fiber-enriched cereal.

When the children are asleep and the only light in the kitchen is the bulb in the range hood, I pull on the gloves once more, and carefully pull out the advertising page. I cut the picture of the plate out carefully, with the same concentration my littlest one exhibits when creating snowflakes from coffee filters. I fold the almost perfect circle ("image shown smaller than real size") in half and slip it into an envelope. Again I type a label. I place the envelope between several bills that I must mail tomorrow. I wad up the cut bits of magazine and stow them carefully down the side of the garbage, dumping a used tea bag over top of them for good measure.

In the bath, as I am contemplating the shower head high above me and the article I've just read on energy efficient plumbing ("Save pennies all over the house"), it occurs to me to analyze what I've been doing. What am I hoping to accomplish by mailing anonymous whales to my ex-husband? Are these the actions of a sane woman? I slide down so that the hot water laps around my shoulders, sighing as the tension lessens. Sanity is an over-rated virtue, I think to myself, and settle in to shaving my legs.

I begin to see whales everywhere. I keep a folder of cut-out photos, since I can't send them all at once without losing some unconsidered effectiveness. I mail a tape of flute and whale songs that I find in a discard bin at the drug store, after washing the wrapping in Windex. Envelopes with a picture go out every week or so. The children mention that their father is getting whales from someone as a prank. He apparently suspects an old college roommate. The youngest plays with the first plastic whale in the tub on their weekends there.

His lack of fear doesn't bother or deter me. I continue to find whales, as if God and Carl Jung are gaming, with me as some latter day Job. I parcel up a used copy of Paul Quarrington's *Whale Music,* an old coaster from a flea market, a picture of the singing whale from a Disney flyer. Every time I close the mouth of the mailbox I feel lighter, and I am laughing more these days. I don't think it's a malicious laugh.

I pick the children up. The youngest announces that their father is growing a beard. I realize I haven't noticed this fact while I was asking if their shoes were packed in the duffel bag. I strain to see him, but I can't bring his face into my mind. We go out for fast food and decide to stay there and play in the playroom. My eldest says she is too old to be allowed on the slide. There is no one else there. I promise to stand guard and tell her to drool if anyone in a uniform pops in. She looks shocked. I wink.

I am sitting on my eldest's bed. The young one has been asleep for ages, but it seems that sleep eludes the other. She wants to talk. We talk about her friends at school, about my new part-time job, and finally she gets around to what she wants me to know.

It seems her father has been seeing someone. This is someone he knew from university days, someone before I appeared. This someone is now a marine biologist. He may move to where she lives, which is, of course, on the coast.

I tell her that he will always be her father, no matter where he lives. She seems at ease, now that I know the score, and turns into her pre-sleeping position on her side, clutching her stuffed rabbit. I smile and pat the covers around her still tiny frame.

I smile as I pad down the darkened hall. I can see the scenario as clearly as if I had been there. Him straining to figure out the source of the whales, hitting upon the old girlfriend, looking her up. Her denying her participation, him thinking it coyness. So, he will soon be moving toward the sea.

It's a start.

Janice MacDonald *is the author of the Randy Craig mystery series set in Edmonton, Alberta, which is also where she is settled. Much like her fictional heroine, she teaches writing and English literature when not writing mysteries, children's fiction, university textbooks, short stories and essays. She has two beautiful and accomplished daughters, and one amazing husband. She sneezes in threes, she plays the banjo and she is nervous of the ocean.*

Glass Eats Light

Susan C. Gates

In one of those weird boomerangs life throws your way, I found myself schlepping out to Yvonne Bellinger's suburban Mississauga home on a Friday evening. As a freelance journalist, I'd been assigned to write my first feature profile on Yvonne's pioneering thirty-eight-year banking career. I had an "in" with my subject—she'd been the lead instructor at the Dominion National Bank's training centre when, fresh out of business school, I'd started my own short stint as a banker.

This job for the *National Business Review* was an opportunity to break into the ranks of their staff reporters. Yvonne had deflected my requests for an interview; she was too busy winding up her affairs at the bank and preparing for an extended trip. I found this odd, because the Yvonne Bellinger I knew had never shied away from sharing her successes. But my piece was due Tuesday, so I'd used another contact in the bank's public relations office to secure this meeting.

I'd wondered if Yvonne would be annoyed and uncooperative, but she smiled broadly when she opened the door to me. "Sandra, thank you for coming."

Could this woman be almost sixty? I was fifteen years younger, yet she had fewer wrinkles. She'd probably been as disciplined in using sunscreen and keeping her figure trim as she'd been in her work life.

Even in her own home, Yvonne Bellinger was dressed formally in a knee-length blue tweed skirt and a periwinkle sweater set. As she took my coat, a subtle waft of Chanel No. 5 tickled my nose.

"Come this way, won't you?" Yvonne said, inclining her elegant white head ever so curtly, managing to appear commanding, yet genteel. "Let's make ourselves comfortable."

I cast a glance at my wrinkled khakis and ten-year-old tweed blazer in the hall mirror. Déjà vu threatened to swamp me. Even tending my babies hadn't made me feel as inadequate as I did in the company of this imposing woman.

My cellphone rang. "Sorry," I said, mortified. "Do you mind if I take this? My girls are still at the sitters."

"As you wish." Yvonne disappeared through a doorway to the right of the foyer.

I pressed the talk button, "Hello?"

"Coleman? Bob O'Donoghue here." Bob was a senior reporter at the *Review.* "I hear you're meeting with Yvonne Bellinger tonight."

"Just about to start the interview, Bob. What's your interest?"

"I'm tracking a rumour about an embezzlement case at the DNB. Can't get anybody at Head Office to comment. Makes me think I'm on to something." I could hear Bob take a long drag on a cigarette. "Millions, I hear."

I lowered my voice and moved closer to the front door. "You think Bellinger's involved?"

"Hell, no. Just thought you might pump her for information." Bob coughed. "I'm told you know their Security Chief."

"Vandenburg? He's more circumspect than a priest at a deathbed confession."

"Then what about your other DNB sources?"

"Shared byline?"

"Depends on what you bring me, babe." With that, Bob disconnected, and I went looking for Yvonne.

I found her in an intimate sitting room. Two teal upholstered arm chairs were drawn up to a smoked-glass coffee table facing a leather loveseat. Above the sofa hung a tall oil painting splashed in vivid strokes of royal blue, red and yellow on a churning background. I found the choice of modern art curious for a woman who'd maintained a lady-like appearance throughout the eras of Women's Liberation and Casual Fridays.

"So you didn't stay with banking, Sandra?" Yvonne appraised me through sharp blue eyes. "I thought you had the right stuff."

"Except for my face!" I said, taking the seat she'd indicated.

Yvonne's back stiffened, and both her expertly pencilled eyebrows shot up. "Pardon me?"

"When you assessed my performance, you told me I could be successful, but I 'needed to do something about my face.'"

"Oh heavens, yes." A delicate laugh followed. "You asked if I was recommending plastic surgery. Such a sensitive young woman. But that was exactly my point, your face was far too expressive. You needed to master your emotions, so staff and customers wouldn't gain the upper hand."

"I took up poker."

"Really?" She didn't sound convinced. "Let's have a drink, shall we? Come." Yvonne rose and walked into an adjoining room, stopping in front of a console table beneath an open stairwell.

She fixed me a scotch on the rocks and poured a glass of sherry for herself. The room was cavernous, with a twenty-foot vaulted ceiling sliced by long skylights that admitted shafts of waning, natural light. A solid sheet of thick glass laid across a pair of sturdy bronze "Xs" created the dining room table. Above it hung a massive chandelier fashioned from frosted cubes of glass. The windowless walls were lined with shelves displaying glassware and crystalline art objects, dazzling in a combination of sunlight and recessed halogen spotlights.

"Heavens, I've seen Macintosh & Watts shops with less display space and inventory."

"Ah," Yvonne said, handing me my drink in a heavy, squat tumbler. "The object of my obsession—Bertil Vallien." She swept her free arm to the far end of the room, where three narrow, squared columns of bronze metal commanded attention.

The outer posts each held a luminous oval head, placed on its ear. These faces, crafted from glass, were more alien than humanoid. Pricks of clean, white light served to create exclamation marks above them. The taller, central stand stood empty.

"My interest in Vallien's work was ignited when Richard and I chose items for our bridal registry," Yvonne said. "The glassware offered by Kosta Boda, where Vallien worked as a designer, enchanted me. Richard preferred the sturdiness of their stemware."

She directed my attention to some of her favourite pieces, a clear glass tile inlaid with a smiling primitive mask and a suspended ship's hull, embedded with a mummified figure. She lifted a medieval-looking crucifix down from its prominent position on the staircase wall and handed it to me.

"Pendulums, masks, bridges and ships are all recurring themes in Vallien's work. He likes to play with opposing concepts of connectivity and isolation, revelation and intrigue."

I'd sooner have guessed Yvonne Bellinger was a dominatrix than an admirer and collector of Swedish glassworks. I'd always imagined Chippendale or Georgian antiques and pastel Chintz would fill her home.

"Why can't I see through the glass?" I asked, as I ran my fingers along the rough surface of the cross.

"It's sand cast," Yvonne explained. "Vallien's famous for his expression: 'Glass eats light.' Conventionally, people expect glass to reflect light, but he prefers to play with its light-absorbing qualities, creating something truly startling and mysterious."

"So are some of these pieces valuable?"

"The earlier pieces aren't. They're considered mere decoration, mass produced. Some of my later acquisitions— reflecting Vallien's concentration on art over industrial design —are." Yvonne nodded toward the sideways faces on the poles. "My first bust was a gift from Lions International after I managed one of their vision care projects in the Caribbean."

Hefting the crucifix in both hands, I began to realize why I always felt so frumpy next to this woman. The only item of Swedish design I owned was an IKEA lamp.

"In retirement, I plan to visit galleries and museums in Europe and Tokyo, where some of his best work resides. After Richard died, I filled my time travelling to Vallien's exhibits in the United States." Yvonne extended her hands to retrieve the cross.

I grasped the piece tightly to hand it back to her.

"Careful," she said, but not in time. Blood spurted out of a gash in the web of tissue between my thumb and forefinger. Dismayed, I watched as red droplets splashed onto the pristine cream broadloom.

*   *   *

By the time Yvonne had dressed my wound and sprayed stain remover on the rug, I'd managed to collect myself. And drain my drink. Time to get control of this interview. With what I had so far, I could write an excellent article for *Art In America*, but it wouldn't get me a spot on the *Review's* roster.

"What our readers want to know, is how you broke through the glass ceiling in this male-dominated field."

The question stilled Yvonne. "What makes you think I did?"

I counted off her accomplishments on the fingers of my left hand, including her appointment as the first female branch manager in Ontario. "All this with a secretarial school education."

"Ah, well. One's education is never an indicator of one's intelligence, is it? Mind you, most of my male contemporaries had no post-secondary training. But yes, compared to the women who went before me, I did benefit from greater opportunities." She picked a minute speck of lint from the weave of her skirt. "It helped to start my career at a time when there were social pressures to create greater equality for women in the workplace. It came from the commercial side of things, too. Women were demanding personal and business credit. The bank didn't want to lose out on their share of this new market."

"So, good old-fashioned capitalism was responsible for busting the glass ceiling?"

"Perhaps for raising its height." Yvonne placed a palm on each knee and leaned toward me. "Look, I made the best of the opportunities that presented themselves. And," her shoulders relaxed, "sometimes it can be an advantage to be underestimated."

"Has that happened a lot?"

Yvonne shifted in her chair, crossing then re-crossing her legs. "Really, Sandra. I fail to see how my little career will be of the slightest interest to your readers. With the state of branch banking these days, I sincerely doubt that exceptional young women would find it a challenging career."

"Because?"

"Customer service, administration and lending even, all rely heavily on computerization. There's so little expectation that staff will think for themselves." Yvonne's pitch had climbed a notch or two. "Machine-generated scores have replaced human judgement."

"Would it surprise you to learn there are rumours the DNB has uncovered a large embezzlement scheme?" Bob better appreciate my legwork on his story.

"Where on earth did you hear that?" Yvonne's cheeks pinkened.

"So it's true?"

"I'd find that very hard to believe." She stood. "The DNB has the lowest rate of misappropriation of all banks."

The interview was over. Loyal to the bitter end, I thought. Before I let Yvonne shut the door behind me, she reluctantly agreed to a follow-up interview on Monday.

Climbing into my dusty Caravan, I realized I'd garnered little insight into the career of the legendary Mrs. Bellinger. Sure, she'd done relatively well, but less capable men at the DNB had exceeded her. Perhaps she could have secured a corporate position with a hefty stock option if she'd traded some of that loyalty for advancement at other institutions or in another industry. Had loyalty entombed her in a block of frosted glass, or had the glass ceiling been that confining?

*   *   *

Yvonne Bellinger's had the best turnout of any retirement party I'd ever attended. Saturday night found me in a crush of bank officials—from all strata and from several institutions—in one of the larger downtown banquet rooms.

The majority of arriving guests were headed to the right, where Yvonne held court in a receiving line. In this sea of sombre serge, she'd dressed to be seen. Resplendent in a tailored skirt suit of lilac silk, an orchid corsage on her right lapel, the guest of honour was a vision of female charm.

As she turned to greet her next guest, Yvonne caught sight of me. She gave me a small, gracious smile, and that tiny nod of her head. I'd been effectively greeted and dismissed. She said, "How lovely of you to come," giving her full attention to the next person in line. Guess a reporter didn't warrant a fulsome welcome.

I cast about for a remotely familiar face and followed the stream of dark suits flocking to the bar. If any of my former colleagues had come to honour Yvonne, I'd probably spot them near one of the watering holes.

Drink in hand, I turned to shoulder my way back through the thirsting throng. A square hand clamped down on my forearm, "Sandra! Christ, you haven't changed one wit, girl."

"Damn good thing I'm right-handed, Chaz, or you'd be replacing this drink and taking the dress to the cleaners." I had to look up a good foot to see into the face of my old friend Chaz DeCicco. Same devilish brown eyes, but now his massive crown of wavy hair was shocked with silver. "Gadzooks, Chazman, lose your Grecian Formula?"

Chaz roared. "At least I still have hair. You should see Vandenburg. Besides, the matrons in Rosedale dig the distinguished look. I'm getting all their trust work—it's great for business."

"And great for your social life, too, I bet." I'd heard Chaz's second marriage hadn't taken any better than the first.

Chaz slipped his arm around my waist, feeling warm against the thin fabric of my black cocktail dress, and guided me through the crowd. "So, you've come off the Mommy Track," Chaz bent his head to speak into my ear. "But a reporter? Come on!"

I'd known this evening wouldn't be easy. Bankers are a

clannish bunch. Yet it's a business built on checks and balances. As much as you might like the people you work with part of your job, in a management position, is to watch out for the teller who's constantly short in her till or the accountant who can't balance his foreign exchange account. It makes you wary and, after a stint on the audit team, more than a tad paranoid. A familiar prickle swept my shoulders.

We'd stopped in front of a man with the body of a long distance runner, his back against the wall.

"Sandra, you remember Jon Vandenburg, don't you?" Chaz said, saluting Jon with his glass. Vandenburg tore his gaze from the crowd to shake my hand.

"How could I forget?" I said. No way would I have recognized this guy, even though we'd been colleagues for several years.

"Jon's head of corporate security these days," Chaz said. "Big responsibilities, big bucks. Must be what happened to the hair, eh?"

"You forgot the big headaches." Vandenburg ran a hand over his head, once a mop of blond hair, now a knob of burnished and bronzed skin. "What's a reporter for the *Review* doing at a banker's retirement party?"

"I'm writing a feature article about Yvonne. But I hear there's a juicier story to report. Care to comment?"

"About what?"

"Embezzlement."

Vandenburg wiped a trickle of sweat from the side of his face. "The Bank of Montreal in trouble again?"

My follow-up question was quashed by the arrival of a skinny, twenty-something brunette with round, far-set eyes and shiny hair. She greeted Chaz with a big hug. "I hoped you'd be here," she said, oblivious to the presence of others.

I cocked an eyebrow at Chaz as he extracted himself from her embrace. He introduced her as Jennifer Lewicki. "She's Yvonne's loans assistant. Graduated from Western."

Jennifer's round head bobbed towards Vandenburg then me, giving her the look of an animated Kewpie Doll. "Mrs. Bellinger is just so great to work for. She does all her own paperwork and computer inputs, you know?" Jennifer wrinkled a freckled nose. "Unlike most of the male managers I've had."

"You're kidding, right?" Chaz said. "Nobody was more macho than Yvonne. We called her the Iron Lady."

"Maggie Thatcher was her role model," I agreed. "She even dressed like her, right down to the helmet hair."

Jennifer asked Chaz, "Who's Maggie Thatcher?"

I rolled my eyes. "Have current procedures completely done away with the need for two-party verification within the branch?"

Chaz grunted. "Software programs generate random audits of our accounts now. Cheaper than paying auditors' salaries."

"There most certainly are still policies regarding in-house verification," Vandenburg said, sending a stern glance at a reddening Jennifer Lewicki. "Shareholders can have every faith that their investments are secure with the DNB."

I persisted. "But is that faith misplaced? Aren't losses way up due to fraud from both inside and outside the bank?"

"Computerization has been an incredible productivity tool for the industry. You'd be staggered by the volume of business we process now." Vandenburg sounded more like a public relations wag than a former auditor. "The downside has been some increase in the rate of fraud. But it is by no means a serious problem for us." He buttoned his suit jacket, nodded toward the room's entrance and excused himself. "The boss has arrived."

Following Vandenburg's departing dome, I saw Cameron Walters, the Division's hulking General Manager, shaking hands with Yvonne. The full force of her personality was trained on him. Vandenburg interrupted them, and the two men disappeared back into the lobby.

"When'd you first meet Yvonne?" Jennifer asked Chaz.

"Let's see. We started, what? Twenty years ago?"

I nodded. Jennifer cast an appraising glance my way, presumably to verify for herself I was that ancient.

"She trained us as rookies."

"She trained you and just about every other snot-nosed kid that came along." This from a voice so low and gravelled it sounded like a man's. A squat woman in a navy polyester pantsuit and with hair like steel wool extended a gnarled hand.

"I'm Helen MacLean. I was Head Teller when Yvonne started in 1966. Too sharp for her own good. Every damn bloke they hired learned at Yvonne's feet." The sentence was punctuated with a snort. "Then she ended up reporting to them, when she was every bit as good, or better, than the lot of them."

No one voiced a reply. I recognized the truth in Helen's remarks, had seen the same scenario repeated everywhere I'd worked. It amazed me the chartered banks made so much money, when they were so foolishly run.

Helen was on a roll. "And now she's getting the Tin Handshake." She took a swig of beer. "I saw the writing on the wall and got out myself. But not Yvonne, she's a loyal one, she is."

"What do you mean?" I said. "Isn't retirement her idea?"

"Still four years away from a full pension! She's getting the bums' rush just like all the other old-timers." Helen groped through her gigantic purse.

"Nobody makes it to full retirement any more," Chaz interjected. "Too expensive for the pension fund. Cheaper to hire younger staff to replace them."

"How do they get away with that kind of behaviour?" I

asked. Chaz shrugged his linebacker shoulders.

"It's been her whole life," Helen huffed. "She gave up having kids to do this. Then had a tough go of it with Richard sick so long and off work. Heart disease. They'd stopped promoting her then, said her husband needed her at home." Her upper lip curled back, and she stuffed an unlit cigarette between her teeth.

*   *   *

The emcee had announced dinner would start in fifteen minutes, and I needed to find a bathroom. Leaving Chaz to get fresh drinks and find us a table, I headed to the lobby only to discover the line to the ladies' washroom snaked several metres down the hall. Waiting was never my strong suit. Setting off around a corner, I spied Jon Vandenburg huddled nose-to-nose with Cameron Walters.

There were wild arm gestures and red faces. I could hear the occasional curse word, but when I caught Vandenburg saying "reporter", I sidled down the wall and hid behind a large pillar to better eavesdrop.

"What the hell am I doing here, then?" Walters seethed. "The last thing I need is to have my picture in next week's paper with an embezzler."

Bob was right!

"We only have suspicions at this stage. No proof," Vandenburg said.

Suspicions of whom?

"When will you have proof?"

"Give me till Monday to follow my leads. I've got people working the paper trail." Vandenburg shot a look down the hall. I held my breath. "Best you leave."

"You bet your ass." Walters stalked past me, Vandenburg jogging to match his stride.

I followed them through the lobby and watched as Walters got into a chauffeur-driven Town Car. Vandenburg took off in a dark-coloured Chrysler sedan, tossing the valet a five-dollar bill.

With a little digging, I might break Bob's story wide open.

* * *

I returned just as Yvonne was introduced to a standing ovation. Her smile was dazzling and, in the spotlight, the sheen of her silk jacket glowed.

I sidled up to Chaz and whispered into his ear, "So what have you heard about the embezzlement?"

His head snapped to face me. "I've only heard rumours."

"Who's under the gun?"

"Haven't heard any names. Have you?" His handsome face clouded. "If it's an insider, heads'll roll. The public's sick of cover-ups. The bank'll drop the hammer."

"Is it you, Chaz?" I asked with a twinkle in my eye.

He faked a hound dog expression and raised both wrists together. "Lock me up!"

The rest of the evening consisted of insipid chicken and wilted broccoli served up with the usual tributes from divisional managers, young enough to be college students. Not much of it was quotable, so I made an early exit.

* * *

I drove to the Bellinger home late Sunday afternoon, figuring an unannounced appearance might shake Yvonne up a bit. I needed to make sense of this woman's career. Had it been a success or not? I had nothing to lose—I didn't have enough for a decent article at this point anyway—let alone a lead on the fraud case. Now that Yvonne was officially retired, maybe she'd set aside her loyalty to the Bank to tell me how she really felt.

Pulling into the driveway behind a dark green Sebring, I noticed a silver Integra inside the garage. Had she kept her husband's car, or did Yvonne have company?

When no one appeared after a third ring of the doorbell, I ruled out the company theory. A twist of the knob told me the front door was locked. Emboldened by training that valued answers over privacy, I decided to do a little snooping.

I was disappointed to find the doors of the Sebring locked, but noticed a man's sports jacket on the back seat. Perhaps Yvonne had a visiting relative? The Integra was unlocked, the only content of note a suit bag filled with stylish women's sportswear.

Inside the garage, a set of stairs led to a steel door. None of my reporting assignments, to this stage, had involved unlawful entry. I tried the doorknob, adrenaline coursing through my body when it turned in my hand. Holding my breath, I opened the door and walked into a laundry room, the rhythmic whoosh of a dryer covering my steps. Someone must be home.

"Hello? Yvonne? Hello?" I didn't shout, but it wasn't a whisper either.

Moving into the kitchen, I listened for voices but only heard water running from somewhere upstairs. A navy leather handbag sat on the counter directly ahead of me. I rifled through it and found Yvonne's passport, her photo starched and perfect, and an Air Canada folder containing a ticket to Buenos Aires for a flight departing this evening.

Did Argentina have a Vallien collection? Why had Yvonne moved up the date of her departure? Had she lied to me when she promised to meet me on Monday?

I scanned the rest of the space and spied a carry-on bag on the floor. A collection of envelopes peeked out from the tote's side pocket, beckoning my examination. I slipped them out and walked into the dining room, where I'd be in a better position to listen for any changes to the activity upstairs.

A new face, last night's retirement gift, had assumed the place of honour on the centre post. This one was milky, virtually featureless and fixed in an iron vice. I couldn't see the beauty in such a bizarre creation. It struck me as a particularly cruel present if Yvonne Bellinger was being squeezed out of the career for which she'd subjugated the rest of her life. Walking closer, I peered at it, its semi-transparent surface refusing to divulge a clear view of some inner image.

Enough art criticism. If I was going to break laws in the service of my craft, I'd better not waste time. I shuffled through the business-sized envelopes in my hand, noting the logos of Crédit Suisse, Deutsche Bank, Citibank, with return addresses in the Cayman Islands. Why would she have correspondence from foreign banks? I opened the envelope from the Swiss bank to find account statements in Yvonne's name with a balance of over two million dollars, American.

The sound of running water stopped. I hadn't thought this far ahead. Should I call out? Get out? Turning to check for movement on the second floor, I scanned the contents of a second envelope. I heard an upstairs door open. Startled, I raced into the sitting room, hoping to escape out the front door before anyone came downstairs. I didn't make it.

Face down between the armchairs lay the body of Jon Vandenberg, a massive depression in the back of his bare skull. Blood seeped down his neck and pooled under his head. A large octagonal vase of clear glass, reflecting shades of deep claret, lay at his feet.

Blind with horror, I stumbled backwards, hitting the frame of the archway. Fighting a wave of nausea, I willed my body to run, but only a deep moan escaped.

"Sandra?"

I swung around to see Yvonne Bellinger gripping the upper balcony's railing with bloodless knuckles. Naked of makeup, her browless face had a vacant look. Confusion flitted across it, followed by a rapid tightening of muscles that etched heavy lines in the corners of her mouth.

"What on earth...?" Yvonne seemed to struggle for words. She gathered a terry bath robe around her waist. A hand fluttered up to smooth the usual impeccable coif of tamed waves, now a cluster of damp spikes.

The steeliness returned to her tone. "What is going on here?"

My heart wrestled my brain for control of my face. I squeezed a smile through trembling lips. "I was worried about you when no one answered the door bell. And then I saw a man's coat in the car outside, so I..."

"You what?" Yvonne stalked to the head of the stairs, stiff and menacing. "Decided to break and enter? To interfere where you're not welcome? You never could accept 'No' for an answer."

Her blue eyes, cloaked behind heavy hoods and dark circles, bore lasers through me. A chill raced down my spine.

"Yvonne, it's not that bad. Let's call 911," I sidled towards the table, its bevelled edge pressing into my thighs. "Get him help, and it'll be okay."

She descended four steps. Her hand rested just above the top shelf on the partial wall along the staircase. Yvonne's lip curled like a Doberman confronting an intruder.

"Did Vandenberg tell you his suspicions?"

"About what?"

"Don't toy with me, you uppity little bitch," Yvonne hissed. "Do you have notes in your office, in your car?"

I was gripped by fear, and all those poker lessons abandoned me. Squeezing my eyes shut, I grappled for a response that would save my hide. They snapped open when a heavy object struck my forehead. I grabbed the table to steady myself, head swimming. A decanter lay on the floor. Something wet streamed into my eyes, and I reached up to wipe it away, shaken to see blood.

Yvonne snatched a glass nude from another shelf and hurled it. It bounced off my forearm. My feet welded to the carpet, I could only watch, stunned, as Yvonne raced down the staircase, grabbing the crucifix on her descent. She paused on the lower landing long enough for me to see her mask of fury.

"I won't go to jail." With that, she charged me.

A banshee screech filled the air as the weight of her body on mine tipped the tabletop. It cracked beneath us and we crashed to the floor in a splintering shower.

Bursts of white light thundered through my brain. I struggled for breath. Shards of glass surrounded us. I was petrified to move, for fear I'd be pierced by one.

A gasp shuddered through Yvonne and she rolled off me, groaning, the broken cross just beyond her reach. Deep-red rivulets streaked her hands and robe. Dazed, I turned my head to the left. A pair of metallic, wire-caged eyes stared back at me. Screaming, I pushed a cold blue bust away and struggled to sit up.

Yvonne's body hummed to life. She roiled up on her knees like a fern unfurling in fast forward. Seizing the jagged crucifix in both hands, she plunged, aiming at my chest. I grasped a chunk of the shattered table and thrust upward.

Yvonne didn't do any jail time. The shard I'd used to defend myself had pierced a major artery in her abdomen, killing her. I'd escaped with a deep laceration to my palm, a variety of cuts and bruises, a concussion—and more material for my article than I could have imagined.

I'd even managed to scoop Bob.

The story of Yvonne Bellinger was one of a highly capable woman who had sought, in the first instance, to break through the glass ceiling then, in the second, to use it as a shield to seek her revenge. While underestimated by the corporation, she'd managed to embezzle over seven million dollars in the years since her husband's first heart attack.

Investigators discovered that Richard's poor health, complicated by depression, had led him to amass heavy gambling debts. Yvonne had written her first fraudulent loan to bail him out. The frequency of the loans had increased after his death and as she was passed over for executive positions. Her insider knowledge had been her weapon, Jon Vandenburg an innocent victim.

A light of her generation of career women, Yvonne was crushed by the glass ceiling. Glass had, indeed, eaten light.

Susan C. Gates *is an Ottawa-based writer, a recovering public servant and a reformed banker. Trading the creation of public policy for the fabrication of crime fiction has proven to be an easier transition than initially imagined. Susan emphasizes that, to the best of her knowledge, none of her family or friends in the banking industry has been convicted of embezzlement or murder. She serves on the executive of Capital Crime Writers.*

"Glass Eats Light" is a comment of Swedish glass artist Bertil Vallien and the title of a book by Gunnar Lindqvist (Carlsson Bokforlag, Stockholm, revised 1999. Translation by Angela Adegren) about the artist's life and work.

My Husband the Dead-Head

"I want to go to Woodstock,
I want to hear them play,
I want to see Jerry again
Alive as he was that day.

"I want to hear old Mikey
Beating on his drum
And 'Pig Pen' blowing on his harp,
Boy, it would really hum."

Oh you were always complaining
A never-ending reminisce,
Sitting around and moaning
About the good times that you missed.

Well, Garcia's taken the Golden Road
And his group has fallen apart
This world is no longer Truckin'
And I know how that broke your heart.

Sure it was partly all that moping
That made me bash your head
But I feel like I did you a favour
You should be Grateful you are Dead!

Joy Hewitt Mann

How to Make a Killing in Real Estate

Pat Wilson and Kris Wood

Summertime and the real estate's selling,
Suckers are buying and the prices is high…

Gavin smiled at his take on the old Gershwin standard. July was a good time for a real estate agent in Nova Scotia, especially for a young, handsome hot-shot entrepreneur who knew how to reel them in. He swung his new black Subaru Outback into the airport short-term parking lot, slotted a couple of loonies into the meter and headed for the arrivals area.

"Margo Blackthorn". The name on the curtesy card was all he knew about his prospective client, aside from the fact that she wanted a summer hideaway in Nova Scotia. Didn't they all, he thought. Baby boomers from Winnipeg to Montreal, not to mention Americans by the hundreds, thought buying a little house on the ocean would alleviate their collective mid-life crises.

Inside the terminal, Gavin positioned himself in front of the exit doors and held up the placard. The third person through the doors started towards him. A good sign. Business class always got off first. His adrenalin started pumping. He knew prime prospect material when he saw it. Italian bag and shoes, silk and cashmere pants and sweater, salon-perfect hair in an improbable shade of red, manicured nails, exquisite make-up job, Rolex watch, and a diamond ring that could buy a small country. She had to be in her early fifties, but money and willpower kept the visible advances of time at bay.

"Mrs. Blackthorn?" Gavin put a little honey into his voice and allowed his eyes to linger a touch longer than necessary on her generous cleavage. The older ladies always liked that.

She held out her hand. He shook it warmly, being careful not inflict bruises from the rock she wore.

Once they were settled into the Subaru and on their way back to Halifax, Gavin got ready to put out the bait. He had several properties in mind, each well into six figures, pulled up from the MLS listings. Now, he wondered if he should have looked at some of the seven figure properties as well. Before he could even throw his line into the water, she turned to him and began to talk.

"I know just what I want," she told him, her blue eyes glittering with excitement.

Gavin's heart dropped. Shit, he thought. He hated clients with a checklist. Made his job a lot harder.

"A little fisherman's cottage," she said. "Something small and quaint. A hideaway, really. On the ocean, of course. Very private. With wonderful views." She looked at him as if he could conjure such a thing up out of thin air right there and then.

"A fisherman's cottage," he repeated. Before he could stop himself, his mind jumped to his own private game, a game where he created truthful descriptions of the real estate he sold, rather than the flowery phrases that appeared in the listings. *Fisherman's cottage,* he thought. *Built like an upside down boat, right on the road, with sixteen sheds between the house and the water, blocking all possible views of the ocean.*

"Will you be able to find me the little hideaway that I have in mind?" Margo Blackthorn shifted in her seat so that she faced him.

"Absolutely!" Gavin said, his voice betraying none of the anxiety he felt. This wasn't going to be as easy as he'd hoped. He reached across and patted her hand. "You're in good hands with Gavin James." He noticed that she flushed as he touched her. Good sign, he thought. She's one of the hungry ones. All part of the job, and a little charm goes a long way in reeling in the big sale. Not that it ever came to anything personal. I'm too smart for that, he thought, humming under his breath.

"Summertime and the wishers are dreaming,
That the next one they look at is fine.
Facing south, looking out to the ocean..."

Margo slid her hand out from Gavin's and glanced at him from under her lashes. Early thirties, she decided. Not much more than that. Slim, but not skinny. Good suit and shoes. She always noticed shoes. Nice manners, too. Hair a little long, perhaps, but not thinning. The gold stud in his ear gave him an edge that she rather liked. In fact, she liked everything about Gavin James, if for no other reason than he represented something as different from George as day from night.

George. Florid-faced, paunch hanging out over his belt, the comb-over beginning to lose the battle with the bald spot, loud, rude and abrasive, much too rich to care about looking well-groomed or exhibiting good manners. George. Marrying him had seemed like a good idea twenty years ago when she'd been newly-divorced and looking for an easy meal-ticket. If it hadn't been for the pre-nup, he would have been history long before now.

He *should* have been history, she thought with an edge of anger. After all, he was sixteen years older than her, had a tricky heart, high blood-pressure and a penchant for fast food, cigars and single-malt whisky. By rights, he should have keeled over within the first five years of their marriage, and she should be living as the grieving, but rich, widow. That had been the plan.

Instead, he showed no sign of obliging her by dropping dead. Even with his sexual acrobatics, like the Energizer bunny —he just kept going and going and going. In the meantime, she got older and older. Opportunities were fewer and farther between. Her life was slipping away. Soon, she'd be old. Dried up. Dessicated. Even beyond hormonal replacement.

She had to make the most of the few good years she had left by snatching what little bit of pleasure she could find. Hence, Nova Scotia and Plan B.

She glanced at Gavin and licked her lips. If she needed any incentive to carry out Plan B, here he was.

Married, she wondered? No ring. But that didn't mean much these days. Look at George. One affair after the other. Not that she really cared, but it rankled that he didn't even bother to hide them.

Gavin shifted the Subaru's gears, and she noticed the long lean muscles in his thigh flex beneath the thin cloth of his summer suit. She sucked in her breath. It had been a long time since she'd felt that trickle of warmth in the middle of her stomach. Not since George had fired Bennet, her tennis coach. Typical George. Liked to play around himself, but expected her to be the faithful wife.

"Summertime, and the client is picky
Wanting something that won't pay me well…
Thinking cheap when the market is climbing
But she's a buyer and I'm just the guy who can sell."

Gavin hummed as they drove past the Ocean Vista Realty sign and bumped down a narrow, overgrown driveway.

"This is the only fisherman's cottage on the market in this area right now," he said. Out of the corner of his eye, he watched her as she took in the small, one and half story box, painted a virulent purple. Several sheds dotted the scrubby yard, two of them leaning haphazardly against each other. Three rusting vehicles graced the patch of grass in front and an old oil tank sagged against the side of the house. The front door stood several feet off the ground with no steps or porch for access.

"We have to go around to the back door if you'd like to see inside," he said.

"Where is the ocean?" Margo asked in a small voice.

"It's a 'distant view of the Atlantic'," he told her, trying to sound reassuring, while his brain played the game. *Distant view of the Atlantic: if you're in the bathroom, standing on the toilet seat, in the winter, at sunset.*

"Oh." She made no move to get out of the Subaru.

"Generally speaking, fishermen don't care to look at the ocean. Having spent all day battling the waves, they want to come home and look at something more relaxing, like traffic on the road in front," Gavin explained.

They sat for a moment. Only the shrill cries of the seagulls foraging in one of the large garbage bins on the edge of the driveway broke the silence.

"If you'll forgive me for making a personal comment," Gavin began, slipping his hand on hers again. "I really don't think this is for you. I see you in something a little more prestigious, more in keeping with your style. Say, something like a 'sea captain's house'." *Sea captain's house: same as fisherman's cottage, but bigger and usually over-priced.*

Summertime and the agent is handsome
Young and good-looking and ready to play...

This time, Margo didn't pull her hand away. Instead, she sat back and contemplated Gavin's suggestion. A "sea captain's house." It had a romantic ring. Gingerbread trim, arbours, ocean vistas from the gazebo, a boat moored at the bottom of sloping lawns. Spacious rooms, high ceilings, multi-paned windows, wood wainscotting and that wonderful air of Victorian elegance. Yes, she could see herself there. Pouring champagne for Gavin. In the drawing room. Just the two of them. In front of the fire. Alone.

She felt the heat again, only this time it began at her head, prickling its way down her body, leaving her limp and perspiring. She pulled out a tissue and dabbed her cleavage.

"A sea captain's house." She liked the sound of it. So much better than her original idea of a quaint little fisherman's cottage by the sea. After all, size didn't really matter, at least not in *this* instance. She smirked. Whether George set off for his final earthly journey from a fisherman's jetty or a sea captain's wharf made little difference. The same cold, bone-chilling, heart-stopping Atlantic waters washed against them both.

She turned to Gavin and laid her other hand over his. "I'm putting myself entirely into your hands," she said. "You seem to know me so well."

Summertime, commissions are hefty
Clients buying though it takes so much time
Holding hands and pretending to like it
I do what I must as long as the money is mine.

A week later, Gavin began to feel desperation creep over

94

him like mould on a bathroom wall. Would she ever make a decision?

One day, she had to have "access to the beach". *Sixty homeowners have a narrow right of way to a fifty foot stretch of communal sand*

The next day, she wanted a private beach. Any kind of beach, she said. "Shingle" beach is fine. *Small rocks.* Or even a "bold" beach. *Big rocks.* But not an "active" beach. *Appears and disappears at the whim of various storms and tides.*

It must have a wharf, she told him. *Any structure, any size that goes out any distance into the water.* And a boathouse. *A garage built too near an active beach.*

She didn't mind a house that needed some work. One of the ones that advertised itself as being in need of a little "TLC". *Bottom line: cheaper to pull down and build a new house.*

She kept talking about a "hideaway." Twenty miles down a dirt road. Something "quaint." Pokey and inconvenient. "Surrounded by trees." Impenetrable forest all around.

During all of this, Gavin had to bear with her far-from-subtle advances. She insisted upon a succession of cosy lunches and intimate dinners that slowed down their progress. He dreaded the long drives from property to property. Her knee became permanently velcroed to his, her cloying perfume filled the small confines of the Subaru, and to his horror, her hand often insinuated itself onto his thigh, where, at the most inopportune moments, it would stray upwards.

So far he'd managed to get her back to her hotel and into her room without compromising himself any further. However, he had no illusions. She had every intention of luring him into her bed. He broke out in a cold sweat at the thought.

Towards the end of the week, he began to suspect that she saw the two of them in a continuing relationship. In a desperate bid to remind her of her married state, Gavin brought up the absent Mr. Blackthorn.

"What kind of home is your husband looking for?" he asked her, edging his leg away from hers yet again.

"He doesn't care. I doubt he'll come here very often." She gave him a hot glance. "He won't be any bother to us. Don't worry."

Gavin's heart sank.

"Won't be here often?"

"No. He's too busy with his affairs in Toronto." Her hand stroked his thigh.

Gavin caught the slight emphasis on the word "affairs" and knew he wouldn't be rescued by the arrival of a jealous husband.

"So you'll be alone most of the time?"

She took that as an invitation. "Yes," she purred. "Unless of course, I have company." Her hand tightened on his knee.

"I'm surprised you'd want an out-of-the-way property then," Gavin continued, trying to sound brisk and businesslike. "Wouldn't you be happier with a property in town? Neighbours nearby? Close to shopping? I have a few very nice heritage homes on my list." *Heritage home: usually in a town, must conform to the Historical Society guidelines for buildings in the area. Don't plan to put on new aluminum siding.*

"No," she snapped. "Nothing with neighbours close by. I want privacy at all costs." She settled back in the seat and sucked in her mouth. "I hate busybodies watching every move I make."

Finally, they found a property that suited her: an isolated older home, perched at the end of a rocky peninsula. Gavin smiled as she ooohed and ahhhed over the "hand-hewn beams". *Uncle Pete built it.* She liked the fact that it had many "recent upgrades". *Uncle Pete fixed it up.* That the wainscotting was "original woodwork". *Great Uncle Pete built it.* And that most of the rooms had been "fully restored" to their original Victorian splendour. *Oncle Pierre fixed it up.* She loved the idea that it was "over a century old". *So old we can't remember who built it or fixed it up.*

Things looked good. Gavin knew all the signs. Her flushed face, little coos of delight and constant chatter of where the dining room set would go, plus numerous ideas for new wallpaper and paint made her interest plain. She talked about the colour of the drapes she'd have in the living room and how cosy the fireplace would be on a cool evening.

However, more than one fish had come this close to being landed then had slipped away at the last moment. The time had come to set the hook and reel her in.

"Wait until you see the widow's walk," Gavin told her. "It's phenomenal. You can see for miles from it."

"What's a 'widow's walk'?" she asked.

Suicidal deck. "It's a sort of platform on the very top of the house where the sea captain's wife used to go to watch for her husband's ship to come into the harbour."

"How romantic!" she trilled. "I can't wait to see it. How do we get there?"

"There are stairs out of the attic. Follow me. We'll have to be careful when we go outside. The railing still needs a little work."

Gavin began the long climb, all too aware of Margo panting behind him. They emerged onto a weather-beaten ten-by-ten asphalted platform, surrounded by an intricate but peeling wrought-iron railing. The wind buffeted them, cold and chilling off the water. Gavin shivered. The roofs slid precipitously away on every side, ending at a three-storey plunge to the ground. On one side, the drop continued to a rocky beach far below, now exposed at low tide.

He hated heights. What he did for his clients. He comforted himself with the thought of the fifty-thousand dollar commission. He figured he'd earned every penny of this one.

Margo's lack of fear surprised him. She did a quick circuit of the widow's walk. Her eyes narrowed as she glanced down over the edge of the railing. A look of calculation crossed her face.

"I'll take it," she said. Her voice hardened. "It's perfect."

Summertime and the searchin' is over
Found a dream home and a dream of a guy
Got them both for the price of a condo...
Gonna have fun under the Maritime sky.

"Widow's walk". How apt. Humming under her breath, Margo turned, pretending to admire the breathtaking views. She ran her fingers along the crumbling railing. Perfect. She'd bring George up to see the view. A little shove in the right direction at low tide, and her troubles would be over.

She looked at Gavin standing beside her. There would be no need for him to restrain himself any longer. So often during the week, she'd been aware of his drawing back from her. He's such a gentleman, she'd thought, as she longed to tell him that his scruples were unnecessary. Only the thought of the time that stretched before them once George was out of the way had kept her from taking the initiative. For now, it took every ounce of restraint she could muster to keep her hands off him.

She knew that the strong physical attraction was mutual. Everything he'd done had encouraged her to expect so much more. His warm glances, his silky voice, his lingering touch, his constant attendance to her every need. Such a far cry from George's continuing indifference.

She couldn't wait any longer to tell him how she felt.

"Darling Gavin," she began, pressing a hand against his chest, where she could feel the strong beat of his heart, which quickened under her touch.

Out of the corner of her eye, she saw a small red car careen up the driveway and screech to a halt in front of the house, spewing up clouds of dust and gravel.

The man who flung open the car door wore bright yellow pants topped with a pink and orange striped T-shirt which vied for attention with his magenta hair. He stood with his hands on his hips, his head flung back, and bellowed, "Gavin, darling, you've done it again!"

Margo felt Gavin suck in his breath. "Bruce!" he croaked. "What are you doing here?"

"You old silly. How many times do I have to come tearing after you because you don't pick up after yourself?" The man pulled something from his pocket and waved it at Gavin. "You haven't even missed it, have you? I found it on the dresser this morning. What am I going to do with you?"

"What?" said Gavin in a strangled voice.

"It's your wallet, silly. I'll bring it up to you. There must be a divine view from up there." The man disappeared into the house.

Margo felt the anger leap through her body, followed by a wash of heat like molten lava that poured from her head and left her dripping with sweat. Gavin had played her for a fool.

"You bastard!" she hissed and pushed hard against his chest, putting all the frustration, fury and anger of the past twenty years into the shove.

He stumbled back several steps, hitting the railing hard. It crumbled behind him, and he went over the side like a child's slinky toy, end over end, rolling with satisfying speed down the roof, then dropping onto the bare rocks below. Just as she'd expected, it worked perfectly.

Such a shame she'd wasted this particular opportunity. Now, she'd have to see what Prince Edward Island had to offer in old homes with widow's walks. She opened her mouth for a suitably horrified scream.

Summertime, and the game is all over
Lost the deal, lost the client and all...

In his last split-second of awareness, just before his body began the long drop, which he'd advertised as "sloping to the beach", Gavin played his game for the last time.
Sloping to the beach: a high cliff.

Pat and Kris *have been friends and co-writers for over thirty years. As well as being regular contributors to the Ladies' Killing Circle anthologies, they are also known for their humorous looks at life in the Maritimes. The "definitions" in this story come from their latest book,* Extreme Sports of the Maritimes: Lobster Suppers, Fire Hall Bingos, Flea Markets and All the Rest.

A Little Bit Easy

Therese Greenwood

L ally Thibodeaux didn't seem the kind of girl people shot at. Oh, she was different, I'll give you that, but she was a pretty, well-mannered little thing. I took to her the minute she stopped in about renting the old place on the point.

I always thought the point was the nicest spot on Wolfe Island, maybe the nicest in the Thousand Islands, with the old frame homestead on the hill about thirty feet from the St. Lawrence River. Grandpa Allen had built it before they dug the well; back then they hauled water up the riverbank. You can see clear down the channel from the kitchen window, watch the lakers steam up and down, and there's a fine stand of birch over on the American shore. There's a nice pasture out back, too, ten acres you could hay as long as you keep an eye out and don't let the tractor wheels get too close to the river bank. It's pretty, gone to clover and wild carrot and mustard flowers. I wouldn't mind looking out at it every morning, but the wife says I'm too sentimental. She likes the bungalow we built out near the road after our girls left home. But I liked the idea of renting out the old house. Someone ought to live there, although I wasn't sure Lally knew what she was getting herself into.

She was just a slip of a thing. I could barely see her behind the steering wheel of her big red truck the first time she stopped on our road. She hopped down to the ground, tumbling out like the last peanut in the bag and pointing her little black remote control, click-click, to lock up her truck tighter than a drum, even though the wife and I were the only people for miles.

"We aren't much for locking vehicles here," I said.

"I find you can't be too careful," Lally said. She had a funny drawl, slow and twangy, and looked about the age of our youngest, in her middle twenties. Her sweet face had a tad too much make-up, but she wore clean clothes, not like some of those young people with ripped jeans and dirty shoes. She had on a nice blouse and pressed shorts like the women in banks wear, and her nails were a rosy pink. I noticed her hands because she was holding the For Rent notice we had put up at Mosier's store in early spring. Since it was into June, and she was the first person to ask, we'd likely rent it to her. But for the life of me, I couldn't figure out why she'd want to live out there all by herself.

"Are you sure it won't get too lonely for you?" I asked.

"Potable water in-house, clear view for a thousand yards, slight incline to slow invaders, and limited access points to the island," she said. "It's the perfect defensive position."

"Planning a party?" I asked.

"Not if I can help it," she said with a smile. I could tell I tickled her, and I like tickling a pretty girl, so I laid the yokel thing on thick.

"We had a family reunion out there on the long weekend last August," I said, hooking my thumbs in my suspenders. "People who were supposed to stay Saturday night were still staggering around on Labour Day. But you can't pick your family, can you?"

"No sir, you can't," she said, not smiling any more, her drawl so strong you could hardly make her out.

"That's quite an accent you got," I said. "Where you from?"

"South," she said.

"A Yankee?" I nodded across the shore at the top of New York state. They call it The North Country, but it's south of me.

Lally smiled again, like I was a real comedian. "In New Orleans, we'd call you a Yankee for living north of the Mason-Dixon."

"Most people call me a Canuck for living north of everything Yankee," I said. "But you can call me Jim. You sure are a long way from home."

"As far as I can get, Jim."

I fished around, but I couldn't get any more information out of her. Lally always was tight-lipped. That's another reason I was surprised when those bullets tore the place up. I couldn't believe she'd open her mouth long enough to make anyone want to shoot her, let alone cut loose with a machine gun. We're still picking bullets out of the old kitchen. I found one yesterday in the old radio next to Grandma Allen's wooden rocking chair.

You never would have guessed Lally would be mixed up in that kind of a hullabaloo. After she got settled in, I dropped by a couple times to make sure she wasn't finding it too lonely, and she always kept everything clean as a whistle, even the wife said so. You could've eaten off the floors, and Lally gave the old place some touches of her own, although they weren't what I would call girly. First thing she did was put her shotgun on the rack on the kitchen wall. You're supposed to lock away your firepower these days, but that rack has been up there since Grandpa Allen shot his first mallard and, anyway, it wasn't like anyone would be around to check.

Lally kept a few more of her treasures on a corner table in the kitchen along with a bunch of wildflowers she picked fresh every day. There was a picture of a small, determined-looking woman squinting into the sun on a cement stoop, gripping a clutch purse in a hand that looked too big for the rest of her. Next to the photo was a black candle in a fancy ivory holder and a crazy statue of a skeleton in a suit. I figured it was left over from a childhood Halloween, and Lally put it out as a joke because we were just getting to summer.

"That must be a photo of your mother," I said one afternoon as I dropped off another of the wife's rhubarb pies. "There's quite the resemblance around the eyes. But she's even tinier than you. Looks like she couldn't hurt a fly."

Lally laughed. "Tell that to the crack dealers who moved next door to her. They never knew what hit them when Mama Marie put the mojo on them."

"Crack dealers, that sounds like a bad neighborhood," I said. "Your mother ought to move."

"She doesn't live there any more," said Lally, her laugh gone. "Mama Marie's passed over."

"You're young to have lost your mother," I said, thinking of our girls.

"I didn't lose her," said Lally, taking a sulphur match and lighting the black candle by the photo. "Someone took her. Shall I cut you a slice of your wife's fine pie?"

And that was all she said. She wasn't one for spilling the beans, but otherwise she was a good tenant. She was determined to bring the place up to speed, with two hundred amp service and a backup generator to boot. She even put in those big halogen lights to show off the place. Too bad she picked the ones with motion sensors, the raccoons tripped them all night. I didn't say anything at the time, though. I figured when she got done, the old place would be better wired than the Memorial Centre in town, and it wouldn't have cost me a cent.

She got in her own electrician, and that's when Gord McKillop met her. We thought Gord was a confirmed bachelor. He was a nice-looking lad, tall and strong as an ox, with a good job. One of the Huff girls set her cap at him for a spell, but he never took the bait. We thought maybe girls weren't his cup of tea, if you catch my drift. But Gord took one look at Lally and fell like a ton of bricks. He'd find excuses to come by, little things he'd fix for her. Sometimes he'd get a job half-done and realize he needed a doo-dad he had to go all the way to town for, just for an excuse to come back the next day.

It was Gord who found the first voodoo charm. Lally and I were watching him set up an automatic skeet-shooting thing out in the pasture when he found a heart-shaped rock, polished smooth. It looked like the letter "L" had been carved into it.

"Fancy that," I said. "Nature sending you a valentine."

"It's not natural, Jim," said Lally, looking across the field, squinting so her pretty face twisted up like a monkey's. "Supernatural."

"Pardon me?" Gord and I said together. Sometimes we didn't quite follow her accent.

"It's a vengeance mojo," she said. "My mother was a Creole. She practised voodoo."

"We're United Church," I said.

"I'm a Presbyterian," said Gord. "I saw a movie about voodoo. This corpse got up and did the limbo. It was pretty funny."

"Nothing funny about it," Lally said. "Someone put that mojo there."

Gord and I tried to tell her that a person could find all kinds of comical-looking rocks in these fields, dumped off the glaciers a million years ago. But she wouldn't hear any of it.

"Vengeance was Mama Marie's speciality," she said. "People hired her to get back at folks who wronged 'em. She'd hex a husband who laid one beating too many on his wife, or a gang-banger who shot a nine-year-old in a drive-by, or even on the butcher for keeping his thumb on the scale."

"That's one heck of a town you're from," I said. "Don't people there ever call the law?"

"In New Orleans?" Lally laughed, but it wasn't the pretty girl laugh Gord and I liked. "The police down there aren't in the justice business, Jim. They're in business for themselves. They don't call it The Big Easy for nothing."

"I saw that movie," Gord said.

Lally sighed and wouldn't say any more, but she was wired for sound. When Gord finished hooking up the skeet thing, she got out her shotgun and went at the targets like nobody's business. She used her little black remote control—it amazes me how you can set almost anything to remote these days—to launch ten targets, and she hit every single one. I never saw anything like it.

"Where did you learn to shoot like that?" I said.

"Daddy was a Recon Marine." Click-click. BAM! Another target took to the air and was blown to smithereens. "Vietnam. Every marine a rifleman." Click-click. BAM! "Didn't you pass anything on to your girls, Jim?" Click-click. BAM!

"Are you kidding?" said Gord with a grin. "You should've seen those girls on a tractor. You never saw anybody plough so straight."

"I don't like to brag," I said. "But Laura, our youngest, was Queen of the Furrow at the ploughing match three years running."

"You taught your girls to grow food to make people big and strong," Lally said. "My daddy taught me to kill people with advance reconnaissance and the element of surprise." Click-click. BAM!

I guess I shouldn't have bragged.

Lally shot and shot that day, and all night with the big lights on. You aren't supposed to shoot at night, but on the island there's no police to stop you. We're too small for our own force, and it takes a big deal to get the provincial police over from town. In fact, the last time I saw them was when the place on the point got shot-up. They didn't do a hell of a lot then. I suppose we're better off without them. Maybe we are a little bit like New Orleans. Maybe you could call us "a little bit easy".

We didn't see much of Lally for a while. She kept herself busy, clearing brush near the house, white-washing the picket fence and honing the points on the stakes so they looked tidy. I thought she went a bit far putting up the electric fence along the waterfront. It didn't do anything for the view. She practiced her shooting, too, until she burned out the target-shooting thing. I watched her kick it one day and haul it into the house. Since I don't go duck hunting any more, I got to use the binoculars for something.

I kept an eye on the mailbox, too. She didn't get much mail, just the Hydro bill and a magazine called *Soldier Of Fortune*. The wife thought maybe it was about how to win the lottery. When both came in at end of the month, Lally saw the flag up on the box and roared out in her big truck. She hopped out and click-clicked the door shut while I hustled over, and I was just hitching my thumbs into my suspenders when I saw the chicken bones at the foot of the rusty milk can holding up the mailbox.

"Damn cats," I said, reaching down to pick up the bones, which had been picked clean.

"Wait," Lally said, squatting down on her little ankles as easy as you please. She picked up a twig and poked a bone.

"Worried about rabies?" I said. "We don't get much of a scare, this being an island. We're isolated that way."

"It's a message," Lally said.

"A message I ought to get out the .22 for those cats."

"It's for me," she said. "He's coming."

"Who?"

That's when Gord McKillop rolled up in that disaster area he calls a van, but I didn't figure she was talking about him.

"I'm worried about you spending too much time out here alone," he said to Lally through the van window. "You deserve some fun. Why don't we go over to town for dinner and a movie? There's a pretty good show at the Odeon that would cheer you up."

I liked the way Gord pretended to be doing her a favour, but he should have had the sense to turn the engine off and maybe even get out of the van. No wonder he was still a bachelor.

"I'm not up for town," Lally said.

That's when the wife came out with a plate of her butter rolls and homemade strawberry jam. The mailbox was a regular Grand Central Station that morning.

"Darn cats," the wife said. She handed Lally the plate and squatted to pick up the bones. Lally started forward, but the wife said, "Tut, tut." When the wife tut-tuts, you stop in your tracks.

"Lally Thibodeaux, don't you dare say you can't take those rolls," she said, picking up bones and handing them to me. "This isn't the big city, we do things different here. We don't lock our vehicles, we don't put hexes on our neighbors, and if those neighbors give us homemade rolls, we take 'em and like 'em."

"Homemade jam, too," said Gord, eyeing the plate. "You don't see that every day."

"Lally, it wouldn't hurt you to get out a bit more." I put in my two cents, because I was starting to wonder at the voodoo talk. It didn't seem normal. "Excuse me for saying it, but you tend to mope. A pretty girl like you ought to be out having a high old time."

For a minute, Lally just stood there looking at us like we had two heads each. "Are you people for real?" she finally said.

"Beg your pardon?" we said together.

"What's with the baking and the jam and the worrying and the advice? Why do you care?"

"Don't be silly," the wife said, handing me the last of the bones. "Why wouldn't we?"

Lally looked at us, at the plate in her hands, then tilted her head for a better look at Gord. "You people slay me," she said. Then she smiled her pretty smile and said, "I guess I could use some civilized company. Dinner tonight. I'll cook."

Bingo! Gord was thinking. Then Lally said, "Jim and Missus Jim, y'all come, too. I'll make you a real Creole dinner."

"Good enough," says I, putting the bones in my pocket. "With four, we can get up a game of euchre. We aren't The Big Easy, but we know how to have a little fun."

"Euchre," muttered Gord. "Hmmm. Maybe I'll come by early, finish setting up that generator for you, Lal."

"Why not?" she said cheerfully. "You could look at my skeet machine, too. The launch mechanism is off by ten centimetres."

"I've been thinking about getting a generator," I said. "We lost power for a week in last winter's blizzard."

"I don't know why anyone with a woodstove needs a generator," said the wife, and I knew I wouldn't be getting one any time soon. "We'll see you two tonight."

I hardly recognized Gord when we got to the point that evening. He had on a clean shirt and a tie, and his hair was wet. He had an awful big grin, too.

"Got a little dirty working on the skeet launcher," he said. "Lally let me take a shower and change before dinner."

"Nice of her," the wife said.

I noticed the skeet launcher on the floor by Lally's side

table. There was a screwdriver still in the barrel, like Gord had left off fixing it in a big hurry. It looked spotless to me, like all of Lally's things, not a speck of dirt or oil.

"I didn't quite get it the way I like it," Gord said, then blushed. "The mechanism, I mean. Might have to come back tomorrow with a little doo-dad to get her up and running proper."

"You don't say," said the wife.

Lally looked extra pretty. Her nails were a bright red, and her blonde hair curled within an inch of its life. She was dressed to the nines in a snazzy yellow suit that reminded me of Jackie Kennedy. Gord thought the getup was for him, but I got the feeling she just liked to dress up. It was the first time I saw her having fun.

Dinner was different, all right. Spicy like you wouldn't believe. She even put spice in the rice, and a bottle of hot sauce on the table. Lally ate it down like it was ice cream. Gord made a go at it.

"What is this called?" he said, chewing slowly.

"Jambalaya."

"Crawfish pie and a filet gumbo," I sang. "'Cause tonight I'm gonna see my ma cher amio."

Lally smiled again, and the wife smiled, too. "You old flirt," she whispered. "Give Gord a fighting chance."

We were a friendly party, four people sitting around the old pine table finishing dessert—the wife's butter tarts, best on the island—and talking about the weather and the garden and the neighbors. We were just getting up a game of cards, me explaining trump to Lally, when the power cut out. The only light in the room came from the black candle in the corner. I hadn't even realized it was lit.

"No problem," said Gord, his face spooky in the candle's flicker. "The generator will kick on in about ten seconds."

Lally jumped up and grabbed her truck keys from the ring on the wall, tossing them on the table where the rest of us sat in the candlelight. I figured she was telling Gord to take a ride for his half-assed wiring, and I guess he did, too.

"Missing that doo-dad," Gord mumbled. "To get the generator going."

"Un-huh," said the wife.

"Hush," Lally hissed. "He's right outside."

That was when the kitchen door flung open, and a flashlight cut the darkness, shining into our eyes. I squinted at the silhouette of an army man, with an army hat and army boots and a big army gun.

"Your perimeter fortifications are pathetic," said a voice with an accent like Lally's.

"I let my defences down," said Lally. She stood like a gunfighter, back straight, hands at her sides, fingers bent.

"You three at the table, let me see your hands," the man said. We laid our cards face up on the table and fanned them out. Hearts were trump, and I noticed Gord had the left bower. It's funny what sticks in your mind.

"Not the cards, you idiots." The man swore. "Put your palms on the table."

We put our hands on top of the cards and looked into the flashlight.

"They're civilians," said Lally.

"They're collateral damage," said the man. "I didn't come all this way to neutralize one witness, just to leave three more."

"There's no need to neutralize anybody," Lally said. "If I was planning to testify, I'd have stayed in New Orleans. There isn't a *REMOTE* chance you'd get the needle now. Not the *REMOTEST*."

The wife and I didn't look at Lally's remote lying on the

table. We looked at Gord, hoping he wasn't giving anything away. He wasn't. Good old Gord was staring at Lally, his mouth wide open.

"This is your fault, Lally," said the army man. "Why'd you run to the police?" He said po-lice, like in one of Gord's movies.

"She was my mama," Lally said, "and you killed her dead, Daddy."

"Now Lally, you know the way things go." The man's voice was soft, the same voice I used to tell my girls the rabbits chewed up the pumpkin vine, and we'd have to buy a jack-o'-lantern from the store. "Your mama had no business putting the voodoo on me. Psychological advantage is the principal weapon in a soldier's arsenal. I had to eliminate her."

"You beat her for twenty-five years." Lally's voice was as bitter as his was soft. "One day you killed her. You lost *CONTROL*."

That was when I lost control, too. I must have been crazy, carrying on like some hero instead of a retired dairy farmer from a little island. But I was mad as spit at this fellow who took other men's wars out on his wife and his little girl, and I heard my voice say. "You ought to be ashamed of yourself, mister."

"Ashamed of myself?" he said, and I never heard a man so astonished in my life. "I'm a decorated war veteran. I served my country with distinction."

"Tell it to the Marines," I said.

"Now you are both out of *CONTROL!*" Lally said. "Now. *NOW!*"

The army man was turning the gun towards me, and I guess that should have been it, but the wife hit the remote control with her little finger. Click-click.

I've heard people say, "All hell broke loose," but I never realized what they meant until that night. The skeet machine launched out the screwdriver end over end. I expect Lally meant it to be a diversion, but I must live right because the point hit the army man right in the eye. He screamed, and the old kitchen lit up like the fourth of July, sparking and popping and smoking, the machine gun bursting with bullets that flashed along the old tin ceiling. Lally kicked over the table, leaving the three of us behind it. I was glad I never bought that dainty, spindly-legged item the wife wanted from the furniture store in town. The thick old pine stopped bullets, or at least slowed them down, although the wife got hit in the leg and was bleeding like crazy. It was her scream that made Gord jump up to go for the gun. He took one in the shoulder and fell back down. He needn't have bothered, because Lally pulled her shotgun off the rack and blasted both barrels smack into the army man's head.

"So much for the element of surprise, Daddy," she said.

The man looked dead to me, but Lally wasn't taking chances. She kicked away his gun and frisked his body, pulling out handguns and knives and crazy-looking weapons I didn't recognize. Then she used my suspenders to throw a tourniquet around the wife's leg, pressed a tea towel on Gord's shoulder and called the ambulance.

"She should have told us," I said to the wife as her blood soaked through my fingers. "We could have helped her hide better."

"You old fool," the wife said through gritted teeth. "She wasn't hiding from him. She was waiting for him."

Then I saw how Lally made her stand. She hadn't lit the black candle to keep that bad man away. She wanted to draw him to her. She hadn't made the old place a fortress, it was a giant booby trap, and she waited in it like the last sentinel, ready to use anything or anyone at hand when the final assault came. She had taken her old man's lesson about the element of surprise to heart, and she did him proud.

I still think we could have swept it under the rug, most of it anyway, but Lally wouldn't take the chance. She waited until the paramedics loaded up Gord and the wife, and I drove off with them for the ferry and the hospital in town. The island has its own ambulance, always ready to go for heart attacks and farm accidents and allergic reactions to peanuts. But the police have to come all the way from town, and Lally took off before they got there. I guess she slipped away in whatever boat her father used to sneak onto the shore. But what do I know? I certainly couldn't tell the police anything helpful. I'm just a dumb yokel, overwhelmed by shocking events.

The wife is enjoying her stay in hospital. No one on the island ever got shot before, not on purpose anyway. She's a celebrity, had her picture on the front page of the newspaper, and you wouldn't believe the people stopping by. This afternoon Gord was in, his arm done up in a sling, and he gave me a ride home after visiting hours. On his dashboard he had a heart-shaped rock with an "L" carved on it. Gord doesn't believe in voodoo charms, but I guess he figures what the hell, maybe it will draw her back. Good luck to him, I say. I wish it was that easy.

Kingston, Ontario, writer **Therese Greenwood** *grew up on Wolfe Island, the largest of the Thousand Islands, where her family has lived since 1812. The region forms the backdrop for her historical crime fiction. She has twice been a finalist for the Arthur Ellis Award for Best Short Story. She is co-founder of the annual Wolfe Island Scene of the Crime Festival, online at www.sceneofthecrime.ca.*

A Graceful Retirement

Cecilia Kennedy

On her first morning of freedom, Margaret woke at dawn, brewed a pot of coffee and, still in her nightgown, sat with a mug on the back porch step. Surveying the garden, she thought, this is where I'll spend my time, then decided that the purple-blue delphiniums needed moving back behind the primroses. This is what she'd do. Every morning she'd sit on the step, breathing the mixed odours of coffee, damp earth and flowers, planning her next bit of nipping and pruning, trimming and moving, and when winter came she'd take a nice trip to England or France. Or maybe Italy.

Not behind the primroses.

The hectoring words arrived on a light breeze. Margaret shivered into her flannel sleeves, wondering how long it had been since she'd last heard the deep rasp of her husband's voice, the nagging, the constant correction and fault finding. And why should it come back today of all days, the first day of deserved happiness? It had been a long haul since Des had died of a heart attack at forty-one, leaving her with three young children and no profession. But she'd managed. Got herself through university with the insurance money, taught school for twenty-five years, put her boys through school and even managed to save a bit on the side so that when this day came she'd have the chance to sit on a porch step feeling contented. Happy.

"Happy," she said to the breeze. "Go away. I'll be happy if I like."

She had a house, books to read, and a garden. What more could she want? Des had planted that birch tree the day before he died, and now it danced silvery green in the morning sun, but he hadn't lasted the way a tree lasts. He'd been like the day lilies along the north fence, in flower for a day, then gone. And thank heavens for that.

Later, on the first morning of her retirement, Margaret set out for a brisk one hour walk. She'd promised herself to stay fit. Trekking downtown to pick up the newspaper everyday instead of having it delivered; that was part of the plan.

The walking felt good. No knee problems like so many of her friends. Her legs swung in an easy rhythm, and her mind ran free. Margaret's mind, she knew, had always been a disorganized place in which thoughts that managed to reach a logical conclusion always followed the most circuitous route to get there. As Des had been quick to point out.

"You've got a mind like a gerbil cage," he'd say. "Head like a rat's nest. Where common sense goes to die."

"Shut up," she told the memory. How she thought or let her mind wander was her own business now. Just like that novel she'd started reading last night. It didn't matter if she finished it. Cheap beginning, insulting really, starting with the body laid out on page one. A big ugly hook meant to fish you like a pike, but once you got past that vulgarity you kept reading, partly because choosing another book meant climbing out of bed. Besides, by then the curious character with red hair, freckled hands and the Italian name had claimed the attention.

Just like Pat DiAngelo, from the second year of night

classes after Des died. Pat DiAngelo (really Pasquale) had freckled hands. A jazz fan. They'd had coffee together a few times, but he was married, and that was that.

At the bank corner, she waited for the light to change and wondered how her mind had led her there. It was years and years since she'd thought about Pat DiAngelo. Decades.

The mind is a strange thing. Holds all sorts of bits and shreds, like a kid's pillowcase at Halloween, reach your hand in and you never know what you'll grab. Might be yesterday. Might be Pat DiAngelo.

The light changed. Should she stop at the Muffin Man? No, best to start with good habits. Get the newspaper, straight home, move those delphiniums. Behind the primroses.

*　　*　　*

When Margaret's son Peter came the next day to take her out for a celebration lunch, she walked him first around the garden.

"Those are better in the back." he agreed, looking at the tall blue purple stalks. Then he bore her away for Coquille St. Jacques at the Café de Paris, where he presented her with a gift in honour of her retirement, tickets for France. "From all of us." he said. "It was Mike's idea. John's made the hotel reservations too. They wanted to be here, but..."

"Too far. I know," she said, smiling at him across the red-checked tablecloth and white carnations. How she loved her boys. What a hardship it had been when the "don't touch" phase had arrived, and she had to keep her hands from stroking their long arms or resting on the warm and vulnerable back of a grimy neck.

"How did I get to be so lucky?" she asked.

It was a line she'd repeated all their growing years. "How did I ever get to be so lucky?"

The boys had always blushed and skipped the conversation ahead two tracks. Just as Peter now filled her wine glass and changed the topic.

"You're looking great," he said, frowning at her over his lifted glass.

"What makes you so serious?" she teased.

"Nothing. It's just, all that heavy gardening...you're not doing too much?"

"Goodness, no."

"But you're retired now. You should take it easy. Don't overdo it."

She looked him over critically. He was getting a settled middle-aged look, even a few wrinkles, but surely that anxious frown wasn't a permanent fixture. "What's gotten into you?"

He shrugged. "It's just these stories you read. Retire one day, heart attack, cancer, the next. I don't want you keeling over into the roses. After everything you've done for us, you deserve some time to enjoy life."

She laughed. "It's men that happens to. They don't know how to slow down. Anyway, I wouldn't pick the roses for my death dive. I'd have scratches all over my face for the viewing."

Her son refused to find that funny. "The guy I'm thinking of, Pat DiAngelo in human resources, he was like that. Just go, go, go. Always pushing."

How interesting, to have Pat mentioned like this, when she'd thought of him just yesterday. She said, "I went to night school with Pat. Greek philosophy of all things. Is Pat retired then?"

Peter shook his head. "That's just it. He didn't make it. Three months to go, and he died in his sleep last night. Family called the office this morning."

"That's terrible," Margaret said, feeling a pang for the memory of those hands across a table and the wish she'd once felt to be held by them. "Proves my point though, doesn't it? Men don't know how to retire gracefully."

"Maybe you're right." Her son made an effort to look more cheerful. "Maybe I'll watch how you do it and take notes. Write up a guide for the newly retired: *Chicken Soup for the Retiring Soul.*"

"Oddly enough, I thought of Pat DiAngelo yesterday for the first time in years, and now you tell me he died last night. There's a coincidence for you."

"Weird." Peter swallowed the last creamy scallop and signalled the waiter they were ready for dessert.

Later, still in her going-out-for-lunch dress, Margaret stopped at the garden centre for some bone meal and an extra bag of peat moss. While she wandered among the tempting flats of annuals and out into the rows of trees and shrubs, she thought how fragile it all was. She could be dead, like Pat DiAngelo. Instead, she was here, wondering if a pink Martin Frobisher were the best climbing rose for the back of the white garage. It could easily have been an affair with Pat, and how often she'd wondered if she'd made the right choice. And how strange that she'd think of him the day before he died.

Yet, on the whole, she found that comforting. Maybe we're all more connected than we know, she thought. Maybe Jung was right, and there's an unconscious we share, and maybe Pat was thinking of me for the first time in years, and maybe the energy of two people thinking of each other at the same time connects and creates its own energy. Maybe I'll get one or two of these Saskatoon bushes to make the birds happy.

Two shrubs, a flat of impatiens and four new shades of day lily later, the clerk sent a boy out to load her purchases while Margaret watched, most of her mind dwelling on whether or not a hanging basket of trailing lobelia would work with the blue siding of the porch. It wasn't until she tipped the boy that she really looked at him.

"Thompson?" The ground seemed to tremble slightly under her white pumps. He had the dark seal-like hair, the black eyebrows, the face that made the girls glance sideways at him when they should have been studying the notes for *Twelfth Night*. But shouldn't he be older? Thompson McBride, the terror and bane of her first teaching season, had to be in his forties. Disconcerted, she pressed the coins into the boy's hand.

"Thanks." He grinned and said, "He's my uncle."

"Pardon me?"

"Thompson's my uncle."

"Ah. Well. Thank you then."

Really, she scolded herself as she pulled out onto the road and turned toward home. The boy'll think you're doddering, mistaking him for an uncle he probably considers as ancient as you. Then a smile played across her face. Did that boy have the joker-is-wild personality to match the looks? Her first class of Grade Nines, and the Superintendent had showed up for her first inspection, and there was Thompson's group standing on top of the desks performing a scene from *The Chrysalids*. Thompson McBride and a "streaker costume" at the Halloween dance. The appendix he'd added to his Shakespeare essay, recommending various improvements to her wardrobe.

Where in life would a boy like Thompson end up?

Two mornings later, Margaret walked downtown for her newspaper, succumbed to temptation and the Muffin Man, and read that Dr. Thompson McBride had died in a fiery four car pile-up on the Burlington Skyway. On his way to work the night shift at the hospital emergency. Instead, an ambulance had brought his body in. Cause of the accident unclear. Police still investigating. Call for witnesses.

It's enough to make you stop reading the news, she thought, splashing coffee as she looked away from the wretched newspaper. And she'd been thinking of him just a day or two ago.

Only this time, she took no comfort from it. What was the point of thought and remembering if they only brought you pain? Perhaps he thought of me, and therefore I thought of him, and I do hope his thoughts were kind, but I'll pass on such connections in the future, she told the cosmos. *Maybe there's no pass,* the carping voice whispered in her ear, *No free ride on the cosmic railroad...*

She shivered, in spite of the warm coffee and the cheerful clatter of cups in the Muffin Man.

"Stop it!" she told herself firmly. She was acting just like that silly cousin of Desmond's. Rose-Ann, that was her name. Believed in all kinds of nonsense, meditation, crystals; set up shop as a heath food expert with a sideline divining water. The world has room for all sorts, and she supposed the world could take a herbalist or two lest humanity get so sensible it start to bore God himself. But let a woman think her own thoughts, thank you very much. And she went home to water the garden.

Yet even there, among the lilies and the hollyhocks, from which she attempted to drive a creeping rust of ragged leaves, she felt anxious and restless. It took two days of heavy digging and path building to reclaim her peace. Only a week until Paris, she thought, as she surveyed her work with satisfaction.

Des had stuck the wrought iron bench in the middle of the lawn, and it had always looked lost and lonely, usually just a resting place for the mugs of coffee he expected her to bring him through the day. Now it waited to receive visitors under the birch tree, the destination of an inviting meandering path.

When the phone rang, a portable model she'd propped in the Y of the maple, she was tempted not to answer. Then she remembered she'd asked the travel agent to find out how many of those Euros it would cost to take a taxi from the Paris airport to her hotel.

But it wasn't the travel agent, it was Desmond's elderly Aunt Marie, family conduit of news.

"Has Krista had her baby then?" asked Margaret, trying to sound interested.

"Not yet, dear. I'm afraid it isn't good news."

"Oh, dear." For Aunt Marie that could mean someone's cataract surgery postponed, or heavy repairs needed on the aging Honda, or even a divorce in the clan.

"Do you have a pen and paper handy, dear?"

"I'm out in the garden, Auntie. But I'm sure I can remember."

"I'm sure I couldn't," quavered the thin old voice, "but then you're chicken compared to me."

"You're only eighty-four and younger than most."

"Well, then. Visitation will be from two to four on Friday. That's at Patterson's. And seven to eight thirty in the evening, and the service will be at St. Mark's on Saturday. Of course, you make up your own mind, dear. I just thought you'd like to know. And she and Des were famous friends in the old days, always into mischief, those two."

"I appreciate you letting me know, Aunt Marie, but you didn't say who. Whose funeral is it?"

"I didn't say? I'm sorry, dear. It's Rose-Ann. Had a massive stroke last night."

Margaret's hand froze on the receiver, but even through the blood pounding in her ears, she could hear the tinge of vindication in the old woman's voice. "Only sixty-seven.

Shows where your health food will get you. Just eat healthy and in good variety, that's what I always say."

"Yes. Thank you. I'll be there. Bye, then."

The garden was anything but silent. Birds, of course, not just whistling and chirping, but the hum of their wings and the whirr of the mourning dove as it landed. Insects too, the cicadas just beginning to rehearse for high summer and the dreaming whine of the mosquito hiding in the shade. Skin thick and throbbing with heat. Wind in her ears whispering harsh and rasping: *Mind like a gerbil's cage. Rat's nest. Where thought goes to die.*

It was too bizarre to contemplate. Too true to deny. Three times her mind had lit by chance on the memory of some old half-remembered acquaintance. Three times death had followed remembering like a shadow.

"Don't be foolish," she said to the garden. It's just coincidence. People think their thoughts, people die, both happen all the time. But she turned and stumbled to the house, feeling older than she had on any day since she had found Desmond dead under the birch tree.

"Foolishness." she muttered. "Claptrap and nonsense. Alzheimer's setting in."

Of course, that triggered a panic of its own. It took a long hot shower to wash away the first layer of fear, restore enough calm so she could think through the problem rationally and with at least a veneer of composure. Nothing like a cozy bathrobe and a cup of hot tea to restore perspective, she thought, as she settled for the evening with her latest borrowings from the library.

She'd think about the other business later, just settle her mind first with a bit of reading. She picked up a historical mystery, set in Paris, brought home to help her get ready for the trip. Thinking about another century would be just the thing to shake morbid ideas from her mind and silence that whisper, that carping voice.

It was a wonderful gift, this trip the boys had given her. Of course, the greatest gift any mother wants is her children's love, but it's nice to have a concrete sign of it from time to time, and it doesn't have to be Paris. Upstairs in the cupboard sat the just as precious box full of handmade cards and bookmarks, pencil holders, pens with silk flowers carefully taped on, Mike's tearful letter of apology when he had lost John in the aisles of Canadian Tire, so mesmerized he'd been by the feathered fishing lures, he never noticed his little brother's departure for the bikes. What a frantic fifteen minutes before they found him interviewing the mechanic in the service bays. Which he could only have reached by going outdoors and around the store where anyone might have snatched him.

The one who'd needed the most consolation hadn't been the oblivious John, but Mike, who looked for the rest of the day like he hadn't seen the sun for a year. She'd had to tell him again and again that life had it's risks, and you couldn't be perfect all the time and...

A hand clapped over her mouth, as if silence could quell thought. Tea splashed in the saucer as she set it down. She'd been thinking of Mike. John too. She'd been thinking of her boys. Remembering.

She wouldn't think of it. It couldn't mean a thing. It was nonsense.

Not nonsense, said the whisper, the nasty murmur, the invitation.

"Nonsense!" she said firmly, but still, she went to the telephone and called all three of the only numbers she knew by heart. None of her boys were at home, but she listened to the strong male answering machine voices rumble confidently with life, then hung up without leaving messages for Peter, Mike or John.

What could she say? "This is your mother, and I've got this crazy idea that when I reminisce about people, the next thing that happens is that I hear they've died. And I hear your father whispering that it's all my fault."

Cause and effect...you think of them, then they die.

She forced her eyes to travel slowly around the room, focussing on the small, the ordinary things. The clock ticking on the mantel. Petals of delphinium fallen to the polished mahogany table top. Steam rising from her cup. It was all so everyday, so much as it had always been and was meant to be for years, and yet she stood here thinking such absurdities about remembrance and death, death and remembrance.

She sat down, took up her book, stirred milk vigorously into the tea. You'll just read your book, Margaret, she told herself. Just keep your mind on the book and the present. It's just a strange set of coincidences, she told herself, and not the voice. She refused to acknowledge the hearing of any voice. The boys are fine and will be fine and this will all look so stupid in a day or two. But for now, just to ease your mind, there'll be no thinking about the past. Just keep your mind on the here and now for a change. It'll be good discipline, goodness knows. Just drink your tea and read your book and it will all look so different in the morning.

But staying in the present tense turned out to be hard to achieve. Within another paragraph, her mind drifted willy-nilly from the lover's quarrel on the page to a scene in the high school hallway not two years ago. Had those two scrappers, (what were their names?) gone to the altar after all...

Name them! Name them! said the whisper, *Name them and they're next.*

Cutting off that line of thought, she tried television, chose a program she'd never watched, a game show that promised huge amounts of money for answering the most inane questions. The second contestant reminded her instantly of Mike's grade school soccer coach.

"He's dead already," she told the darkness. Had an asthma attack in the prime of life, right there in front of the kids at the side of the playing field. But she snapped the television off, thinking that things were in a pretty state if she had to be glad that someone was already dead.

You were glad I was dead.

"Yes, I was."

In the long hours of the night, she tried knitting, a tiresome pattern that required strict attention and endless counting of stitches; telephone conversations with people she'd known only for the briefest time; and finally, sleep. No matter what she did, the more she tried to govern her thoughts, the more her mind crept and crawled beyond control. Again and again she lurched out of a half remembered scene, yanking herself back from the brink of recollection like a woman balanced on the edge of a crumbling cliff.

She didn't sleep at all. By the time morning came, Margaret realized there was only one way to test the proposition. The voice. Herself.

Feeling gritty and rubbed all the wrong ways by a night of twisting between the sheets, she climbed out of bed and made that first pot of coffee. Optimistically, she brewed the usual three strong cups, poured in her milk and carried a mug out to the back porch step. Sat there and watched dawn arrive in the garden.

It'll be easier here, she thought.

She sipped the strong warm coffee, picturing Des on the

same porch step, sipping the first of many she'd hand him through the day, not that he'd ever thanked her. Her coffee was always too weak for him, until she'd brewed him that last excellent mugful of exactly what he deserved.

How sweet it had been to shake her head in sorrow that dear Desmond, usually so precise, had miscounted the doses of heart pills he'd taken that day.

Think you're smart, do you?

I do, she replied. *It was nice to have you dead. Even nicer to make you look a fool in the process.*

Then she ignored him and concentrated her thoughts instead on choosing a test subject. She couldn't let herself dwell on anyone for long, but she'd always thought there were some people that the world would do better without. Maybe that woman at the bank, said to be driving the doctor to drink. Maybe that fellow who'd just been arrested *again* for driving drunk. If he died, it might even save a life or two.

Aunt Marie? Be nice to live without those gossiping phone calls. But she was so old, it would prove nothing, might still be just another coincidence. No, it had to be someone fit and strong, who had years of life left to live.

And anyway, she was only playing a game, avoiding the inevitable. Really, she'd known all along that there was only one way to satisfy the whisper.

Dew glistened on unfurling lilies that would bloom only today for a single bout of glory. What had she to complain about, who'd had so many days, and her boys, and their love?

So, within a single boundary, Margaret let her mind run free. She named her self. She remembered the doll who had become as real as any person, and the black checked pants it had worn, and the house she'd made for her under the cherry tree. Remembered the blue church dress with the big bow at the back she'd loved. Games of hide and seek in the dusk from which no one had ever wanted to come in, the grown-ups calling from the porch, "It's time to come in, Margaret!" while the fireflies flickered in the gathering dark. The swing in the backyard from which Margaret had fallen and broken her arm, the feeling as vivid as ever of whumping hard onto the ground and the numb oddity of a bone going the wrong way.

And while she sat on the step, remembering and remembering, the silver branches on the birch tree danced.

Cecelia Kennedy *lives and writes in Brampton, Ontario. Her Tony Aardehuis stories have appeared in* The Grist Mill *and in* Storyteller, *where she won the Great Canadian Story contest for both 2001 and 2002. Her collection of Tony Aardehuis stories,* The Robbie Burns Revival, *was recently published by Broken Jaw Press.*

The Black and White Blues

He either loved me or he didn't,
There were no shades of grey,
Not like that Philco TV set
I used to watch all day.
It was black and white, with no remote.
You had to get up to change it.
And there he sat with our remote
As if he bodily owned it.

So...

He either loved me or he didn't,
There were no shades of grey,
Not like that plasma TV set
He sat and watched all day.
"It's black or white. Give me that remote.
You do not blinking own it!"
And he just sat and ignored me
Not knowing that he'd blown it.

So you see officer...

He either loved me or he didn't,
There were no shades of grey,
Not like the Philco TV set
I used to watch all day.
Now he's black and blue and so remote.
I had to try to change it.
There he sits with that thing down his throat
And he truly bodily owns it.

Joy Hewitt Mann

The Red Pagoda

Day's Lee

The responsibilities of the eldest son are clear: marry, provide an heir to carry on the family name, and assume responsibility for the family and the family business if necessary. That was my mother's firm belief, a belief rooted in Chinese custom and tradition.

So, when my father passed away over a year ago, my mother insisted that I assume his position of managing the Red Pagoda, the restaurant my parents owned for over forty years, while she continued as head cook. Two years earlier, with a yearning to run my own business, I'd left the banking industry to join Peter, my younger brother, in his publishing venture. With my parents' consent, we'd converted their basement into office space. The magazine had seen black ink for the first time when, one evening, before we left for the funeral parlour, my mother stood between stacks of the next month's issue and informed me that I had an obligation. At forty-seven, I was still single and, to my mother's consternation, dating Caucasian women. I had not been living up to expectations. My mother was certain this was because I was cursed with her brother's good looks and affable character, a combination that, if history was being repeated, meant I was adverse to responsibility. Thankfully, Peter had ensured the family lineage by having a son a year after marrying his mail-order bride from Hong Kong. However, family friends would expect me to do what was right: take care of my mother and assume my position as head of the family.

I agreed. My parents had made a number of sacrifices in the name of family responsibility. Owning a restaurant was synonymous with living in one. I don't have a family memory that doesn't take place in the Red Pagoda. The cooks, waiters and waitresses became extended family. The restaurant had provided me with a couple of trips to Hong Kong and a Masters degree. The time had come for me to make a sacrifice for the family. Peter would now be able to hire a part-time assistant for the magazine while I ran the restaurant.

The Red Pagoda is a fixture on The Main, a few blocks north of Chinatown. Not much had changed since it first opened its doors in 1961. Vinyl green and yellow booths and Formica tables formed aisles over a faded linoleum floor. I used to joke that it was the Chinese version of "Happy Days", but the aging furnishings didn't look so funny any more. It was time to update the restaurant.

My mother was appalled that I planned to destroy my father's legacy only a month after his death. We had many arguments. In private, she was resolute and enforced a punishing silence. But in the restaurant, she gave a performance that rivaled any Peking Opera star. To anybody who didn't understand Chinese but was literate in gestures, it was the story of a son who was the reason for his mother's tragic heartbreak.

It finally dawned on me that I hadn't explained it properly. I wasn't destroying my father's legacy; I was ensuring that it would survive and thrive. That clinched my argument. Minutes later, I was on the phone making appointments with renovators.

Telling my mother that we had to close for a month for renovations was not an easy task. Her fears that the Red

Pagoda's doors would be closed permanently were obvious. To placate her, I let her have a say in the décor. I agreed with her decision to keep the huge embroidered picture of one hundred birds, a Chinese good luck symbol, but cringed when she insisted on keeping the gold plastic lanterns with red tassels, which she deemed classy. And there was no way I could talk her into giving up the grotesque framed plastic skyline of Hong Kong, which my father had purchased for the restaurant's twenty-fifth anniversary. She never ceased to admire the fireworks that lit up its nighttime sky when it was plugged in. The interior designer did her best to incorporate my desire for a more upscale look with my mother's reluctance to let go of the past.

The result was Calvin Klein meets Suzy Wong.

Customers and restaurant critics loved it.

The review was the lead story in the *Gazette's* restaurant section one Saturday. My mother beamed as I read out loud the critic's praise for her authentic cuisine, translating phrases with which she was unfamiliar. The staff congratulated her, and everybody's spirit was lifted by this public declaration of success. While she sat at the table basking in the glow of the restaurant's triumph, I felt relief. There is a certain amount of pressure in taking over the family business. Comparisons to my father would be inevitable. Could I, the son with all the advantages of higher education, match the success my father had achieved with only a grade school education? The following months would tell, but this was a good start. I continued to read through the pages of the newspaper as my mother chatted about the new dishes she wanted to add to the daily menu. Suddenly, she grabbed the newspaper and turned back a couple of pages. She pointed at the caption underneath a black and white picture and asked me what it said.

"Violet McIntosh, CEO and president of McIntosh Enterprises, hospitalized after falling down the stairs at her home in Westmount."

The woman in the photo was anything but matronly. She looked to be in her sixties, one of those women who aged gracefully, perhaps more due to her station in life than nature itself. Her no-nonsense look and confident smile probably reassured thousands of shareholders from the pages of McIntosh Enterprises' annual reports.

The accompanying article explained that she had fallen down the concrete stairs in front of her house. She was unconscious when the ambulance rushed her to the Royal Victoria Hospital. With serious wounds to her head and a couple of broken bones, doctors described her condition as life-threatening. Her son, Michael, was with her when the accident occurred.

My mother didn't say anything for a few seconds. What was it about the photo that had caught her attention?

"I used to work for her family," she said, as if that explained everything.

"When?"

"A long time ago, before I married your father."

The news wasn't shocking, but it was news. My mother was generally disinclined to discuss her past. For instance, I had never known we had relatives in Hong Kong until one day, out of the blue, she announced that my high school graduation present would be a trip "back home" to meet relatives. Then, there was my uncle, her brother, who had moved to New York before I was born and was never heard from again. He was mentioned infrequently, but served as a warning of what happens to people who aren't responsible. Even the circumstances surrounding my parents' marriage were fuzzy. I suspected, but never tried to confirm, that I was already born when she married my father. The loss of face in those days would have been great, and I felt the memory of the shame was still vivid in her mind.

Violet had been a teenager when my mother was hired by her family to serve as a domestic. They lived in one of the stone mansions in an area known as the Square Mile, close enough for my mother to make the trek from her parents' apartment in Chinatown. She was provided with two uniforms, consisting of a white jacket and black trousers, so that she would be suitably dressed when answering the door. She was allowed meals and earned only a few dollars a day.

My mother inhaled deeply as she recalled the first time she had seen the sumptuous surroundings. At thirteen years old, she had marvelled at the velvet curtains, silver serving trays, and a dining table long enough to seat twelve people. Every week, she sheathed the beds in soft clean cotton sheets and blanketed them with silk coverlets. She hung wool carpets over a clothes line and beat them clean, dusted heavy wood furniture, and washed and ironed fine European fashions.

Her acquaintance with Violet hadn't started right away. There was too much work to do, and there was also the language barrier. My mother barely spoke enough English to understand instructions. Violet took it upon herself to expand my mother's vocabulary. Thereafter, for a few minutes each day, Violet had taught her a new word or phrase. Their bond as employer and employee became so great that when Violet's parents sent her to Hong Kong for a year, ostensibly to work in one of her father's banks, they'd sent my mother along to look after her.

I was caught off-guard by her story. Questions erupted in my mind so fast that I couldn't get the words out. I hesitated too long. With a sigh, my mother shook her head and said it was all in the past. Then she got up, ambled down the aisle and disappeared behind the kitchen door.

The "sweet and sour" smell of success, when associated with a Chinese restaurant, is a good thing. Long-time customers couldn't believe they now needed a reservation on weekends. At least once a week, a celebrity was spotted in our dining room. The purchase order for ingredients to create popular dishes such as Sweet and Sour Pork, General Tao's Chicken, Pan Fried Dumplings, and Bird's Nest Soup doubled. Every Tuesday morning before the restaurant opened for the noon crowd, delivery trucks dropped off boxes of Chinese vegetables, noodles, sacks of rice and fresh pork and beef. A local farmer delivered a couple of crates of live chickens. That my sixty-five-year-old mother could lift one of these crates on her own astonished both me and the delivery men. She waved off my concern. She knew what she could and could not handle.

Slaughtering chickens was one of them.

The chickens fought right down to the last second of their lives. My mother would snatch one from a crate and slam the lid down before the others could escape. Plopping her prey into the deep sink, there would only be a few seconds of desperate squawking and a mad flutter of wings before a quick slash of a chopping blade across the throat took the fight out of it. Then, she'd hold the chicken upside down for a few seconds as the blood poured down the drain, pleased that we would serve fresh chicken that week. I tried to convince her that buying frozen chicken would save her a lot of time and work. She'd just shrug and say she had nothing else to do with her time, and besides, since her chicken dishes were so popular, she had no intention of changing what were obviously winning recipes.

Friday evenings are the noisiest of the week, as people welcome the beginning of the weekend. Groups of office workers often fill the tables and keep the bartenders at the newly installed bar busy. On the wall behind the bar, surrounded by a display of liqueurs and aperitifs, a stream of fireworks light up the plastic Hong Kong skyline. The constant chatter is punctuated by the tapping of the hostess's high-heeled shoes on the hard, blond wood floor as she escorts customers to their tables. On one such evening, I happened to overhear lewd praise of the hostess's legs. I scanned the new arrivals. After all, the hostess was only eighteen, in university, and from what I'd seen and heard, a good girl. The remark came from a small group of men who were dressed as if they owned the world.

At least one of them did.

I recognized him immediately. His photo had been in the papers over the past few weeks, along with reports of his mother's condition. The heir apparent to McIntosh Enterprises looked as if everything was going his way. The tabloids nicknamed him "The Heir Most Likely to Lose the Family Fortune," capitalizing on rumours of his gambling habit. The news reports that morning stated he was deciding whether or not to pull the plug, since Violet's condition had not improved. As her only child, and with the death of his father in a sailing accident years ago, it was all in Michael's hands. Right now his hand held a glass of wine, which the waiter had poured for his approval. Something about the scene was distasteful. Maybe it's just the way I was brought up, but if my mother were hovering between life and death in the hospital, I'd be eating day old sandwiches from the hospital vending machine.

When one of the waiters tapped me on the shoulder later that evening and said one of the customers wanted to meet the chef, I wasn't surprised. It had become a regular event, happening often enough for my mother to arrange for a standing weekly appointment with her hairdresser. He pointed out Michael

McIntosh's table. Normally, I'm pleased whenever a customer wants to congratulate my mother, since the restaurant is her life's work. But I just didn't trust that cheeky Cheshire cat's smile. I told the waiter I'd handle it and headed over to his table.

"Mr. McIntosh," I extended my hand, "I'm Roger Chiu. I understand you'd like to meet our chef."

"Yes, it would be an honour." He stood up and gripped my hand with both of his, like a politician on a campaign. "Have we met before?"

"No, but I've seen you in the news. I'm sorry to hear about your mother."

"Ah, yes." He dropped back into his chair. "It's awful, but when people get to that age, they start to lose their balance. Accidents start to happen." A murmur of agreement went around the table. I excused myself to get my mother, not because I didn't want to keep him waiting, but because I didn't want to say something I'd regret later.

My mother was curious about the son of her former employer; she scrutinized him from behind her image as a simple immigrant cook. Her coiffed salt and pepper hair was carefully tucked underneath a hair net. She'd put on a clean white chef's jacket to cover her splattered apron, something she'd seen on the cooking channel, thinking it would make a better impression on the customers. She smiled at Michael's comments, but when she asked me to translate phrases I knew she understood, I wondered why she didn't want him to know.

"Better he not ask too many questions," she explained later as we were closing up for the night.

"Questions about what?"

"Anything!" She threw her hands up in exasperation.

After that, Michael started to dine regularly at the Red Pagoda. He was usually accompanied by men in business suits or a pretty woman. He always shook my hand campaign style, and he would always ask me or the waiter to send his compliments to my mother. But the day he had the gall to stroll into the kitchen, unaccompanied and unannounced, was the day I wished he would take his expense account elsewhere.

"Sorry, I didn't mean anything by it." He swivelled around, taking in the stainless steel refrigerators, the back door where deliveries were made, the assistant cooks stir-frying in woks over gas lit stoves, and the busboy loading up the dishwasher. Maybe if he hadn't chosen lunch hour to invade the kitchen, I would have been more patient. Maybe if he hadn't looked as if he was checking out the kitchen. Maybe if his apology was at least as sincere as the words were meant to convey.

I planted myself in his path. His six foot plus frame towered over me, and it was obvious he was using it to intimidate. At five foot eight, I consider myself of average height for a Chinese man. I had encountered a few opponents in the bank's board room who tried to use their physical size as an advantage, and I had no trouble taking them down a notch.

"Mr. McIntosh," I said firmly, looking him in the eye. "This is not a good time for a tour. The kitchen is like a steam bath at this hour." I stepped towards him, attempting to usher him out, but he ignored me and continued to survey the kitchen. When my mother emerged from the basement around the corner, it was as if he'd found what he was looking for.

"Mrs. Chiu, I just wanted to pay my respects. You and your team created a lovely meal as always." My mother nodded in acknowledgement, but didn't reply as I moved Michael into the dining room. "Roger, I'm sorry about that," he said, contritely. "Other restaurants don't mind, and I had just assumed…"

I wasn't in the mood to listen to his excuse. "Understandable," I lied.

"Listen." He stopped and reached into his jacket pocket. "Actually, I wanted to show this to your mother." He pulled out an old black and white photo. It was square with a white border trimmed with ridges. A young pregnant woman had her arm around the smaller woman's shoulders. They were poised on a hilltop overlooking a seaside city below. I wasn't sure who the pregnant woman was, but I recognized my mother, who must have been in her late teens then.

"Know her?" Michael pointed to the pregnant woman. I shook my head. "That's my mother," he said.

I blinked twice. Violet had been a beauty; a young Marilyn Monroe without the heavy makeup. She must have been pregnant with Michael at the time. My mother had been thin in her youth, unlike the sturdy figure now who could hoist a sack of rice with ease. But, if my mother had known Michael when he was born, why did she act as if she'd never met him before?

"I came across it when I was going through some of my mother's things," he explained. "You know, she might go any day now, and I thought your mom would like to have it as a memento."

It was a sincere gesture, and a pang of guilt hit my gut for doubting his intentions. I thanked him and took the picture, assuring him I'd give it to her. He looked grateful. We shook hands and parted without another word.

By mid-afternoon, the lunch crowd had dispersed. The staff chatted away in the nearly empty restaurant as they went about getting their lunch. I was sitting at the bar examining the photo when my mother came over to ask what I wanted to eat.

I showed her the photo. "When was this taken?"

She stiffened and stared at it for a few seconds. "Who gave that to you?"

"Michael McIntosh. He wants you to have it."

"Aiyah," she exclaimed softly. "How did he get that?" A worried look came over her. I put my hand on her shoulder just as she turned away to head back to the kitchen. There were too many secrets in our family.

"Ma, tell me, where was it taken?"

"Long ago. I don't remember."

"When you worked for Violet's family?"

"Yes, long time ago. I'm too old; don't remember too well." She shuffled off, mumbling something about Singapore fried rice.

I remained at the bar for a few minutes, staring at the photo. Something was familiar about this seaside city and the view from that hilltop. As I stared at the photo, I noticed several boats on the water, their sails indicative of no other: sampans. I looked at the plastic skyline above the bar and compared it to the photo.

The picture was taken in Hong Kong.

I didn't bring up the subject again until the next morning, when I drove over to my mother's house, as usual, to pick her up. I thought I'd give her time to think things over, but getting her to talk could be maddening. Peter had already arrived and was working in the office. My mother was rushing around, putting things away, when I brought up the subject.

"There's nothing to tell," she said, firmly. "I already told you I went to Hong Kong with Violet."

"You never said she was pregnant. And, if she was pregnant when you were in Hong Kong, why did you pretend not to know Michael?"

"Not pretending. I never met him before."

"Well, Violet was pregnant in the photo."

"Yes, but not with Michael."

The photo was taken in the late 1950s. A beautiful, unmarried, pregnant woman was sent to Hong Kong. There was a reason for this sketchy picture. It's easy to forget that things were different back then.

"Her family sent her away because she was pregnant, and you were supposed to look after her?"

My mother nodded.

"What happened to the baby?"

"She could not keep the baby." She hung a black purse over her arm and headed for the porch to put on her shoes.

Of course, the family would have insisted that it be put up for adoption. Having a baby out of wedlock in those days would have put the entire family to shame. Sending Violet to Hong Kong to give birth seemed a little extreme to me, but then, things were not as they are now.

There's something about opening the restaurant that I enjoy. It's like unwrapping a gift again and again. My mother and I were the first ones to arrive. A few minutes later, two of the cooks announced their arrival with a cheerful "Good morning" as they walked through the door. I went into my closet-sized office and snapped on the radio as I prepared the till for the day. When the news announcer stated that Violet McIntosh had died in her sleep, I almost scattered a roll of quarters all over the desk. Hospital authorities deemed the death suspicious, as her condition had improved a few days earlier, and they would be investigating further. I decided not to tell my mother until the end of the day. Since she didn't want to talk about the photo, there was no telling how the news would affect her.

As people are less inclined to stay out late early in the week, the restaurant closes at midnight. It had been a moderately busy day, enough to make me forget about Violet. I locked the door as the last customers faded away down the empty sidewalk. The dining room staff had already left, so I cleaned up the table and brought the dishes to the kitchen. The stoves were cold and the countertops clean. The back door was ajar. One of the cooks was probably hauling the garbage to the dumpster. I assumed my mother was downstairs getting ready to go home. I went back to the dining room to wait for her. A few minutes later, when the assistant cook came out, he looked relieved to see me.

"Hey, Roger, when I didn't see your mom, I thought I was locked in!"

"What do you mean? Isn't she downstairs?"

"Didn't see her, man."

As soon as the lock bolted behind him, I headed back to the kitchen. The back door was locked from the inside. With one sweeping glance at the rectangular room, it was obvious she wasn't here. As I headed down to the basement, I heard the unmistakable metallic click of the walk-in refrigerator door. I got to the bottom of the stairs in time to see my mom come out of the fridge, with Michael right behind her. It didn't look like she was giving him a tour. Her eyes were wide with fright, and his hand was clamped on her shoulder.

"Michael! What're you doing here?"

He was dressed like a bad guy on a cop show: black turtleneck and black leather jacket. The fact that he was also wearing black leather gloves in June made me uneasy.

"Hey there, Roger, just having a chat with your mother about my family," he said, in a manner that reminded me of a corporate shark planning a raid.

"The fridge isn't as comfortable as upstairs."

"Just wanted some privacy."

"Well, we have to get going. Come back tomorrow. We'll have lunch together, just the three of us." I approached slowly, and as I reached for my mother, he yanked her back. She shouted, then elbowed him in the stomach. He grimaced, but didn't let go of her.

That was enough.

I grabbed his jacket with the intention of kicking his ass out of my restaurant, when he reached over and pulled a chopping knife out of the butcher's block. "I didn't plan to do it this way, but if I have to, I will." He held the edge of the blade under my ear. I released him and took a step back. My mother was frozen in terror. "All I wanted were some answers. If she had cooperated, this wouldn't have been necessary."

"Answers? You mean about that picture?"

He nodded. "Where's that baby?"

"She doesn't know. It was given up for adoption."

"Like hell it was! I found the birth certificate dated Hong Kong, 1958. I found the cheques!" His face turned purplish red as he became enraged. "My mother wrote cheques to your mother for over forty years with a note saying it was for Renji. Renji's birthday! Renji's high school graduation! The same name on the birth certificate!"

I was dumbstruck. It couldn't be.

Michael held the knife threateningly. I was certain he had no intention of welcoming Renji as a sibling.

"I hear the hospital is investigating your mother's death," I said, scrambling to stall for time. A gasp escaped from my mother. "Did you have anything to do with it?"

"What do you think this is, TV? That I'm going to confess to the good guy before I kill him?" His words chilled me to the bone. "Nobody is going to find out about that baby. I thought only your mother knew, but now, I'll have to take care of you, too."

Knives are dangerous, but they can't accidentally go off like a gun. I grabbed a roasting pan and slammed it against his hand. He cried out in pain, and the knife flew out of his hand. I lunged at him, and we both fell onto the concrete floor. He was getting the upper hand when suddenly, his head jerked backwards and a long, sharp blade was firmly pressed against his throat. My mother had him helpless in her grip, like the chickens she slaughtered every week.

I quickly got up and reached for the phone on the wall. "I'd advise you not to move, Michael. You know they lose their balance at that age. Accidents happen."

It took almost a year before Michael's case was heard in court. His battery of lawyers tried to suppress every piece of evidence and challenged every witness's testimony: the hospital doctor, who said Violet McIntosh had been asphyxiated; the CFO of McIntosh Enterprises who swore that Michael had ordered him to fix the books, inflating the company's shares, and that only days before her accident, Violet, suspicious of the numbers, had ordered an investigation.

And then there was my mom, the only person alive who could confirm that Violet gave birth to a baby boy in Hong Kong in 1958. Violet's Last Will and Testament clearly stated that the bulk of her estate, including the controlling shares of McIntosh Enterprises, were to go to her eldest son. As long as the world didn't know about that baby, Michael stood to inherit everything. The prosecution maintained that Michael had planned to destroy all evidence surrounding that birth— even if it meant committing murder. He had discovered the photo when he broke into his mother's safe and recognized his mother's maid as the chef pictured in the *Gazette,* the same issue that had reported his mother's accident.

As for me, the eldest son, I have many new responsibilities to assume.

You see, Renji is my Chinese name. I am Violet's son.

The morning after Michael's arrest, my mother sat Peter and me down for a talk. Violet had had an affair with my uncle, the one who had disappeared. He had fled to escape her father's wrath and responsibility for the situation. Violet's parents had sent her to Hong Kong, not only to hide the shame of her unmarried state, but to hide the fact that the baby was half-Chinese. The plan was for her to leave the baby there for adoption, but my mother could not abandon her nephew. The two women made a secret pact: my mother would raise me as her own with Violet's financial support. A fake birth certificate was paid for, and I returned to Canada as my mother's son. My father knew I was a product of one of my uncle's affairs, but had nonetheless raised me as his own. A year later, Violet had married into the McIntosh family, and Michael was born in 1960.

It was Violet who had sent me on those trips to Hong Kong and who had paid for my education. She also gave my parents the money to open the Red Pagoda.

My mother had kept the secret out of loyalty to Violet, and out of the fear that I'd leave her for Violet's lavish lifestyle.

Peter runs the restaurant these days, having sold the magazine to his assistant for a small profit. I visit at least twice a week, whenever I can get away from the office. It's going to take a lot of time and work to win back shareholders' confidence. Michael was found guilty, and his lawyers are filing an appeal.

My mother says she is lucky to have two eldest sons.

Day's Lee *has been short-listed in several contests, including the 2001 CBC Radio Short Story Contest. Her first children's book,* The Fragrant Garden, *will be published by Napoleon Publishing in the fall of 2005. She is a member of the Quebec Writers' Federation, is a recipient of a grant from Conseil des arts et des lettres du Québec, and is currently working on a novel.*

Life Sentences

Joan Boswell

Banging bars, clanging gates, shouting—the noise drove Foster crazy. He sat back on his bunk. Fifty, the big five-o—no birthday parties in the Big House. What kind of a life was this? How many times had he been in and out? Too many. Thirty-one months done; five months left until he was eligible for parole. Maybe this time, he'd stay out. Now that was an original thought. How many guys had he heard say, "never again", and six months later the wagon pulled in, and guess who got out?

Maybe if he'd been to university when he was young, he'd be a household name, one of those financiers he read about in the paper. Those guys made millions and hardly ever went to jail and, even if they did, they stashed money away and lived like kings when they came out. If he'd taken commerce and headed into that world, he could have made those Bre-X guys look like amateurs.

He'd aced the Queen's University TV courses he'd taken while he was in jail. Psychology had been a joke. Separating the gullible from their money, playing on their greed and hope, that's what he did professionally; he could have written a how-to book, but why let others know his methods? Not that they'd worked last time, but how could he have known the woman's daughter was a cop? Instead of writing a book, he'd taken more courses. Although he enjoyed learning, what he really loved was being in the quiet library. He had time for one more before they sprang him.

The big five-o—when he got out, he needed one final score, and he'd retire.

*   *   *

Pre-Confederation Canadian History: he picked it because the instructor, Dr. Mary Beth McNab, was a woman, and there weren't too many in his life. Taking a course on TV was okay, but for him the hook was knowing the instructor would visit the class several times a term.

He liked to learn the background of his professors. He figured you did better if you got an idea of what they'd done, what made them tick. None of the other six cons taking the course knew or cared. Since he did, he researched her in the university calendar and online.

She'd written five books, four of them on Canadian Arctic history and one, *The Montreal McNabs,* about her family. He remembered reading in the business pages how the McNabs differed from other Canadian families whose involvement in their companies tapered off as grandchildren lost the work ethic that had made their grandfathers rich. The fourth generation McNabs continued to run their enterprises and rake in the dough. The librarian ordered the book from interlibrary loan. After he skimmed it and studied the genealogy charts, Foster concluded Dr. McNab rated as one very rich woman.

*   *   *

Pen and paper in front of him, Foster turned on the TV to catch the first class. Professor McNab was probably about his age, and not bad looking. Not a beauty, but not bad. Better if she'd cut her scraggly hair, wear a little make-up—those blue eyes needed some help. She was walking back and forth, making notes on the board. Those shoes, what were they called, Birkenstocks. He couldn't be sure, but she probably didn't shave her legs. What was it about feminists and hair? No ring, but that didn't mean anything. She wore a brown saggy skirt and some kind of striped top. If she was on a TV make-over program, they'd do a job on her. Hell, with her money, she could hire a pro to fix her up.

Two essays a term, a test and a final exam. "You may write your essay on any topic on the list you received earlier," she said.

His eyes scanned the twenty topics and brightened when they settled on "Franklin's Arctic Voyages—Lessons to be Learned". The Arctic was her field; it might be risky to trespass, but he'd bet that if she was like most "experts", she'd be pleased a student was interested. And it was a no-brainer. The *Toronto Star* had run an article on Franklin and lead poisoning a couple of weeks before, when somebody discovered the grave of one of Franklin's sailors. The permafrost had preserved the guy. They did an autopsy and found he was full of lead. In those early days of canned food, the lead used to seal the tins leeched into the food, poisoned it and made those who ate it raving mad. The phrase "mad as a hatter"came from hat-makers, who also used lead to do something to the felt for hats. Lesson number one; don't eat canned food.

With the librarian's help, he decided on the books and journals he needed.

*   *   *

"I skimmed several of your books. You'll really relate to the crew," the librarian said when the volumes arrived.

Foster knew his eyebrows had risen. "How so?"

"You won't believe this, but on Franklin's second expedition, his ship stuck in the ice for three years; the ice never broke up. You know what three years in here is like; can you imagine what it was like in the Arctic?"

Foster collected the material and moved to a quiet corner, where he thought about those guys up there surrounded by miles of quiet; nothing to see or hear, except on the ship. All of them stuffed into a tiny boat in the middle of nothing. Hundreds and hundreds of miles of white nothing. When they decided the ice would never break up, they'd left the ship and set out to find land, but by then with all the lead they'd eaten, they must have been crazy as coots. No one ever saw them again. Now that was what you'd call a "cool" jail break. He laughed at his own joke, but he felt for those guys; what a rotten way to die.

Later in the term, Professor McNab returned their essays and scheduled a ten-minute discussion with each student. Foster couldn't believe he felt excited about talking to a middle-aged woman about Franklin: it showed you what happened to a guy after three years inside. He didn't have much of a wardrobe to choose from, but he did visit the barber.

Sitting in the barber's chair, he studied himself in the mirror, imagining what kind of an impression he'd make on Professor McNab. What would she think? Pretty good looking guy for five-o. Not all that tall. Who was he kidding—short, but probably taller than her, although it was hard to judge her height on TV. Working out kept his muscles toned and made his tattoos look good. Tattoos, but not anywhere she'd see them. He'd been smart enough to know little old ladies didn't trust men with snakes twining around their arms, and he specialized in scamming the old dears. No glasses yet, and he wasn't, what did the jokers say, follically challenged. Lots of grey curly hair on his head, his chest, his arms; if she liked hairy, she'd love him.

Professor McNab, accompanied by a guard, strode into the room set aside for meeting the students. She parked her battered brown briefcase on a table at the front of the room and took a moment to study the seven men sitting on folding metal chairs. When their eyes met, Foster knew as surely as if she'd sent him an e-mail that she found him attractive. And to his surprise, she looked better in person than on TV, thinner for one thing.

"I have your essays, and you impressed me with the amount of work and thought you put into your writing. Of course there's room for improvement, but some of the essays, particularly Foster's on Franklin and JC's on Henry Hudson, were very good." She handed the work back. She'd written, "Excellent, but you can do better. You have a gift for research and writing."

He laughed to himself; good con artists specialized in good communication skills.

Interview time. They talked about his paper.

"If you haven't finished your degree, you should," she said.

"I haven't. Are *you* giving a course next term?"

Her turned-up lips and slightly raised eyebrows told Foster his remark had pleased her.

"Queen's has many excellent professors. Actually, I'm taking a leave of absence." She pursed her mouth then gave a small, neat smile. "It's probably immodest to say this, but I'm considered *the* expert on Arctic history."

Immodest his ass; she wanted to brag. "And I have been invited…" Again the smile. "Invited by the government to act as one of the go-betweens in the Department of Indian Affairs Land claim negotiations in Ottawa. It will mean doing quite a lot of research and attending meetings to substantiate the claims made by either side."

"Sounds fascinating."

"It's a great honour to know that both the Dene and Inuit trust me."

A germ of an idea wormed its way into Foster's brain. "Congratulations. After the research I did on Franklin, I find Arctic history truly fascinating. I'd like to hear how your work is going." Would she buy it?

She tilted her head to one side and considered him. "Why don't you write to me?" she said.

*   *   *

Dear Professor McNab, Please do not answer if you're too busy, but I would like to hear about your progress with the negotiations, Foster wrote shortly after she left.

Her reply arrived within the week. *Dear Foster, Please call me Mary Beth.*

Following three single-spaced pages describing who had said what, she wrote, *Now, tell me about yourself…*

Given the green light, Foster created a wonderful sympathetic repentant man intent on reform but worried about re-entering the labour force.

The letters flew back and forth.

When you're paroled, I realize it will be difficult for you to land a job. Is there any chance you'll come to Ottawa?

I'm amazed. You've read my mind. I've already applied to locate there, Foster assured Mary Beth.

I don't think I've mentioned my health problems, but they drain my energy. Since I arrived in Ottawa, I've found there's more material than I can handle in the time I have. I need an assistant. If you're interested, I have grant money, although not enough to pay you very much.

Eureka. The big enchilada.

*   *   *

It was a piece of cake. She was lonely—he was grateful and attentive. From their first meeting, he'd known she found him attractive, and she responded to his overtures.

After three years inside, regular sex was great, even if the quality wasn't the best. Mary Beth lived in the dark ages in terms of experimentation and variety. Maybe it was because she believed she'd saved him that she insisted on the missionary position to the exclusion of anything else.

"It's crazy. We're so different, but you make me happy," she said one night.

"Me too, what would you think if I proposed?" Foster held his breath. This could be the answer to everything.

"I'd accept," Mary Beth said. Three days later, after Foster signed a prenuptial agreement, they trotted off to City Hall and tied the knot.

*   *   *

Foster had landed in another prison.

During their brief courtship, he hadn't seen the "real" Mary Beth. As a husband, he discovered she held fixed opinions on many subjects, and he didn't share most of them.

It began right after their wedding, when they went out for a celebratory dinner, and he ordered spareribs.

"Foster, how could you? Don't you know that pigs are close genetic relatives? In fact, we already use pig heart valves for humans. Eating pork is tantamount to cannibalism."

She launched into a long spiel about the virtues of a vegetarian diet combined with an attack on his food choices.

She said it was for his own good. She claimed her diet kept her from dying from the after-effects of a bout of childhood rheumatic fever that had damaged her heart.

Hoping to cook food he liked, he offered to take over in the kitchen. Mary Beth enjoyed his pancakes, bread and trail mix but refused to allow even a whiff of meat or poultry. Foster, a confirmed carnivore, hated tofu, yogurt, stir fries and vegetables. He'd never known there were so many vegetables, and when he sneaked away for a food fix, he rejected all of them except fries and ketchup.

Once they settled into a regular life, he also discovered her obsession with her health. A sniffle, and she worried about pneumonia. A cough and TB threatened. A class-A hypochondriac, she bored him with her endless preoccupation with health and diet. It did occur to him that in some circumstances, this could be a plus. If she died, suddenly no one would be surprised, and her trust fund, house, cottage and stocks would all go to her spouse, who would become a rich man.

He certainly wouldn't be one while she was alive. She might have a trust fund, but she required a detailed accounting of the money she doled out.

And if he'd wanted quiet, he got it—Mary Beth spent her evenings reading, usually about the damn Arctic. One night he snapped on her small, antiquated TV to catch *Law and Order,* the educational program for cons.

"Foster, I can't concentrate with all the noise. TV is mindless. Don't shows like that bring back unhappy memories?"

He turned it off and bought headphones. The next night it was *CSI*, another instructional show.

"Foster, the flickering gives me a headache."

He gave up and rented DVDs to watch on the computer while she read, and before she asked him to share a cup of camomile tea, a snack, a walk or to hike off to bed for more sharing. Once in a while he broke out, saw some of the guys and played pool, but mostly it was dullsville on the Rideau. He'd wanted a normal life, but this was like being buried alive.

It got worse. One spring weekend, they drove to her home thirty clicks outside of Kingston. The whole way, Mary Beth hummed under her breath. Of all her habits, he hated this one the most.

As they bumped up the long rutted tree-lined driveway, she stopped humming. "Aren't the trees beautiful? We'll always be alone here; this is my sanctuary. I never invite anyone to visit. There will be lots of things for you to do. You can putter in the barn, cut the grass and plough the lane. It'll be an idyllic life for us."

Idyllic death, he thought as they entered the old farm house where floorboards squeaked, windows rattled and dead flies clogged the windowsills. Solitary in the pen would be better than this.

She brushed the flies off the kitchen table. "You'll love my cottage even more than this house. It's on an island, and there isn't any hydro or plumbing. The view from the outhouse is to die for."

God, he could just imagine.

He could have bailed, probably should have, but once a gambler, always a gambler. She wouldn't last forever, and when he inherited, he'd buy a condo in Toronto and live the good life. He could wait.

His time frame altered on a May morning.

Sent up to the Departmental library with a list of material to pick up for Mary Beth, he discovered forensic books shelved in the science section. Pulling one out at random, he thought back to the things Reggie the Rat had gone on about while they'd exercised in the prison yard—poisons and how the modern ones were undetectable. At the time, poison hadn't interested him; he'd identified himself as a con man, not a murderer. But now…

After he'd collected the volumes Mary Beth required, he continued to think about what he'd read. Walking into her office carrying the pile of books, he collided with a young woman and dropped them. As she helped him pick them up, her straight fair hair swung around her face, and she looked up at him with worried-looking blue eyes.

"I'm so sorry. I'm Cindy. I'm new, and I'm typing for Professor McNab."

"I'm Foster, her husband and research assistant," he said. Her effect on him was immediate and shocking. He told himself to cool it; he had a good thing with Mary Beth and was old enough to be Cindy's father. But when had that ever stopped anyone? Look at guys like Michael Douglas that you read about in the *National Enquirer*.

Having a great little bit on the side would make living with Mary Beth easier.

He launched a campaign to seduce Cindy but soon realized she was different from other women he'd pursued. After he drove her home from work on Friday, he knew that with this pigeon, he would need to lay his trail pretty carefully, or he'd scare her off. And it might be all or nothing, the old "not before marriage" bit.

Bigamy wasn't an option.

"Great morning. Isn't spring the best? How about going down to the cafeteria for a coffee?" Foster said, sticking his head around the half wall dividing Cindy's cubicle from the rest of the office. He gave her his "I'm just a regular, harmless kind of guy" smile.

Cindy looked up from her computer screen and blushed. Catching her lower lip with her teeth, she shook her head and turned a deeper shade of pink. "Thanks, but I don't know if I should."

Foster moved to stand in front of her. He inhaled the light scent of perfume and something soft like baby powder. He couldn't believe a twenty-three-year-old could be such an innocent. "You mean because of…"

Cindy nodded.

"Hey, it was just a kiss."

"I know, and I appreciated the drive home when it was raining, but it's wrong to kiss a married man. I don't want it to go any further."

"No problem. It won't." Foster flashed his "disarming little boy" grin. "But we both work here." He produced a barefaced lie. "Mary Beth suggested I take you, because she's off to an all-day meeting, and you won't have much to do."

"Mary Beth's nice," Cindy said. "Well, if she said to go, I guess it's okay."

Later, as he let himself into their apartment, he thought about Cindy; about how much he'd love an ordinary wife who liked beer and movies and barbecues. He thought of Cindy's round smiling face and cap of blonde hair. His fingers tingled, and his breath quickened. He shook his head and checked the answering machine.

"Foster, I have to work on the Inuvialuit claims for tomorrow's meeting. I'll be late."

Inuvialuit, Inuktitut, Herschel Island, Holman Island, Coppermine—Mary Beth's world revolved around the negotiations and her research.

"We shouldn't go for coffee every day," Cindy said when he popped into her cubicle next morning. The way she looked at him told him as clearly as if she'd spoken the words that if he was single, she'd be his.

"Mary Beth told us to. She feels bad because she's busy with negotiations," Foster lied. As he breathed in her light, flowery smell, he looked at Cindy's smooth rosy cheeks and round blue eyes and knew he had to have her.

Cindy locked her purse in the bottom drawer of her desk and smiled up at him. "It's my turn to take coffee in to them."

Foster's brow furrowed. "Who?"

"The negotiators. Our guys, a bunch of Inuit, Mary Beth and the lawyers are in that huge boardroom up on the seventeenth floor."

"Let me give you a hand."

He realized he'd made a mistake when he pushed the cart with the coffee urn through the door. Mary Beth's gaze moved from him to Cindy and back to him. Her lips thinned, and she stared at him. Talk about stupid; the last thing he wanted was for her to figure out he was making a move on Cindy.

Discussions continued while they organized the coffee.

He looked around the room. The negotiators were gathered around the biggest map he'd ever seen spread. Several of the Inuvialuit had focused attention on a particular bay.

"It may be the nesting ground of the buff-breasted sandpiper, but I can't see why it's significant," a young sandy-haired bureaucrat with a tiny moustache and a voice that expressed aggrieved disbelief was speaking.

Cindy whispered, "He's the senior government negotiator, Martin Anderson."

Foster heard something in her voice. He stared at her.

A blush spread up from Cindy's neck to her cheeks, which turned a deep pink. She met his eyes and looked down.

"You're going out with him," Foster said in a low voice.

Cindy gave a tiny affirmative nod. "A couple of times."

"According to the *Checklist of North American Birds,* there is no positive confirmation that the buff-breasted sandpiper nests on the northern coast of Banks Island," Anderson continued.

The Inuit and their lawyer stopped talking, considered Anderson and switched to what Foster assumed was Inuktitut. Anderson puffed out his chest and made himself resemble the birds under discussion.

Cindy giggled and quickly put her hand over her mouth.

Foster also thought it was funny. The Inuit could have been speaking a mystery language from Mars as far as the government guys were concerned; nobody understood them. They didn't even have to leave the room to have a conference. Sometimes he'd heard the native guys in the pen speaking Cree or some other Indian language. It had driven the guards crazy.

After they'd served the coffee, he followed Cindy out of the room. In the hall, she smiled at him. "I nearly lost it when I saw how mad it made Marty."

Marty! Time to fast-forward his plan.

The next day, sitting at their usual table in the cafeteria, Cindy sipped her milky coffee and said, "You promised to tell me how you and Mary Beth got together."

Foster returned the smile. "Sure. I took her class at Queen's University. When I moved to Ottawa, I called and asked if she knew of any jobs, and she hired me to help her. To thank her, I invited her out to dinner."

Cindy's eyes shone. "That was nice. Did you bring flowers?"

Foster pretended amazement. "How did you know?"

"And chocolates. Mary Beth loves eating. She told me she never gains weight."

"Right. But not chocolates. She doesn't have a sweet tooth. Nuts, popcorn, trail mix—she loves salty food. One thing led to another. I felt grateful. She was lonely. We ended up taking the plunge."

A puzzled frown replaced Cindy's look of rapt attention.

Before she could ask, Foster sighed loudly and allowed his

mouth to droop. "You're wondering how it worked out." He puffed his lips and exhaled. "It hasn't. Our reasons for getting married weren't the greatest. It hurts me to admit this, but Mary Beth loves the north more than she could ever love me." Foster watched Cindy's face as he spun his tale.

"How could she?" Cindy asked and patted his hand. "How could she with a handsome husband like you?" Her eyes widened. "I'd never do that."

"I know you wouldn't," Foster said softly. "And I wish I'd had more sense. We'll probably get a friendly divorce pretty soon."

As he fed this line to Cindy, he mocked himself. They might get a divorce, but Mary Beth would keep all the assets. Because of the prenuptial agreement, the only way he'd cash in would be if Mary Beth died. Otherwise Foster knew he'd get sweet bugger-all. And he hadn't spent all these months toadying to Mary Beth to come out with nothing. Even in stir, you left with a small stash of cash for the work you'd done inside.

On the way home, he stopped to pick up a pizza. He expected to have the house to himself, but Mary Beth stood in the living room peering at the floor to-ceiling bookcases she'd brought from Kingston and filled with her books.

"I didn't think the negotiations would finish early," he said and held out the box. "Pizza. Sorry, it's pepperoni and double cheese. I would have bought vegetarian if I'd known you'd be home."

"Scrape the pepperoni into the garbage bag and take it outside," Mary Beth ordered before she explained. "That's why we worked late last night. The group flew home today because hunting season begins on Friday, and most of them live at least partly on the land. They'll be gone for a couple of weeks." She waved at the bookcases, "I'm looking for Edgar Christian's diary. They're working on the Dene Indian land claim next, and I have to be sure of the historical precedents for drawing the demarcation line between the Dene and the Inuit at the mouth of the Mackenzie River." She paused. "I don't want to read it again."

High-handed bitch. He'd damn well eat the pepperoni outside. He controlled his rage. "How come? I thought you found something new every time you read one of your books."

"Not this one." Mary Beth hugged herself and shivered. "Christian starved to death when he wintered at the mouth of the Thelon River, where it drains into Coronation Gulf on the Arctic Ocean. You think you had it bad in prison; this was much worse. It was a terrible way to die. Even thinking about the book makes me hungry. The last time I read it, I ate a whole box, a large box, of Laura Secord's mixed nuts. Do we have any of your trail mix?"

"We're out," Foster said and checked his watch. "I'm going to the beer store after supper. I'll stop at the health food store and pick up what I need. Hang on for an hour, and it'll be ready."

* * *

"Coffee?" Foster said, sticking his head into Cindy's cubicle.

Cindy sat clutching her stomach and rocking back and forth. "No, I don't think so." She swallowed and breathed shallowly through her mouth.

"You look terrible," Foster said.

"I feel awful. I think I'm getting the flu. My head aches. I wish I could throw up, and my heart's beating weirdly."

"You should be home in bed. How come you came in?"

Cindy tightened her grip on her stomach and doubled over before she said, "I felt terrific first thing this morning." She groaned. "Whatever this is, it hit me after I got to the office."

Foster stepped closer to her desk. "Get your things. I'll drive you home."

Cindy shook her head. "No, I should go to the nurse's office and see if she can give me something to settle my stomach."

Standing next to her desk, Foster looked down at her waste paper basket. "What have you had to eat today?"

Cindy ventured a pathetic imitation of a smile. "Nothing much. The only thing I had was a bag of your trail mix that Mary Beth gave me."

Foster wanted to swallow, but his mouth had gone as dry as the Sahara.

Sweat coated Cindy's white face. She gasped and held her breath before she exhaled noisily. "Mary Beth said you'd made it especially for her to eat while she read some horrible book. When she decided not to read it..." She clutched her stomach. "She brought the trail mix in for me, because she knew how much you liked me." She moaned. "The cramps are awful."

Foster couldn't form a sentence. Had Mary Beth known what he'd done? Had she set him up? Trapped, his brain ricocheted endlessly, searching for an exit.

Tears rolled down Cindy's cheeks. "Didn't Mary Beth tell you?"

"Last night I called one of my buddies and played pool. I came home really late, so I slept on the couch, and I didn't see her this morning." He didn't add that he hadn't expected to see her at breakfast, because he'd figured she'd be dead.

Cindy punched her fists into her stomach. "If I could just get this to stop hurting and my heart to stop jumping around." She mewed like a tiny pathetic kitten. "I wish I hadn't eaten the whole bag."

Foster thought of how he'd laced the trail mix with the

contents of several packages of larkspur seeds. He remembered the words in the book on poisons, "Death results from increasing the force of the heart's contractions. Too much irritates the heart and jacks up the central nervous system. Death results within six hours."

What should he do?

If he called 911 and told them about the larkspur seed, they'd save Cindy's life. But, not only would he lose her, the police would charge him with attempted murder, and he'd go back to stir.

If he called 911 without telling them the contents of the trail mix, the doctors in the emergency ward might not find out what she'd eaten in time to save her life.

If he did nothing, she'd die and Mary Beth might blow the whistle.

No matter what he did, he'd lose.

Cindy, who had slumped over her desk, raised her head and looked up at Foster. "Please, help me."

Foster picked up the phone. Life inside wasn't that bad—probably better than it would be living with Mary Beth in that godforsaken house. And there was always the library. God knows, he might end up with a PhD.

Joan Boswell's *work has appeared in magazines and anthologies in Canada and the U.S. In 2000 she won the $10,000 first prize in the Toronto Sunday Star Short Story contest. As a member of the Ladies Killing Circle, she has had stories in each of their six anthologies of mystery short stories as well as co-editing the fourth, fifth and sixth books—*Fit to Die, Bone Dance *and* When Boomers Go Bad. *Her first mystery,* Cut Off His Tale, *was published by Rendezvous Press in the spring of 2005.*

An Omen for Gwen

Kathryn Cross

Gwen hobbled from one flower bed to another, deadheading nasturtiums and petunias and cursing the swollen ankle of her sprained foot. She also damned her late husband's quad cane that really didn't provide the support she needed on the uneven ground. And when she shoved the thick-lensed glasses, also her late husband's, back onto the bridge of her nose for the fiftieth time, she cursed those as well. If not for her stupid ankle, she would've driven into town long ago and had her own glasses repaired. "Damn, blast and bloody—"

Gwen tilted her head, brows furrowed, listening. Some idiot of a fool was hammering her front door. What now? she wondered.

"I'm in the back yard!" she hollered. "I'm back here!"

Heavy footsteps crunched in the crushed stone of her walk. Too late, Gwen remembered the JW's who'd been dropping in over the past few months. Nice enough people, but their persistence annoyed. She'd thought telling them of her faith in omens and her interest in Wicca would've scared them off.

He was big, coming round the corner of the house. Big as in tall and broad-shouldered. Formidable looking, especially with that revolver hitched to his hip.

"Mrs. Shire?" From the somewhat perplexed tone in his voice, Gwen knew she wasn't the person he'd been expecting.

Little wonder. Clad in her old-lady gardening clothes, loose at the waist and baggy at the knees, leaning unsteadily on a quad cane, her eyes vague and owlish behind the thick lenses of the glasses, she probably looked ancient and absolutely decrepit, at least to him. "Yes," she said, letting a waver creep into her voice, a mischievous grin tugging one corner of her mouth. Let him think her old and feeble, physically incapable of any wrongdoing. Should she have done anything wrong.

"Mrs. Gwendolyn Shire?" he asked, glancing down at his notebook, the pages ruffled by the morning breeze. When he looked up again from under his hat's wide brim, his dark brown eyes puzzled, Gwen saw he wasn't only big, he was also good-looking.

"Can I help you?"

"It concerns your neighbour, Mr. Watson."

Gwen paused a moment before speaking, in order to keep the venom from her voice. She didn't want the OPP officer suspecting she wanted Watson dead. Just in case Watson already was.

"Mr. Watson?" she asked, not quite sure she'd achieved her objective.

It was B. Watson on his mailbox. She'd christened him Bart, a name she loathed. There'd been a horrific storm the night before he'd moved in. The wind stripping leaves from the trees and lashing rain against the house from every direction. "Bad omen," she'd whispered to Nutmeg, her cat, cowering beneath the bed.

Gwen had tried to be neighbourly, especially since she was Watson's only neighbour for miles around. She'd gone over three days after his arrival with a plate of butterscotch squares, her late husband's favourite.

The door had yanked open at her light knock as though he'd been waiting for her. Watson wasn't big. More thin and wiry. With his hair shaved close to his head so his balding wasn't as evident. In his late forties perhaps, a decade or so younger than herself.

It was his face, though, that commanded her attention. The lines around his scowling mouth and the creases fanning from his narrowed, flinty eyes were deeply etched. As though all his life he'd been smelling something rotten.

"Hello," she said cheerily enough. "I'm Gwen Shire. I live next door." She aimed her finger at her board-and-batten house and the straggling lawn with its collection of trees, vegetable and flower gardens. Admittedly, her property was a bit ragged around the edges, but she preferred it that way— with weeds and wildflowers creeping in, bringing birds and butterflies with them.

Watson's scowl deepened, and she felt the fool standing there with the plate of squares he made no move to take. Gwen tried a different tack, bending down, even though she wasn't keen on dogs, to the miniature collie watching her from behind its masters legs. "What a lovely dog." The dog leapt at her, snapping and snarling. She stumbled back, almost dropping the squares. And a smile flitted across her new neighbour's lips, a twisted little smile Gwen didn't care for.

"Listen carefully," Watson instructed above the dog's growling. "I bought this place to get away from people like you. I'm not interested in being friendly, in being neighbourly. Got it!" He was shouting by then. "So bugger off and leave me alone!" He'd slammed the door.

But not before he'd called her something ending in "itch".

Gwen had turned on her heel, hurt, angry tears starting in her eyes, so missing the lovely family who'd previously occupied the house. She'd flipped the squares into the culvert. She'd almost thrown the plate after them but decided the waste would be ludicrous. She wouldn't throw away a good plate because of *him*.

"Has something happened to Mr. Watson, Constable?" she asked, then glanced at the ID tag pinned to his shirt. "Constable Bradly?" She briefly wondered if his initials stood for Thomas William, two of her favourite names. "Is he in some sort of difficulty?" She restrained the impulse to express the wish she hoped Watson damn well was.

"The fact is, Mr. Watson has lodged several complaints against you."

"What?" Her voice spiked. "What complaints could that, that..." She barely managed to shut her mouth against the epithets that leapt to mind. "...possibly have against me?" Her hands trembled in outrage.

"Perhaps we should go inside." Constable Bradly took her elbow to steady and guide her, as if the trembling of her hands was a symptom of a debilitating disease. She would've enjoyed his touch and the wide expanse of black-shirted chest temporarily filling her field of vision—she wasn't that old!— but her fury over Barty Watson spoiled that.

"Would you like something to drink, a coke or something?" she asked, once they were seated around her kitchen table, once she had her anger under control. It wasn't the officer's fault, and she didn't wish to alienate him. "I could make coffee..."

He was polite enough to accept the coke, taking the can from the refrigerator, refusing the offer of a glass. "This is fine," he said snapping the lid, shifting a coaster so he could set the can on top. The chair creaked a little under his weight, but not alarmingly so. Then he flopped his hat down on the table next to the coke and re-opened his notebook.

Gwen leaned back in her chair, the palms of her hands

pressed flat against the surface of the table. She'd tossed her straw hat into the kitchen sink and knew her greying hair now stood up every which way. Her nuisance of glasses she'd impatiently shoved, once again, to the bridge of her nose. "So what exactly are Mr. Watson's complaints?"

"He says you've been trespassing."

Gwen squeezed her eyes and mouth tightly shut. Yes, she supposed she was guilty of that heinous crime, occasionally treading three or five feet over the property line.

"He claims he sees you every morning dumping a wheelbarrow-load of cat scat onto his lawn."

"What?" Gwen snapped her eyes open. "It's not cat scat! It's his dog's business that I dump where it belongs. His dog's over here constantly, dirtying my lawn, digging up my flower beds, chasing my cat!" She realized she was waving her hands. She took a deep breath and placed them back on the table. "I don't know how many times I've asked him to control his dog. He said he'd moved to the country so his dog could have more freedom, and he'll be damned if he'll chain it up."

If Gwen had secretly applauded her ability to keep her emotions restrained, she was truly in awe of Constable Bradly's. "I see," he said, lifting his brown eyes, completely devoid of expression, to hers. A better poker face Gwen couldn't imagine. Then he bent his head again, turned to another place in his notebook and began writing, or at least gave the semblance of writing something on the blank page.

"I assume," Gwen said, "that is not the full extent of Watson's accusations."

The constable reached for the coke, took a sip, then cleared his throat. "Well, no."

If Gwen had been the sort of person who swore in front of police officers, she would have and in a very explicit fashion.

"Mr. Watson feels you're responsible, in some way, for the grubs and caterpillars infesting his lawn and trees." Constable Bradly didn't raise his eyes this time, but kept them decidedly fixed on the page of his notebook. "He also claims you've been driving snakes onto his property."

"What does he think I *am?*" Gwen demanded through gritted teeth.

Maybe Bart Watson thought she was a witch, maybe witch was the term he'd used when he'd slammed his door in her face. Was that possible? Was the man more than mean, was he crazy?

"Constable Bradly, this has been a bad year for lawn grubs and tent caterpillars. And if Mr. Watson would let nature take its course instead of saturating his property with herbicides and pesticides, he'd be better off. In addition to killing the insects he dislikes, he's killing the good insects that prey on them, not to mention the beneficial birds he's poisoning." Should she tell the constable that Watson used his sprays indiscriminately, that the poisonous mist often settled on her vegetable gardens and bird baths? That she'd cautioned Watson on numerous occasions, but he'd persisted. That, the last time, as soon as she'd turned away from him, she'd heard the hiss of his sprayer and then been enveloped in a choking fog.

"As for snakes..." Gwen sighed. "This is a great area for snakes, lots of frogs for them to eat, lots of fissures in the granite rock where they den over winter. I've no control over where they wander, for heaven's sake. And they're mainly little garter snakes, absolutely harmless."

Even though they were harmless, she'd seen how terrified of them Watson was. Had witnessed his little two-step of avoidance—one she used herself to avoid treading on a snake—turn into a frantic, panicked dance that had ended with him stumbling to the safety of his front porch, his hand clutched to his chest. She'd hurried over—he was still her neighbour—and found him grey-faced and sweating, fumbling from his shirt pocket a small, bright-pink vial of liquid that he spritzed under his tongue. She'd retrieved the vial when it tumbled from his shaking hand and rolled beneath the porch steps. When her attempt to return it to him failed, she'd tucked the vial into the pocket of her cardigan in order to free her hands. "I'll dial 911!" she'd told him, over the snarling of his dog, and tried to loosen the collar of his shirt.

He'd broken away from her, arms flailing. "Get off me! I don't need your help." The back of his hand had caught her across the mouth, the shock of the blow blinding her with white light. She'd staggered back, blood trickling from her cut lip. "See what happens when you get in the way!" he'd said, snarling like his dog.

"He has a gun, you know," Gwen told the constable, not quite sure why she volunteered this information.

"A gun?"

"Well, a rifle. I've seen him sitting with it on his back deck." Gwen wondered if Watson had purchased the rifle as a defense against snakes. The idea might have amused her if she hadn't seen old Barty searching his lawn through the sights of his gun.

"Has he threatened you with it?" Constable Bradly asked, flipping back to the section in his notebook where he'd been writing.

"No," she answered with a laugh, a nervous little laugh, it seemed to her. Watson wouldn't threaten her with a gun, would he? She'd not been sure if he'd been targeting her cat, that day, tracking her as she strayed across one corner of his backyard. "Nutmeg!" she'd shrieked in alarm, startling both her cat and Watson—she'd thought. Watson had looked over the end of the gun, as though surprised Nutmeg was there.

But, then again, what of his warped little grin?

"It isn't illegal for him to own a rifle. Supposedly it's registered." Constable Bradly took another small sip of coke. What emotion was he concealing with his coke this time, Gwen wondered. "He said he needed the rifle to control the vermin overrunning his property. No thanks to you, he said. Disease-ridden, probably rabid, a threat to himself and his dog—"

She laughed outright. "Isabel and her little ones? Josie? Josie's fawn?" What was wrong with Watson, anyway? She hadn't thought people like him actually existed, except as cartoon characters, stereotypical villains in some animated TV series.

"I assume these are the raccoons you feed. The deer."

"I feed the raccoons because it was something my husband did. And there's no creature quite as vicious as a deer, is there? Especially when compared to that wimpy, backbiting mutt of *his*. Besides, it isn't illegal, either, for me to feed the wildlife." She was sure she wasn't imagining Constable Bradly's crimped mouth and dancing eyes, even though he wasn't looking directly at her. "Well, it isn't," she said in a justified tone.

The constable shook his head, his scant grin—if there'd been one—gone. "What about building a privacy fence between your property and Mr. Watson's? That might be a solution."

"Do you know how much a project like that would cost?" she asked, incredulous. "I'd have to fence the whole ten acres to keep his dog out, and it would keep out the wildlife as well."

Constable Bradly flipped his notebook closed and released a breath.

"I feel you need to know something, Mrs. Shire." He hunkered forward, leaned his weight on his forearms resting on the table. "I've dealt with Mr. Watson before. And I honestly don't know what it is with this guy. Badgers his neighbours until... Quite frankly, I was relieved when he left my jurisdiction." Constable Bradly uttered a little grunt. "Then I'm reassigned, and who do I run into first thing." He drummed his fingers on the table for a moment. "The kicker is, he has an influential friend."

"A friend?" Well, she supposed it was possible. Even the worst person in the world had to have some friends. What sort of friend did Watson have, though, she wondered. Was that where Watson went, dog in tow, every other Wednesday? To his friend's?

"One who's capable, it seems, of pulling important strings. So I'm obliged to keep Mr. Watson out of as much trouble as I can *and* to deal with his complaints." He ducked his head and glanced out her kitchen window. "He's sure to note my cruiser in your driveway."

Constable Bradly hitched his chair back with one hand and rose to his feet. "You might consider that fence. One long enough to separate the two yards, at least." He stood for a moment, his hat in his hands, staring at a point somewhere above her head. "And, Mrs. Shire..." He looked down with those dark brown eyes. "You might want to mark, quite distinctly, the boundary of your property, all along the length of it. You might want to do this as soon as possible. Mr. Watson mentioned something about hiring a bulldozer, about harvesting trees and clearing the brush on his acreage."

Gwen's own eyes flashed wide. "But birds nest there, the deer sleep in a sheltered grove, the wildflowers... Why would he do such a thing?"

"He considers it the ultimate solution. Eliminate the habitat, eliminate the vermin, as he calls it. And hardwood trees bring good money. You wouldn't want that bulldozer 'accidentally straying' onto your land."

Two days passed before Gwen trusted her ankle enough to get her into and out of the city. By then she had a million errands to run, including the most important. The purchase of dozens of "no trespassing", "trespassers will be prosecuted" and "private property" signs. Well past dusk, she returned home to Nutmeg's complaints of being kept indoors all day. "Tomorrow, Nutmeg. You'll have to wait until tomorrow to go out."

It was also well past the time she normally set out food for Isabel and her young. Gwen poured nuggets of dog chow into the two dishes on her back deck and replenished the water bowl before she unloaded the car. An hour later she collapsed in bed, her ankle throbbing.

The following morning, when Gwen found the food on the deck untouched, she assumed the raccoons had come at their usual time, discovered the dishes empty and returned to wherever they nested. Besides, she had other worries on her mind. As soon as she'd eaten breakfast, she dumped the collection of signs she'd purchased, along with the wood mallet, into the wheelbarrow. She then pushed the wheelbarrow up the slope behind the house, headed toward the surveyed line that separated her property from Watson's.

Birdsong filled the air, a chipmunk pucked at her in warning, a squirrel nattered from the branches of a tree. She wove the wheelbarrow through the tall grass, the daisies, buttercups and Indian paintbrush. "Why would anyone what to destroy this?" she angrily demanded.

She set the wheel of the barrow in one of the trails the deer had established in trekking across her property, and this made the going easier. A metre short of her property line she encountered the body of a raccoon

Gwen dropped to her knees beside it. "Isabel?" She recognized the distinctive reddish-brown fur touched with silver, the scar across the nose.

The raccoon's masked face was frozen in a snarl, as if she'd died neither quickly nor painlessly. Had she been coming to me for help, Gwen wondered. It had happened once before, to her husband, a raccoon entangled in fishing line. "Oh, Isabel." Then she saw the bloody bullet hole. "Watson!" Had he lain in wait for Isabel, Gwen wondered, along that portion of the trail that cut through his property. He would know the time of day the raccoons normally appeared on her back step.

Gwen pushed herself clumsily to her feet, remembering. "Tac! Guys? Tac! Where are you? Are you all right?" She was sobbing now. She backtracked the game trail until it disappeared into a dense thicket of brush. "Guys?" she wailed. If Bart Watson had murdered the little ones, too, so help him... But what could she do, what recourse did she have?

If only she *were* a witch, she thought. She'd rot Watson's body with pestilence. She'd parch his throat with insatiable thirst. She would summon wind and rain and hail. She would call down lightning and destroy Watson's house, Watson along with it.

In an act of desperation, she spread her arms wide in appeal. "Can't you do something?" She wasn't sure whom or what she was invoking. A cosmic force? Nature personified? "He's evil. You've seen what he's done, what he's doing! He has no care for you, for yours. Can't you intervene?" Gwen desperately wanted an answer, an omen. More than anything, a sign.

When the young raccoons didn't arrive at her back door that night or the next, for Gwen it was her omen. An omen that good would not triumph over evil. Gwen hadn't had a drink in a long time; that night she had two.

Isabel, Gwen buried. She posted her private property signs and searched again, without success, for some evidence of Isabel's litter. She kept constant watch through her kitchen window for a flatbed truck hauling a bulldozer, and she despaired.

The menace of the bulldozer so distracted her, she almost missed seeing him that morning in her driveway. She shielded her eyes against the sun's glare with one hand. "Charlie?" She pushed open her kitchen door. "It isn't that time of year, is it?"

Gwen went back inside and fumbled a dog-eared journal from the junk drawer of her cupboards. She found the page and the date. No, it wasn't that time of year. "Charlie, you're weeks early, what's wrong with you?" For the past three years, Charlie had been very particular about the date on which he made his annual appearance. Was everything in the world now out of balance? She checked through the window again. There was no doubt. Charlie. On a Wednesday, too, when he normally favoured a weekend, for whatever reason.

Then the veil lifted from Gwen's eyes, and she saw Charlie for what he was.

"On a Wednesday!" She glanced through her kitchen window at Watson's house. Not just any Wednesday, but the alternate Wednesday, the Wednesday Barty Watson, with dog in tow, disappeared, not returning until late at night. "Oh, my!"

Hurriedly Gwen retrieved one of the empty burlap bags she used for storing potatoes from the basement. She tugged on her garden gloves for protection. Then she rushed outdoors.

"Charlie, my darling," she greeted him. "Don't worry, I'm not going to hurt you." She had considerable difficulty getting Charlie into the bag, but finally she managed it. She knotted the top and hauled the bag back downstairs into her cool, dry basement. "You'll be fine here."

Gwen readied everything while she waited until sunset, even putting on her cardigan against the coming night's chill. Then, with Watson and his dog long gone, she hauled the aluminum extension ladder out of her garage and lugged it over to Watson's. After laying the ladder down in the grass behind Watson's house, Gwen went back and retrieved a long length of rope, her husband's sheathed hunting knife and the heavy bag containing Charlie. Once she'd deposited these on Watson's lawn, she raised the ladder and extended it until it leaned against the edge of Watson's roof. Then she picked up the bag, the length of rope, stuffed the knife into the waistband of her jeans and clambered up the ladder.

Gwen smiled as she pushed herself up the sloping roof to the chimney. Now she knew the reason she'd invested so much time and effort in her tai chi exercises. "The Force is with us," she whispered and happily hummed the theme from *Star Wars*.

She knew the chimney led to the fireplace in the living room. She'd been invited over many times by the previous owners. And as she used the chimney top to pull herself upright, Gwen also knew, with absolute certainty, that the damper would be open. "Okay, Charlie, your turn." She tied one end of the rope to the top of the bag using the square knot she'd learned in Girl Guides a thousand years ago. Gwen then manipulated the bag until Charlie fit into the flue, drew a long ragged slit with the hunting knife down the bag near the top and lowered Charlie down. Just before the bag reached the hearth, she felt her load lighten as Charlie escaped. Quickly she hauled the empty bag up. "Do what you were created for, Charlie," she whispered into the chimney. "Kill a rat." Then she slid back down the roof and clambered down the ladder.

Gwen sat for a moment in the grass, catching her breath, watching the stars brighten in the darkening sky...feeling quite remarkable. She tucked her hands into the pockets of her cardigan. The fingers of her left hand wrapped round something she'd completely forgotten she'd put there. Another omen. A thrill of elation swept through her.

Once she hotfooted the ladder home, Gwen poured herself

a celebratory drink, then burst into uninhibited laughter as Tic, Tac, then Toe, Isabel's litter, appeared at her back door. *"Salut!"* she offered, raising her glass to whatever force or powers that were out there in the wide wide world. Her ankle...her ankle hadn't felt better in days.

Gwen rose late the next morning, ate a leisurely breakfast, then changed into her old-lady clothes. The ambulance didn't appear in Watson's laneway until noon. The friend, she thought, with a twinge of guilt. But she thought again and wondered if the friend, too, might not be well rid of Bart Watson. What hold might Watson have had on him or her?

Her ankle began throbbing again. Funny that it would. Nor could she seem to lay her hands on that new pair of glasses she'd recently purchased. A puzzle. Gwen fetched the quad cane and her husband's old glasses.

She was ready when she heard the light knock on her front door.

He was as tall and broad-shouldered, standing on her front step, but not quite as formidable looking, now that she knew him a little, even with that revolver hitched to his hip. Still, Gwen kept a firm grip on the object in the pocket of her cardigan, making sure it didn't go astray. It was an object the OPP officer would be obliged to regard as evidence.

"Mrs. Shire," he greeted her.

"Constable Bradly," she responded in kind.

"It's about Mr. Watson."

She invited him in. He accepted the coke she offered and sat down at her kitchen table where he had sat before. "What's happened to Mr. Watson?" she asked

"He's dead."

"Oh." For the life of her, she couldn't utter the words "Too bad" or "I'm so sorry".

"Heart attack, apparently."

"My husband died of a heart attack. It can be very fast." Gwen offered no other comment, relying on a closed-mouth policy to prevent anything untoward from spilling out. But she tightened her grip on the small, bright-pink vial in her pocket. Watson's nitroglycerin.

"There was a snake in Mr. Watson's bedroom. A black rat snake, eight feet long, that even Watson's dog was afraid of." Charlie, Gwen was sure, hardly measured more than six feet. At six feet, with that square-jawed head of a constrictor, Charlie was still impressive.

"What was a rat snake doing in Mr. Watson's house?" she asked.

"It didn't get in though any window or door. Watson had those locked tight."

Gwen arched one eyebrow, hoping she seemed suitably intrigued.

"Up the drainage pipe into the sump-pump well? In through the garage, somehow, or the dryer vent? You tell me."

Gwen did not.

"According to the experts at the Ministry of Natural Resources, rat snakes are excellent climbers. They get into trees, up ladders into haylofts, hunting their prey. They can even climb brick walls." Constable Bradly looked out her kitchen window, and she knew he was estimating the height of the tall brick chimney of Mr. Watson's house. For a moment, Gwen wondered if she were really fooling anyone.

"Rat snakes are a protected species, you know," she said.

"So the Ministry informed me."

Gwen knew, then, that Charlie would be okay.

Constable Bradly finished his coke, picked up his hat and pushed himself to his feet. "About Mr. Watson. I thought you should know."

"Thank you for taking the time to tell me."

He stood on her front step before he fitted his hat to his head and looked up at the bright blue sky. "It *is* a beautiful day."

That it was, and that Constable Bradly had remarked on it, Gwen took as a very good omen.

Kathryn Cross's *mysteries have appeared in* Ellery Queen's Mystery Magazine *and* Woman's World. *Her romance and contemporary fiction has been published, under a name not readily pronounceable, in Australia, South Africa and the* UK. *Her children's short stories have been published, under the same name, in the* U.K. *and the* U.S. *Kathryn lives near Seeley's Bay, Ontario, with her husband and two cats.*

Empty Nest Syndrome

He was her last wee baby,
Her little Bobby Steve,
And although he was past thirty
He really shouldn't leave.

So she let him sit round drinking
And watching TV games.
With her grumpy hubby Robert
Calling him such bad names.

"He's just a big old baby,
He should be leaving the nest;
These years without the children
Are meant to be our best.

"You are such a big old softy,
And he's a parasitic louse
There are one too many Bobbys
In this too crowded house."

Well, her mother birdy mind knew
She couldn't take another fight,
And her heart knew that her baby bird
Wasn't ready for his flight.

Now the nest isn't quite empty
But it's two instead of three
'Cause Big Bobby's in the back yard
With worms for company.

Joy Hewitt Mann

The Day Before the Wedding

Liz Palmer

*A*nd *according to the weather office, the hot humid air mass hanging over Eastern Ontario is going to stay with us for the next couple of days. There's a storm watch for the St. Lawrence area from Kingston to Brockville, so if you're out enjoying the water, be ready to head for safe harbour. And, folks, our electricity suppliers are warning of brownouts and asking customers...*

Catherine switched off the radio. So much for trying to avoid the heat by choosing late August for the wedding. Taking another hard-boiled egg from the bowl, she rolled it between her palms and began to peel off the cracked shell. She hoped there wouldn't be a storm before Charles got back with the cake.

But suppose a major one blew up, a tornado even, and Charles was stuck on the mainland, and the marquee collapsed. The wedding would have to be postponed.

Blast. How she hated it when the white stuck to the shell. She dropped the pitted egg into the discard bowl and picked up another.

A delay would give both Charles and Tracey a chance to change their minds. Not that she disliked Tracey. She admired her courage. She just didn't want her to marry Charles. Tracey's bravado and courage wouldn't make up for her lack of education. Eventually, she would become a millstone around his neck.

Her own millstone, Anna, hunched hawk-like on a stool by the sink, separating paper-thin slices of smoked salmon with her long nails.

"I'm glad we're not at home. Toronto must be unbearable." Catherine wiped her forehead with a paper towel. How did her mother-in-law manage to look so cool? In her apricot linen dress, she could have been presiding over the Ladies Luncheon at St. Matthew's instead of preparing canapés for the rehearsal.

"I can only be thankful Charles chose to have his wedding here, on the island, rather than at St. Matthew's. At least my friends won't have to witness this debacle." Anna waved a piece of salmon at Catherine. "You and Hugh don't seem to care that your only son is marrying that drug addict."

"You're being unfair again. Even you have to admit she has incredible willpower. Imagine the strength it must have taken to drag herself out of the gutter and off the drugs." More strength than she had, or she would have refused to have Anna move in with them after Chuck, Hugh's father, died.

"Once she has him in her clutches, she will revert and take him down with her. I pray every day something will save him." Anna rinsed her hands and dried them finger by finger. "This sink is much too low. It's time you replaced it. You've done nothing to modernize since you inherited."

"We put a new oven in." Catherine looked round the old cottage kitchen. She loved it the way it was, the way it had always been since she had first come to visit her grandparents. After they died, she came every summer with her parents, and now it belonged to her. Her eyes softened as they took in the warm honey-coloured log walls, the old Findlay stove they still lit on cold spring nights and the hand carved rockers, one each side of the stove. She tried not to think of what would happen when she passed the place on to Charles and Tracey.

"It's like history, man." Tracey had stood in the doorway staring around. *"Hey, you wouldn't get me living in this."* She turned to Charles. *"We could make a pile. Put a whole lot of modern buildings up, get some jet skis and motor boats and rent them out to tourists."*

And Charles had laughed.

If there were to be a grandchild who loved the place the way it was, Catherine would rewrite her will.

She wished it were already Sunday with everything over. She ran the tap until the water felt cold and filled a glass, holding it against her cheek for a moment before gulping it down.

"Chuck and I so wanted him to marry Emily. They made a lovely couple." Anna said. "Emily would have accepted him."

"Would she?" Emily with the glossy brown hair and clear, honest eyes. Her family owned the other cottage on the island and yes, Catherine had hoped. She should have known better. Charles had been bringing home waifs and strays since he could walk. The three-legged dog. The cat with one ear and a broken tail. The little boy with the awful limp. And now, Tracey. Catherine put the glass down and went back to her job. She halved a hard-boiled egg and scooped out the centre. "Emily and Charles played together every summer since they could walk. I think they feel more like brother and sister."

"For a would-be artist, you are not very observant." Anna carried the tray of salmon to the fridge, her heels clicking on the tiled floor. "Emily has been in love with Charles for years. What do you want done next?"

"Nothing right now. In love with Charles? How do you know?" She ignored Anna's putdown.

"She blossoms when he appears. She's always eager to do things with him, and she watches him when he's not looking. I haven't noticed Tracey doing the same." Anna looked out of the window. "Where is she? She's not lying in the hammock."

"I asked her to pick some flowers to put in the marquee." Catherine stared at the bowl of dry egg yolks, trying to picture Emily in love with Charles.

Anna spun away from the window. "Not in my garden."

"No, no. I told her not to touch the herbs." Anna and Chuck had spent many summers on the island with them, and over the years, Anna had planted an impressive number of herbs. "Do you think everyone will like curried eggs? Or should I just use mayonnaise?"

"I have no idea. I'm going to check on Tracey. She wouldn't know a herb from a dandelion." Anna hurried to the door. "And had you taken my advice and had dinner catered tonight, you would be free to relax now." The screened door swung closed behind her.

Free to think. The last thing Catherine wanted. She spooned Hellman's mayonnaise into the bowl and began to mash the yolks. "Would-be" artist. That hurt. It wasn't supposed to be like this.

Last summer, she had revelled in the thought of the "studio" waiting for her in their Toronto home. That March, with Hugh's encouragement, she had handed in her resignation, to become effective at the end of the school year. No more lesson plans or late staff meetings. She would have time to follow her passion. Through the spring, she and Hugh had remodelled Charles' vacated bedroom and playroom into an airy, light-filled apartment, ready for their return from the island. Only last July she had felt alive, filled with a bubbling kind of happiness. She ought to have known things were going too well.

Hugh's father had a fatal heart attack in August, and Charles had met Tracey. Of the two events, the death of Chuck had had the most catastrophic effect. She still found it hard to believe she'd agreed to let Anna move in with them.

We can't leave her by herself, Hugh had argued. *She can use the spare room until she finds her feet.* He'd called it the spare room, not the studio.

What about Maggie? Catherine had asked desperately. But Hugh's sister lived in Vancouver and refused to consider it.

And if you've got any sense, Catherine, you'll say no, or your life won't be your own, Maggie had told her.

She hadn't been able to hold out against Hugh's persuasion. The couple of months while Anna got over her loss had stretched to almost a year, and Catherine hardly painted at all now.

She spread some lettuce leaves on the platter and laid out the halved egg whites. Tracey would have banned Anna from the den after the first visit.

I know I'm not an art expert, but surely paintings should please the eye? What is it supposed to be, dear? And why make the leaves that horrid shade of grey?

And she refused to understand the message. *Yes, some people do lead grey lives, but all this psychological stuff is far too clever for me.*

Hugh's sister had been right. But not in the way Catherine had expected. She hadn't expected Anna to take Hugh away from her.

It had happened so slowly, it had taken a while to notice. She was happy, at first, when Hugh escorted his mother to her Thursday bridge evenings, because it made a break for her from Anna's constant *I-know-better-than-you* type of pronouncements, and she knew Hugh enjoyed the game. Even when it expanded to two nights a week, she didn't complain. But then, soon after

Christmas, Hugh and Anna had joined a study group at St. Matthew's, and they were gone for a third evening and part of Sunday. And when they were home, they talked together of things Catherine wasn't a part of and people she didn't know.

He began to beg off accompanying her to art shows or movies she wanted to see with the excuse he needed an evening at home. But it wasn't until a friend asked her if she and Hugh were having problems that she sat down and really looked at why she was so unhappy with her life.

She felt excluded. As though Anna and Hugh were the couple and she the drudge who cooked and cleaned for them.

Before they moved to the cottage in June, she'd told Hugh that things had to change when they got back. *Anna needs to get back to her own life with her own friends. And we need to renew our marriage. When was the last time we did something together, just the two of us?* He'd promised to speak to his mother.

And he had. Catherine had eavesdropped. It was when she heard him agreeing that, yes, there was plenty of room in the house, and it did seem silly for Anna to have the expense of a separate place, that she decided to act.

Hugh still hadn't told her about this conversation with his mother, nor had she told him she had put her name down for substitute teaching. Thirty mutinous teenagers seemed less daunting than spending the entire fall with Anna.

Catherine scraped the last teaspoon of egg mixture out of the bowl and popped it into her mouth. It needed more curry. Too bad. She balanced the filled platter on top of the marinating steaks in the fridge. Time for a swim before she hauled Hugh from beneath the old boat he was fixing and got him to change for the rehearsal.

The phone rang.

Drat. She picked it up. "Hello."

"Mom," Charles said, "I've got the cake, and I'm on my way."

"Keep an eye on the weather, darling, and go back if it looks iffy."

"Don't worry, I'm following the marine forecast."

"I'm just off for a last swim before the hordes descend. Put the cake in the spare fridge as soon as you get here." She hung up. Now to escape for an hour of peace in her special place on the island.

The screen door slammed. Tracey stomped in, holding out blotchy red, scratched hands. "Look at me. It's not going to look good with my dress tomorrow. What'll people think I've been doing?"

In Catherine's opinion, no one would notice if Tracey walked through the marquee naked. All eyes would be riveted on her face.

The first time Charles brought her home, Catherine had been fascinated by the number of rings in her ears. She had wanted to see if the rims would peel off like the edges of perforated paper. She didn't mind the eyebrow rings but hated the nose and mouth ones. At least the tongue jewellery had gone, but it had taken an infection for that to happen.

"Let's see." Catherine took Tracey's hands in hers, turning them over. "Have you been picking the late raspberries up in the field?"

"Yeah. Em showed me the patch yesterday, and we went again this morning." Tracey took her hands away and started to scratch.

"Em?"

"Yeah, the girl who lives in that other cottage on the island. She's friendly."

Not friendly enough to point out the poison ivy.

"You need something to stop that itch. Wash them with

soap while I fetch the calamine."

"How'd you stand it all summer? There's nothing to do and now this fu...stupid poison stuff everywhere and fish and weeds in the water. I'd sell it and buy a condo with a pool."

Be positive, thought Catherine, running upstairs, at least the girl had tried not to swear.

Anna was looking at Tracey's hands when she returned.

"Heavens, Catherine, that stuff is useless for poison ivy. I'll fetch my healing cream. The calendula in it will soothe the skin."

Catherine stared at her. Anna never, ever shared her cream. When the church bazaar committee had suggested she donate some to the Christmas bazaar, she had refused. *I design it for my skin only,* she'd told them.

"What are you staring at, Catherine?"

"I...I'm just stunned. You've never let anyone else use it."

"We have never had an emergency like this before." Anna stalked off.

"How'd I get poison ivy anyway?" Tracey asked studying her hands.

"Hm?" Catherine tried to think what to do for the best. "Probably while you were picking flowers. It's my fault. I should have shown you the plant. I keep forgetting you're a town girl." She wouldn't mention that the raspberries grew in a particularly luxurious patch of the ivy. "I really don't think you ought to try Anna's cream. She makes it from her herbs, and goodness knows what she puts in it. You don't want to risk another kind of allergic reaction."

"Here we are." Anna came in with a small blue jar. She unscrewed the lid. "Smell." She held the jar under Tracey's nose.

"Cool. What's it for, anyway?"

"For the winter. I get dry, itchy skin if I don't put this on every night. And it keeps the skin flexible." Anna held out her hands. "How many seventy-four year old women have hands that look as young as mine?"

Catherine watched the two women. Why did Anna have to choose this moment to do a complete turnaround and become friendly towards Tracey?

"I'll try it," Tracey said, ignoring Catherine's advice. She reached to scoop some out with her finger.

Anna whipped the jar away. "No. Not like that." She took the handle of a spoon and scraped some cream from the jar.

"Why not use your fingers?"

"Contamination. I use rubber gloves when I make it, and a clean spoon each time I remove some. Here." She passed the cream to Tracey.

"I'm going for a swim," Catherine said and went upstairs to change.

For a moment after she dived in, the water felt cold against her sticky skin, but just for that second. Then it was bliss. She swam along the rocky shoreline and climbed onto the flat rock ledge. Her private place. The hot wind blew over her wet skin. She lay back and concentrated on the sultry sky. Don't think about anything. What will be will be. She watched the oak leaves moving gently in the breeze, then closed her eyes and breathed slowly in and out, emptying her mind the way she'd learned in yoga classes.

The rumble of distant thunder above the sound of lapping water intruded into her empty mind. The promised storm, but still far away. She slid back into the lake and swam to the dock.

The grass up the slope to the house felt dry and dusty beneath her toes. She glanced at the glowering clouds and sniffed the air. It smelled of rain.

"Catherine. Where have you been? Charles sent me to look

for you. You're never there when you're needed. Tracey isn't very well, and she's saying some dreadful things." Anna's helmet of white ordered curls was now in disarray. Her hands clutched at Catherine.

"She was fine an hour ago." Catherine ran the last few yards and rushed to the kitchen. Tracey drooped in the rocker with Charles hovering over her.

"Let me see, Charles." Catherine knelt by Tracey, noting her dilated pupils. She felt her forehead. "She's very hot." She took Tracey's hand. "You are having an allergic reaction to something. Did you eat anything other than the raspberries when you were out?"

"It's not what I ate. It's her. The old witch. She never thought I was good enough for Charles. Now she's poisoned me." Tracey rubbed her eyes. "I can't see properly."

"Nonsense. Think back. It's important. What have you eaten?"

"Just the blueberries Em gave me and the raspberries."

Catherine turned to Charles. "Emily knows her berries. Charles, check which flowers Tracey picked."

"You don't think...? Anna looked at Catherine. "Emily wouldn't, would she?"

"No." Catherine turned back to Tracey.

"But she might," said Anna. "She is in love with Charles. Or it could have been an accident."

"Whatever it is, is an accident." Catherine snapped. "She could be super-allergic to poison ivy." She ran a tea-towel under the cold tap, wrung it out and held it against Tracey's forehead.

"She hasn't picked anything that could hurt her." Charles crouched down. "Tracey, we need to get you to hospital. Mom, call 911 and have an ambulance meet the boat at Gananoque. Gran," he turned to Anna, "go and find Dad."

189

"He's in the boathouse," Catherine told her, dialling the emergency number.

"I'll fetch him." Anna almost ran from the kitchen.

"This is medical, and it's urgent." Catherine said. "We need an ambulance to meet us at the town dock in Gananoque. My son's fiancée is having a severe allergic reaction to something."

"I'm not," Tracey screamed. "I've been poisoned by that fucking old witch. I want the police."

"Hush now. You mustn't say things like that." Charles stroked her hair.

"But it's true. She put something on my hands for the poison ivy. That's what did it. I'm going to die, aren't I?" Tracey rocked back and forth, wailing.

"Yes, I'll hold. They're connecting us to the hospital," Catherine said to Charles. "Hello?"

"Ma'am, an ambulance has been dispatched. It could save time if we know the likely cause. Can you describe the symptoms?"

"Her vision is impaired, and she feels very hot." *This isn't supposed to be happening.* Catherine felt unreal, as though she was acting a part in a drama. "Oh, and her pupils are dilated."

"What about her mouth. Is it dry?"

"Tracey, how does your mouth feel?"

"Like my tongue is too big, and my skin is too tight. I want off this island." Tracey clutched at her chest.

"You heard that? The possible causes," Catherine watched a frowning Hugh usher Anna into the kitchen, "are eating the wrong berries or a reaction to a home-made herbal cream."

"No." Anna teetered across the kitchen and snatched up the small blue jar. Using her fingers she scooped out a great dollop and began smearing it up her arms and rubbing it into her skin. "I stand by my cream." She had almost emptied the pot before Hugh wrenched it away from her and put it down.

He looked at Catherine. "I'm taking Mother with us. You'll stay here. The guests will be arriving in Gananoque in a couple of hours. When they call, tell them to wait at the hotel until we contact them." He sounded very stern. "And check the marquee, the wind is getting up."

Thunder rolled across the darkened sky as the procession headed down to the dock. Ten minutes over the open water, and the rest of the trip would be sheltered by the other islands. Catherine watched the boat take off, spray flying from the bow as it bit into the waves, and knew it would be an uncomfortable twenty-minute ride.

She turned and went slowly up the hill again. Why was Hugh snapping at her? And what did he expect her to do? If the damn tent blew away, she wouldn't be able to stop it.

Behind the cottage, the white canvas sides of the marquee hardly moved. They'd chosen a sheltered spot, and it looked safe for now.

Inside, the first thing Catherine saw was a pot of milkweed wilting on the makeshift altar. Tears filled her eyes. *I didn't mean it to happen to Tracey,* she said silently to whoever was listening.

But since it has happened, she told herself, *perhaps it's for the best. You didn't want Tracey to be the mother of your grandchildren. Now you'll be rid of them both and be free in September instead of having to wait for Anna to use the cream in the winter.*

It sounded so easy, but her mind kept seeing the look of terror on Tracey's white face.

A flash of lightning lit the tent, followed immediately by a loud crack of thunder. Catherine covered her ears and ran for the cottage.

The rain came in sheets, pounding on the roof, drowning all other sounds. She rushed around, closing all the windows.

In the kitchen, she poured herself an iced tea and sat at the table. She imagined what would happen now. She would have to testify at the inquest, under oath. She had no need to lie. Anna did experiment with her herbal cream and always kept the ingredients secret.

The coroner's jury would come up with a verdict of accidental death—which was true of Tracey's death, she hadn't planned that—then they would make lots of recommendations on the dangers of using herbs. And that would be that.

"Then there's Emily," she said aloud. Supposing Anna was right. In a couple of years maybe, they would be doing this again, this time with the right bride.

The sound of the phone startled her. She leapt up.

"Yes?" She covered her other ear to keep the drumming sound out.

It was Hugh. "They think she'll be okay."

"What?" Catherine pressed the phone to her ear. "I didn't get that."

"Tracey." Hugh shouted. "She's probably going to be okay. They think she ate some nightshade berries. She's very ill, but it looks really hopeful. Mother is crowing, of course."

Nightshade berries? Not the cream. How could it be? She stretched over to the table and picked up the blue glass jar.

The label read; Anna's Healing Cream, 2002.

It was from last year. Catherine's knees gave way. She collapsed into a chair, her heart thumping.

"Can you hear me?" Hugh shouted in the sudden hush as the rain stopped as suddenly as it had started.

"Sorry. I'm just, just so relieved." And it was true. *I must have been mad. Thank you, thank you, Powers That Be, for saving me.* The heavy lump she'd felt in the pit of her stomach disappeared. She wanted to dance, to raise her voice and sing with joy.

"We're all relieved," Hugh said, "but Mother has been going on about Emily being in love with Charles and giving Tracey the berries. I tried to shut her up, but now it seems the police have been called in."

"Surely Emily wouldn't deliberately…" She didn't finish. She knew Emily would never mistake a nightshade berry for a blueberry.

"No. Tracey probably picked it herself. Um, Catherine, I have a confession to make and an apology to offer," Hugh said. "I don't know how to say this. But remember last month when I came in and you were stirring mother's potion? You had a strange look on your face and…" he went on, but Catherine didn't hear. She was remembering the panic of that moment. Had he arrived one minute earlier, he would have seen her dropping the monkshood into the vat of simmering herbs.

Oh my God. She stared at the phone. In the moment of euphoria at not being a murderer, she'd forgotten this year's batch of healing cream was still sitting in Anna's room. All twenty-five jars laced with monkshood. Each one lethal.

"Catherine? Catherine? Are you still there?"

Liz Palmer's *stories have appeared in the last four Ladies Killing Circle anthologies. Her story "When Laura Smiles", published in* Bone Dance, *was shortlisted for the 2004 Arthur Ellis short story award. Liz writes from Quebec, where her home overlooks the Gatineau River. She is often to be found kayaking on the river but claims she is still working as she plots best whilst paddling.*

Cold Dead

Linda Wiken

It's all right, Mr. Salvatros. You'll be just fine. A patrol car will be here in a few minutes to give you a ride home."

Constable Sylvie Moran checked on her motorcycle, balanced her helmet on the handlebar and looked around for some place the old man could sit down. He hadn't stopped shaking since she'd found him. Hadn't spoken a word, either. The two-foot cement wall would have to do. "Just have a seat over here while we wait, sir." She reached for the old man's arm.

"Don't need your help. Don't need a ride either. You've got some nerve, stopping a law-abiding citizen…" he paused, wheezing… "who's out running his errands. Some nerve. I ain't never been stopped by the cops before." He turned his head to the side, spat, then looked her straight in the eye, chin stuck forward, hands on his hips. Still wheezing.

"Mr. Salvatros, I stopped you because there was an all points bulletin to keep an eye out for you. Someone, your family maybe, thought you were lost. We're just trying to help."

"Well, lady, I don't need your help. I'm doin' okay on my own." Another pause, this time to suck in some air. "I didn't get to be seventy-nine by getting lost and not being able to take care of myself. That's a lot of BS. I'm not lost. Ask my goddam nephew." He flinched, like he thought Sylvie planned to grab him. "I was headin' for the mini-mart, only it wasn't where he said it was. So I'm looking for it. There a law against that?"

"No, Mr. Salvatros. Like I said, someone was worried. We were asked to find you. You're found. Now, in a minute, a patrol car will be here to give you a ride home."

He grunted, slid his hands into his pockets and nodded in the direction of her bike. "Can't you take me on that?"

Sylvie stifled a grin. "Against regulations. I'm sorry."

"I'd sure like a spin on that." He gave in to a short coughing fit, cleared his throat and spit. "What's a pretty young thing like you doing riding that, anyway?"

"I'm on traffic duty, Mr. Salvatros. I asked to be on a bike."

A white patrol car pulled up beside them before the old man had a chance to say anything else. Sylvie gently steered him toward the back door as the officer driving got out.

"Watch your head now, Mr. Salvatros. Constable Drake will take you home. You take care of yourself now."

He'd gone silent again.

*　　*　　*

The call beeped onto the screen of her MVT just before two a.m. The dispatcher echoed the words. "Any available unit...a 10-45 on the railroad tracks just south of Riverside at Pleasant Park."

She automatically reached for the mike. "MC-4. I'll take it."

"10-4, MC-4. Meet VIA Rail Security at the scene."

Another mike flipped on the airwaves. "Delta 410. I'll back up."

Sylvie flipped the switch for the overhead lights. No need for a siren at this hour of the morning. She did the eight blocks in a couple of minutes. No black ice, even though the temperature had dipped below freezing, and there was plenty of frost around. If she'd been on her bike, she would have made even better time, but the bikes had been stored for the winter. Thank God. Just the thought of being out on it in this weather froze her toes.

It took her another minute to walk the distance from the cross street, to where the train idled. She tried to prepare herself for what she'd find. She dreaded these calls. Ten years on the job, and the dead bodies still got to her.

The security officer waved her over. "Bet the poor bugger didn't know what hit him. Looks to be pretty old. In his eighties or so."

"Where's the train engineer? I want to talk to him."

"He's pretty shaken up. Told him to go sit in my car."

"You didn't touch the body?"

"Naw. I know the routine. Looks weird though, like he had a raincoat over the top of his pyjamas."

Sylvie walked back to the marked security car, opened the back door, leaned in and identified herself.

The engineer looked to be in his mid-forties. He gave his name and address at her prompting, his hands clasped together in his lap. Sylvie noted that it didn't do much to stop them shaking. In fact, his entire body shook. Shock.

"This won't take but a minute. Can you tell me briefly what happened?" Sylvie asked.

"I saw something on the track. I…I didn't know what it was…just a shape. I blew the whistle and rang the bell, slammed on the brakes back about…oh, three hundred yards back." He took a deep breath. "But that doesn't do much. It takes a good thousand yards at least to get to a crawl, let alone stopped. I tried. I really tried." He looked at Sylvie, and his face crumbled.

"You just wait here a minute. The paramedics will take care of you." She touched his shoulder, eased the door shut and waved a paramedic over.

Two cruisers pulled up to next to her car, and she quickly filled the officers in. "There's nothing but bushes backing onto this spot. No night owls could see over here. Unless someone was out walking a dog. Can you two do a search of the area? An old man out after midnight, someone must be wondering where he is. I'll check with the info desk and see if there are any reports."

Sylvie knew she should take a look at the body but opted to put it off a bit longer, getting back into her cruiser to radio in. She had her answer within a couple of minutes. The family of Georg Salvatros had reported him missing just before midnight. If that's who it was, she'd met the guy only last month.

Sylvie walked back to the track and braced herself. Regardless of his identity, it would be gruesome. She clenched her teeth and tried not to gag at the sight of Salvatros's crushed body.

*   *   *

Sylvie backed the cruiser into a space in the underground station parking lot, signed off the MTV, grabbed her briefcase and headed for the elevator. The traffic office lacked its usual congestion. Five fifty-five a.m. The patrol shift—the one she wasn't even working—had ended an hour ago. Traffic, her duty, didn't usually work nights. Only when big shots came to town. Escorts between important locations. Like tonight when the visiting ambassador wanted to stay late at the embassy party.

Of course, the other guys in traffic had known better than to answer a late night call. They'd all headed straight back to the station after the escort ended. But good old Sylvie—still trying to score points. Or was it, just trying to be a good cop? Whatever.

She finished typing her report as the seven a.m. traffic shift began trickling in. The last thing she wanted was questions. She filed the report in the Sergeant's basket and left by the back door.

The shower helped. But now, when she needed to be tired, her mind raced, and heading to bed would be useless. She was too wired. Time for breakfast.

She drove a few blocks to a small diner that lured the morning shift with its slate of breakfast specials. Some of the guys would roll by in an hour or so.

She inhaled some coffee and leafed through the morning news while waiting for her eggs. She couldn't concentrate.

What was a little old man doing on the railroad tracks at that hour? More to the point, why hadn't he tried to get out of the way? Why had he sat frozen to the track? She had questions. There shouldn't be any. Write it up as a straightforward accident. But she couldn't let it go. Maybe because she'd met the old guy. He'd wanted a ride on her motorcycle, for frig sake.

The family might answer some of the whys. Let her put it to rest. Give an old guy a reason for dying.

* * *

She had to do some fast-talking to get her partner, Ken Tite, to agree to questioning the family of Georg Salvatros. The traffic accident investigators would do all the blocking off and measuring at the scene. The first officers to respond would sign off their own reports. End of the case. He was right, of course, but she couldn't let it go.

"Mrs. Kronos, you've told me you were sleeping in bed, and your husband had fallen asleep in front of the TV, so neither of you heard your uncle leave the house."

"That's so, Officer. I got up to go to the bathroom, then

turned off the set and shook Peter, then checked on Uncle Georg." She tucked a stray strand of orange hair behind a bobby pin holding the French roll in place. Odd shade for a Fifty-something meek and quiet homemaker, Sylvie mused.

"What did you do after that?"

"We checked the rest of the house, and Peter looked outside in the yard. Then we called the police."

"Can you think of where your uncle might have been going?"

Mrs. Kronos shook her head. The stray lock fell from its perch.

"Had he done this before?"

"No."

The kitchen door swished open, hitting the door-stop. A bulky man, about the same age as Mrs. Kronos, black hair giving way to grey, forearms the size of watermelons, sucked up the space. "I'm Peter Kronos. You are?"

"Officer Sylvie Moran, Ottawa Police. I'm looking into the death of Georg Salvatros."

He snorted. "A waste. Do the police have so much money they can spend time on an old man's accident?" Kronos commandeered a chair, joining them at the kitchen table. He stared at his wife. She got up and poured him a coffee.

Sylvie shook her head at the offer of a cup then answered, "We always like to tie up loose ends."

"What you talking about?"

"Well, for instance, why was Mr. Salvatros out at that hour of the night? And why on the railroad tracks? Do you have any answers, Mr. Kronos?"

"You bet. He was out because that's what he did. Crazy old man with Alzheimer's, gets it in his head to go. Nothing fishy about that. Just crazy." He tapped the side of his head.

Sylvie let the silence build for a couple of minutes. Mrs.

Kronos played with the lace-fringe on her place mat. The husband sat stock still.

"And you didn't hear Mr. Salvatros leave?"

"Not a sound. After the wife's good cooking, my night cap and the late news on the TV... I fall asleep. Right there in my chair. Next thing, she's shaking me."

Sylvie nodded. "But why would Mr. Salvatros go to the railroad tracks?"

Kronos shrugged. "Who knows? He lives in his own world. Who knows why he does anything?"

Sylvie turned to Mrs. Kronos. "What is the name of your uncle's doctor?"

"Why'd you want that?" Kronos asked.

"It's routine."

Kronos finished his coffee in a gulp, slammed the mug on the table and pushed back his chair.

"Seems my taxes should go to catching car crooks or those hoodlums that tramp through my shrubs and break them off. That's where the real crime is these days." He stomped out the back door.

Mrs. Kronos gathered the mugs. "You'll have to excuse Peter. He gets the yard looking just right—it's his pride and joy— and something happens to it. Those kids really upset him."

Sylvie shook her head as she walked out to her car. There's a death in the family, and these folks are worried about the yard?

*   *   *

"I'd like to speak with Dr. Murchison." Not much hope of it, Sylvie thought as she looked around the crowded waiting room. The receptionist probably wouldn't fit her in. No give in that face.

"You don't have an appointment." Small mouth set in an even narrower line. Sharp blue eyes demarcated by no-nonsense round frames.

"No. I'm not a patient. I'm a police officer, and I'd like to speak with the doctor about a former patient of his."

The sign on her desk read Judy Fellows. She moved it over a fraction, as if to get a better view of Sylvie. "Which patient?"

"Georg Salvatros."

"Oh, dear." The face softened. "Oh, such a shame what happened."

Finally, someone who cares, Sylvie thought.

"I heard it on the radio and told the doctor first thing this morning. Such a curmudgeon he was, but he could be quite a flirt. On his good days."

"You said, his good days. What were his bad days like?"

"I shouldn't be saying anything."

"Why not? I'm not asking you to reveal any medical records. I'm just asking for your observations."

"Oh, well, I guess it's okay then. His arthritis bothered him something bad most days, especially when it rained. You'd hear him growling coming down the hall. He couldn't bear to be touched. Sometimes he wouldn't even talk."

"What about his mind? Was he lucid most times? Did he forget things?"

She shrugged. "No more than the rest of us. Never missed an appointment. Of course, his niece always brought him, but he didn't pay much attention to anything she said."

"I thought he had Alzheimer's."

"Not officially. Oh, I probably shouldn't have said that. But you'd hear it from the husband. He used to worry about it. Days he'd bring Mr. Salvatros in, he kept insisting how Mr. Salvatros had Alzheimer's, how he'd keep forgetting things and keep wandering off. He was really worried about him. The niece didn't seem to care about him or wasn't worried about his forgetfulness."

"I thought you'd said the niece always brought him in."

"She had, but these past two times it was the husband. Every two weeks. Standing appointment on Monday afternoons. Like I said, he seemed to be the more worried of the two. It was really touching."

*   *   *

The flip chart covered the upper half of the hall closet door. Sylvie lounged on the sofa facing it and stared. She'd divided it in half. One side labelled "fact", the other "fiction".

Fact: arthritis Fiction: Alzheimer's

Fact: difficulty walking (sometimes) Fiction: wanderer

Fact: sitting on train track

She'd stopped at that. Was there a fiction? No, she'd seen the body. His overcoat had been frozen to the track. Not sure how that had happened, although the temperature had been cold enough for it.

So he'd been walking…wandering…tired and sat down for a rest. Reasonable. But, if for whatever reason, the coat had frozen to the track, why hadn't he gotten out of it when he heard the train coming? Just undo the buttons. Maybe his fingers were too painful? She'd have to ask the doctor when he finally got around to calling her.

Or, had he been sitting? Better check with Ident and see if they could tell his position. Maybe he was already dead and had been dumped on the track. If not, then why hadn't he moved?

How was his hearing? Did he hear the train? Another question for the doctor. She couldn't wait any longer—she'd give him a call. And she'd check with patrol…maybe one of them had seen something that night.

*   *   *

They sat in the patrol car while Sylvie brought her partner up to speed. "So, the autopsy showed sleeping pills, but the doctor said he hadn't prescribed any. The will gives the motive. Now the only question, is it a conspiracy?"

"You've got a plan?"

"Just follow my lead."

They approached the front door. Mrs. Kronos answered on the second ring. As they walked into the kitchen, Sylvie asked her to have her husband join them.

"So, what now?" Mr. Kronos grumbled a few minutes later.

"Just a few loose ends, Mr. Kronos. Mrs. Kronos, do you use sleeping pills?"

"Why, yes. Sometimes it's hard getting to sleep, especially if Peter starts snoring before I sleep. Then I take."

"And the night your Uncle died…did you take them that night?"

"Yes, I think so."

"But why? Your husband wasn't in the bedroom. He was watching TV, you said."

"Yes," she glanced at Peter. "But I didn't think I'd fall asleep."

"Do you take them every night?"

She straightened her back. "Yes."

"So, noises don't usually awaken you?"

She shook her head.

"But you might wake up to go to the bathroom?"

"Yes."

"And did your uncle usually use sleeping pills?"

"No. He always liked his cup of hot milk before going to bed. That put him to sleep."

"And you added a few sleeping pills to his hot milk that night, Mr. Kronos?"

"What?" he sputtered. "You have no proof."

"Proof of what? I merely asked if you'd helped Mr. Salvatros get to sleep that night. Maybe he came in while you were watching TV and complained about not being able to sleep, so you gave him some of your wife's pills. It's a natural enough thing to do."

Kronos sat silent. Sylvie continued.

"And then when they'd worked, you went into his room, picked him up, stuffed him into his raincoat and took him out to your car. Then you drove to the train tracks where you spilled water on the track, set the old man down and left him to die."

Kronos stood up and the chair fell backwards. "You lie. You don't know that. I didn't do it."

"Oh, but Mr. Kronos, I do know that you were setting Mr. Salvatros up over the last several weeks to make it appear he was getting Alzheimer's. That wasn't his doctor's diagnosis. You as much as admitted that you gave him some sleeping pills. And your car was spotted by a patrol officer at the side of the road, at the Pleasant Park crossing at 12:50 a.m. Not much happening that time of night. The officers always take note of cars in no parking areas. So, if you didn't take him there and leave him, why didn't you find him and take him home?"

"Peter, it's not true, is it?" Mrs. Kronos started sobbing, not waiting for an answer.

"Why did you do it, Mr. Kronos? Was it because of all that money, with your wife as sole beneficiary? Was it time for him to pay his bill?"

Her partner moved to block the back door. Sylvie stood in

front of the door to the hall. Mrs. Kronos clawed at her husband's arm. "It isn't true. You wouldn't do that. Not to Uncle Georg."

Kronos looked from one officer to the other. "It's not true."

"I think it is," Sylvie said and went through the scenario again. "You did it, Mr. Kronos. I just wasn't sure if your wife was in on it or not. I think she wasn't. Isn't that so? Or do you want her to be charged along with you?"

Kronos wouldn't look at any of them. His shoulders slumped, the powerful arms limp at his sides. "No. She didn't have anything to do with it. I did it…for her. She was always whining about how she had to do everything for him. Uncle Georg wants this, Uncle Georg wants that. I never got a moment's peace. And the old bastard never paid for anything. He's sitting with all that money from his furniture store in the bank. He doesn't pay a lousy cent. The wife spends my money on the leech and whines. I did it for her."

"No, you got greedy. Trouble is, I did some checking into a police report Mr. Salvatros had filed last year. It seems he got involved in a get-rich scheme and was defrauded. If he'd told you he'd lost all his money, he might still be alive."

Sylvie pulled a set of handcuffs out of her pocket. "But I think he was worried you'd kick him out."

Linda Wiken *is the owner of Prime Crime Books in Ottawa. She is a member of the Ladies' Killing Circle, and her short stories have appeared in their five previous anthologies as well as other mysterious publications. She was shortlisted for an Arthur Ellis Award for Best Short Story in 2003.*

A Nice Cup of Something Hot

Linda Hall

I was sitting in the back seat of a police car, a grey wool blanket around my shoulders sipping hot coffee from a Styrofoam cup. The snow had turned to a kind of sleet, which on the roof of the car sounded like cutlery dropping. I was sitting there because I had just killed someone. That's what they do when you kill someone, they give you coffee and a grey blanket and sit you in the back of a police car.

In the storm, my car had skidded into a drunk who'd staggered onto the road. There was nothing I could do. At least that's what I told the police officers who came and found me crouched over him, my own good wool coat sopping up his blood and covering his neck, which had bent at that awful angle.

Shock does strange things to you. It makes you cold when it's warm and warm when its cold. I sat beside him in the road, in just a cotton sweater and jeans and hadn't felt the cold until later. Until now.

I had told my story at least a dozen times. I hadn't seen him. I'd needed a few things at the drug store, and yes, I *had* gone out on a night like this. I hadn't realized the streets were quite this bad until I was around the block from my apartment, and no, I didn't think to go back. I should have but hadn't. I was half-way to the mini-mall by the time I realized how deep the snow was, how awful the roads were. That's what I told them. They wanted to know what I'd bought. Band-Aids, extra strength Tylenol, Nice 'N Easy Dark Ash Blonde and Nail Slicks nail polish in Perle #820. I showed them the bag. They didn't look inside.

If you're wondering if I was being honest with them here, I wasn't. Shoppers Drug Mart hadn't been my primary destination. Well, yes, I'd been in there. I'd bought all those things that I'd said I bought, but that wasn't until later. What I'd really needed was scrapbook supplies. I'm a mad scrapbooker, totally hooked since taking a "Preserving Your Memories" workshop at the Needles 'N Trims store. They close at nine, and I needed supplies, so I'd gone out. I'm so hooked that when I want string or ribbons or sparkles, I want them now, if you know what I mean. It was only later that I thought about nail polish, and once inside Shoppers I remembered my grey roots and my headaches.

Since my husband left me, walked out of a perfectly good thirty-one year marriage and began shacking up with his bimbo, I've been trying to do things for me; scrapbooking, colouring my hair, looking nice, making the effort.

The front door of the police car opened, bringing in the snow and wind. A new face peered back at me, this one belonging to a cop, so young and peach-faced that he looked like Spanky of Our Gang. I'm talking about the television program, not the music group. I remember them both. When I was little, I was always half in love with Alfalfa. The young cop climbed in and shut the door. He smelled like snow, and I had an urge to touch his jacket, feel the cold on him.

"Mrs. Wilkins? Is there anything you need? Is there anybody I can call? A family member perhaps?" His voice was so gentle that my eyes watered.

I shook my head. "No. I have no family members. Not since..." My voice trailed off. Why had I started with that?

He bent his head at me, nodding, urging me to go on.

"I'm...I'm divorced." A fresh batch of tears. He reached back and patted my shoulder. He seemed so kind.

"They're going to have to take your car for a little while," he was saying. "They need to have a good look at it. I'll be driving you home in the SUV." He was still patting my shoulder awkwardly, like he was unused to such ministrations.

And I was weeping again, shaking my head and weeping. He handed me a Kleenex, and I blew my nose. I wonder if some scientist somewhere has ever measured tears. How much can a person cry before there's no moisture remaining in the body, and it dries to a fine white powder and blows away like sand? I had pretty well not stopped crying since Hal had walked out on me.

"You ready to go home, or do you want to sit some more?" he asked.

"I'd like to go home now."

He came around, got me out, and led me gently, his hand on my arm. "The SUV is better for this weather."

I climbed into the SUV. "I forgot my things," I said. "Can I get my things out of my car before we go?"

"Certainly. I'll get them for you."

"The Shoppers bag on the front seat and my purse."

He left, and through the frosted windows I watched him approach the huddle of police and ambulance drivers. They were moving the body now, lights flashing through the snow.

Of course, I'd been crazy to come out in this storm. Hal always called me crazy. Said he couldn't live with a crazy woman any more... Crazy, crazy. My entire body was trembling. I closed my eyes and pressed my lips together to keep my teeth from clacking against each other.

"You didn't tell us you went to Needles 'N Trims," the young cop said to me accusingly when he climbed in the SUV. I stared at him, open-mouthed. He was smiling. Okay, it was a joke after all, and I saw what had happened. The bag from Needles 'N Trims had somehow fallen out of the Shoppers Drug Mart bag. He handed both to me.

I quickly put my Needles 'N Trims bag inside the one from Shoppers, rolled the top of it down and didn't say anything. My scrapbooks were my private affair. My things. My time for myself.

"Do you do crafts?" he asked, pulling out on to the snowy road. "My mother does needlepoint," he added.

I looked out the window. The ambulance was driving away, slowly, sadly. No need for hurry, no need for sirens now. The lights looked blue against the snow. The dead man was Ernest Rodhever, Ernie to his friends. Bank manager and member of the Rotary. Recently divorced from Rebecca Rodhever. He would probably have a big funeral full of words from kith and comrade. The victim was unknown to me.

"I have a picture in my kitchen she did." He was saying. "It's of a wagon train in snow. Like tonight. Only instead of a car it's a wagon. Framed. You'll have to direct me to your house."

"Down this road a mile or so. At the light, turn left onto Brisbane. It's the Westminster Apartments. I'm on the fifth floor."

"The Westminster apartments?" He turned to look at me.
"Yes."

A few minutes later he said, "Quite a commotion there a few months back."

I shrugged. I knew what he was talking about. Everyone who lived anywhere near Westminster apartments knew that Bruce Searshot had fallen to his death off his fourth floor deck. Some said it was suicide. Others thought it was an accident. The findings by the police were inconclusive.

Outside, the sleet had changed to a kind of half-rain that sounded like hands patting the top of the vehicle. He asked me if I knew the man who'd fallen, and I nodded and said I knew him to see him, that was all.

When we stopped at a light, I asked him his name. He adjusted the mirror and said, "I thought I told you. I'm sorry if I didn't. I meant to. It's Robert. Call me Rob."

"Isn't that interesting. My son's name is Rob. He's a stock broker. Investments. Bay Street."

"Perhaps I could call him for you."

I looked down at my hands, the veins like thick worms crawling across my flesh. When had my hands gotten like this? When had I become this woman with hands like this? I used to be so young. There was a time I was even pretty. "No. Don't call him."

The air in the car was stifling. The young always make it too hot for us. They think we like it that way. I placed the back of one hand against the window, trying to extract coolness from the pane.

Ahead of us, the lights of a twenty-four-hour coffee shop on the corner from my apartment looked surreal through the snow, like a painting on a calendar.

"Would you like a cup of coffee?" he asked.

"What?"

"We could stop for coffee. I think we both need to unwind a bit. Have a cup of something hot."

"That would be nice."

He parked in front of the coffee shop, and he came around to take my elbow as he helped me down from the SUV, as if I was an old woman. Well, maybe I was. Maybe to him I was. And then I thought how nice it would be to have a son who did this, a son who walked his mother into a coffee shop at eleven at night to get her a nice cup of something hot to drink.

There were a few other patrons in there. Two men were at the counter talking about the storm, and a young couple sat together in the far booth and held hands across the table. There was a time, years ago when that could have been Hal and me.

He ordered coffee, and I asked for just a cup of hot water, please. I don't often drink coffee, and certainly nothing with caffeine this late at night. I'd had a couple of sips of coffee in the police car earlier and would probably pay for it later.

Rob was pleasant and talkative. I mostly listened while he told me about his wife and baby at home, about the new house they were building across the river, about how his wife wanted to do the bedroom in a kind of yellow and how he wanted blue. I told him how lucky he was to find love. After a few minutes he said, "Tell me about your divorce. It must've been very painful for you."

I looked down at my cup. They'd given me a tea cup instead of a mug. That was nice of them. "It was very hard."

He looked so serious, so intent, the way he touched my arm, like no son had ever touched my arm, so I told him my sad, sad story.

Later in my apartment, I couldn't sleep. You'd think if I'd just killed someone, that's what would have kept me awake, but no, it wasn't that. It was all that talking about Hal. He shouldn't have left me. It just wasn't right. It wasn't fair. I fell into tears again. Hal. Hal.

I cried as I dumped out my new scrapbooking supplies onto the kitchen table. I had two days worth of newspapers to go through. I cried as I plugged in the kettle. I wept as I went through my papers and added pictures and addresses. I sobbed when I pasted them in, adding coloured string and ribbons.

At around six in the morning, I fell into a restless sleep. In my dream, I was running my car over Hal and his bimbo, the way I'd run over Ernie. Only in my dream I kept running over them, back and forth, back and forth. Then I dreamed that Hal was falling, turning over and over as he fell to his death from the deck. Instead of Bruce Searshot falling the way he did, it was Hal, and it was me who had pushed him.

The ringing telephone jarred me awake.

"Mrs. Wilkens?" I sat up on the couch where I'd slept.

"Yes?" All over me were paste and markers and newspaper cuttings and scraps and scrapbooks. I had left the cap off the red marker, and through the course of my turning and tossing, it had written an elongated Z on the couch cushion. There was also some red on my forearm and a bit on my face.

"Mrs. Wilkens, this is Rob."

I cleared my throat. "Hello."

"I was wondering how you are."

"I'm okay."

"You sure?" He sounded so caring, so son-like. "It was quite an ordeal you went through last night."

"Thank you for calling, Rob."

A few minutes later, I got up and went to the bathroom. I really wanted a bath, a nice bubble one, with candles even, but a sponge bath would have to do. I've been bathing this way for six months now, filling the sink with water, leaning my head into it to wash my hair and then sponging off the rest of me.

Behind the closed shower curtain was the heap of bloody clothes, encrusted and dried to a dark brown by now. I couldn't go in there. I couldn't even move them to a safer place.

Before I washed my hair, I carefully removed the red from my cheek with dabs of cold cream and cotton balls. I'd have to be more careful. I'd have to pay more attention.

In the kitchen, I boiled more water, poured myself some

Kashi, and got out my scrapbooks. The little matter of the red Z on the couch worried me. I hoped the couch wasn't ruined. If I couldn't fix it, it would be yet another thing in my apartment that would be off-limits to me; like my bathtub, my computer case and my 21.7 cubic foot freezer that I kept in my second bedroom. The whole second bedroom would soon be off-limits to me.

I drank hot water from my tea cup and wandered through the day's newspapers, which had come through the mail slot. I get four each day, two in the morning, one in the early afternoon and one at night. I managed to find six more pictures of Hal. These I cut out.

You may wonder that I can find so many pictures of my ex-husband. Well, Hal's a real estate broker, so his picture's in the papers, plus on lots of lawn signs, like he's running for office. When he'd first left me, I'd taken to driving from house to house late at night, parking behind bushes, venturing out and defacing his picture with a black magic marker. I drew mustaches and beards and put round circles around his face with lines through. I thought I was quite clever. No one would suspect me. How could they? A respectable woman-of-a-certain-age writing four letter words on For Sale signs? Think about it.

I'd also managed to find a picture or two of Maura. That's his mistress. It's always a little more difficult to get pictures of her, and sometimes I have to resort to taking them myself. Sometimes I follow her, keeping well behind as she does some ordinary task like grocery shopping, and there I am at the ready with my digital camera. Then I put them on my computer and print them off.

I stacked my scrapbooks on the coffee table. I put Hal's scrapbook on top of Maura's, then I got out my murder weapons one.

I collect murder weapons. Well, I don't really collect the actual weapons, I don't want you to think that, but what I collect are pictures of murder weapons used in actual cases. I follow trials— I sometimes even go to them—and when the murder weapon is mentioned, I look through all my books and magazines for pictures. I've been pretty lucky in finding just about everything I've needed. I've got pictures of guns, knives, pillows (These are easy to find—just go to any Sears ad in any newspaper and you're bound to find pillows!). I've found fireplace pokers and cast iron frying pans in ads for Canadian Tire, but my all time favorite has to be a curling trophy. Yes, someone actually killed someone with a curling trophy! It took me a while to find it, but I lucked out when a rink in our town won some sort of bonspiel, and there was this picture of the skip holding up a trophy right there on the first page of the sports section!

Sun glinted through my window. I got up and closed the blinds. The snow was deep, but at least it had stopped. Down below, Clyde Frodiff was shovelling, and across the way, old Mrs. Gibb was sweeping off her deck. That woman, always sweeping snow, never shovelling, always sweeping. I hope when I'm that old I don't get like that. I looked down to the place where Bruce Searshot had fallen off his deck and onto the ground. Being one floor above him, I knew exactly where that place was. If I squinted, I could almost see him lying there still.

The intercom buzzed. I pressed "talk", thinking it might be the mailman or the courier guy.

"Mrs. Wilkins? It's me, Rob."

I buzzed him up, and while he was on the elevator, I scrambled to shove my scrapbooks under the couch. Then I closed the doors to my bedroom and the bathroom attached to it. Then I turned on the television as if I'd been watching it all along. Old women watch television, and in his estimation, I probably fit that bill.

"Would you like some tea?" I asked him cheerfully when he came to the door. "I have the kettle on."

"I would, thank you."

I knew he was just being polite. Police officers don't usually drink tea. I know this, but on the other hand, I don't keep coffee around. Hal used to drink coffee, but when he left he took with him all the remaining canisters of Tim Hortons along with the Mr. Coffee.

"Are you here with news about my car?" I asked.

"Not yet. I'll keep you posted on that." He stepped into my kitchen, stood there looking around. "I just have a couple more questions for you." While he talked, I looked at the apartment from his eyes and saw the trashcan heaped with paper cuttings, my newspapers stacked in a corner of the living room floor, the scissors, my bottles of glue, my marking pens, bits of cloth, ribbons and colored string. I also saw the dishes in the sink, a loaf of bread on the counter, the cereal box, the butter where I'd left it, the dirty knives on the sideboard. Back when it was Hal and me, I never would've stood for this. I used to have a girl who came in and cleaned for me once a week. I don't have her any more. Sometimes I regret not having her any more.

The kettle whistled, and I unplugged it and got down the tea bags. I'm very fond of Earl Grey.

"It's about your ex-husband, Hal Wilkins," he said.

I turned suddenly, almost pouring boiling water on my hand. "Hal?"

"You told me he left you. I got the impression from you that it was fairly recently, and that's why you weren't yourself last night." His cheeks were flushing purple. "But my information says it's been five years. He's remarried, and they have a child."

"He went and married someone young enough to be his daughter!" I sloshed water onto my counter, that's how much my hands shook. "What kind of a man goes and marries someone half his age? How do you think that makes me feel? And a child!" I managed to still my fingers enough to get two tea bags in the pot and pour water over them. I set the works on the table with the cozy on top.

"You also said you had a son named Rob. I looked that up, too. You have no children, Mrs. Wilkens. You and Hal Wilkins had no children."

"He has a child with that Maura!" I spat out the words. I was shaking now, like last night. "I was mixed up last night. I've been through a lot. I may have said strange things. I don't even know what I said!"

I turned away from him to the sink, pulled off a paper towel from the roll and dabbed at my eyes.

He was holding a bottle of glue, turning it over and over in his hands, looking around, not saying anything. It was making me nervous. Then he sat down at the kitchen table, poured himself a cup of tea and started drinking it, still not saying anything. I asked what colour he and his wife had decided on for their bedroom. Anything to change the subject. He told me yellow. That's a good choice, I said, but he kept looking at me. Finally he asked that if I didn't mind, could he check in on me periodically? His own mother was gone, and he felt a kind of responsibility toward me. Still trembling, still shaking, I said that was fine. Before he left, he asked to use the bathroom. I said okay and led him to the half-bath off the hallway.

He hugged me before he left. Hugged me! Then he said he was sorry. He knew I'd been through an ordeal, he should have been more understanding about Hal.

When the afternoon paper came, I boiled the kettle again and began skimming through the divorce section. Oh, I know what you're thinking, there is no such thing as a divorce section like there is a births or obituaries. But really there is, if you know where to look, and I do. It's the auction section; the legals, those little notices absolving a man—it's always a man—of any encumbrances and debts owing against him. I found a few. Also, I looked for trials and murder weapons to add to my collections.

I found more pictures of Hal. I used my scissors and cut his nose and placed it on one ear, and put his two ears where his eyes should be, and cut out his mouth and placed it upside down. I laughed at that, and you would too, if you'd seen what I'd done to him! I wondered how it would be if I did that for real.

Rob called me the next day, and the next day. And the next. I got my car back at the end of the week, and still he called. Usually he ended up talking about his baby, who was changing every day, he said. He promised to bring me pictures the next time he came over. He always asked how I was doing. No one had ever done that, not even during those early days when Hal left. On Tuesday he called to tell me that his little girl had a new tooth, her first. She was standing too, well, not on her own, but walking along furniture, that kind of standing. I said how nice.

On Saturday, a full two weeks after it happened, Rob called again. "Just tying up some loose ends, Mrs. Wilkins, just trying to get a handle on things." He cleared his throat. "A man in your church, a Thomas Gillian, died of food poisoning a year ago at a church supper? Do you remember that, Mrs. Wilkins?"

"Well, of course, I remember that! I quit going there after that! Something like that happens in a church, you just lose your trust in people."

"Hmm," was all he said.

A day later, he called and asked about Marta, my cleaning lady.

"I had to let her go."

"Her family reported her missing six months ago."

I said, "The day she disappeared, she confided in me that she planned to run away to Vancouver. I told the police as much at the time."

But I have to say that his questions were making me nervous. Why was he asking all these questions, especially when he was so nice to me? Most people aren't, you know. Your husband leaves you, they automatically think something's wrong with you!

When Rob didn't call for four days, I looked up his name in the phone book. I didn't find it. Well, lots of police officers have unlisted numbers. You can't be too careful these days, especially when you have a wife and baby daughter to think about. So, I called in at the police station and was told by some secretary, probably, that Rob was out on a call.

"Poor thing. He works so hard, and especially with his wife and baby at home. I just wanted to invite him for supper."

There was silence, then, "Wife and baby?"

"He promised to show me pictures next time."

More laughter. "You sure you're talking about Rob? Our Rob? That guy's as single as they come. In fact he's more single than they come. He's the party animal to beat party animals. Wife and baby!" And then she laughed some more.

I hung up. All day I worked on my scrapbooks. Didn't eat lunch. Had no supper. No tea. Worked feverishly. I knew what was going on. I didn't just fall off a turnip wagon, not me. I knew the price of tea in China. He was getting like Marta. Steps would have to be taken.

Two days later, he called. "Mrs. Wilkins? I'm sorry I didn't call you. I was away for a few days with Mandy and the baby."

"Oh?" I kept my voice steady, cheerful. *Mandy and the*

baby! "I would love it if you and your wife and baby could come for supper, Rob. That would please me very much. You've been so kind to me."

He told me that his wife and daughter were spending a few day at her mother's, but he'd love to come by himself. Fine, I said, just fine.

The following day he was standing at my door, and I was offering him a nice cup of something hot to chase away the winter cold.

"I have a few more questions for you," he said taking a sip and pronouncing it good. "About that man that fell off the deck here. It turns out he'd left his wife about a month before he died. Did you know that?"

"Hmm," I said, drinking my water and watching him sip tea.

"Also, the man who died in your church, he'd left his wife, too."

"There's a lot of that going around. Men leaving their wives for younger women."

He looked at me curiously. "How did you know they were younger? I never told you they were younger."

I shrugged. "Only a guess."

I'd made my green bean casserole, you know the one—with the frozen green beans and the dried onion rings and cream of mushroom soup. But since I can't use my freezer any more, I had to rely on canned, so it wouldn't be as good, probably. But, it would be highly unlikely that we'd get that far. I'd end up eating that stuff for days and days. He just kept drinking his tea and looking at me. Looking. Looking.

After I put him in the freezer, and that's no small feat with a big guy like him, let me tell you, I boiled the kettle and had myself a cup of Earl Grey.

I'd thrown Rob's wallet and rings into my computer case, which had become the receptacle for such things. I thought about my coat then, my good wool one that I'd used on Ernie Rodhever. I wondered if I would ever get it back. Well, if I did, I'd add it to the others in the bathtub.

Later on, after I put plastic wrap on the rest of the casserole, I pulled out another scrapbook from underneath the couch, the one on serial killers. My favorite. I'm especially interested in female serial killers. There aren't many, you know. Well, there's that one they made a movie about. Did you see that one? I think she got an Oscar. Maybe someday someone will make a movie about me. Maybe they'll get an Oscar, whoever they get to play me.

Linda Hall *is the award-winning author of ten novels and seven non-fiction books. She has worked as a newspaper reporter and feature writer and teaches a popular course in writing fiction at the University of New Brunswick.* Steal Away *introduces her newest series character, private investigator Teri Blake-Addison, who solves cases of missing people.* Chat Room *continues that series. Her next book,* A Good Season for Whales, *is scheduled for release in 2006.*

Hopscotch

Sue Pike

Elizabeth stood in the driveway of the house where she'd lived for thirty-eight years, watching two men manoeuvre her sofa through the front door and into the back of a yellow moving van.

A third man opened the attic window and called down to her. "There's a box up here, way at the back under the eaves. Want me to crawl in there and bring it out?"

"Sure. I'll come up and have a look."

She climbed the stairs to the second floor and waited at the attic door while the man passed her, carrying two small red chairs.

"I've left it on the floor up there. Other than that, I think we're pretty well done," he said. "We'll head over to the apartment and start unloading."

Elizabeth continued up to the small room at the top of the house that many years ago used to be the children's playroom. It was empty of everything now except a large dusty shoebox in the middle of the carpet. She waited until she heard the moving truck rumble out of the driveway, then sat cross-legged in front of the box on the floor and wiped the lid with a tissue until she could make out the words printed in orange crayon on the top: "Property of Rosie Anne Galbraith. All others KEEP OUT!"

She smiled, remembering Rosie's long-ago habit of squirrelling away treasures, but she was pretty sure she'd never seen this particular box before. As she lifted the lid, her breath caught in her throat, and the room seemed to tilt sickeningly. Inside was a pair of very large boots painted a bright blue. She pressed them to her breast and lowered her head to breathe in the faint aroma of paint and old leather. She remembered finding them in the basement on the morning after Brady left. She'd put them in a bag and hidden them on the top shelf of her closet, but Rosie must have found them and added them to her own collection.

After a few minutes, Elizabeth put the boots to one side and lifted the other items from the box—the plans for the basement they'd drawn with orange crayon on newsprint, the stub of an orange crayon, a photo of Brady with seven-year-old Sarah and six-year-old Rosie leaning against his knees and at the very bottom of the box, an old bone-handled penknife.

Elizabeth hugged her knees and howled into the empty house.

* * *

Elizabeth's first view of Brady Keeler was his size thirteen boots stumping down the steps of the bus one Sunday afternoon in late September of 1970. The right sole had split away and caught when it touched the pavement, causing him to stumble.

He was well over six feet tall, thin as an old fence post, with pale red hair poking out from under a faded blue bandanna. The legs of his tattered bell-bottoms were covered with peace signs, and when he turned to collect his rucksack, Elizabeth could read "Hell No", written in laundry marker on one side of the thin material covering his behind and "We won't go" on the other.

"Let's hope that's not him," Elizabeth's husband Walker muttered in her ear. She knew without looking that his lips would be pressed into a hard, straight line. She kept her own mouth shut, hoping another, more prepossessing young man might emerge from the bus.

When there was nobody left but the gangly boy with big hands and wrecked boots, Walker and Elizabeth moved forward to meet him.

He told them his name was Brady. He was from a small town they'd probably never heard of in Ohio, and he'd just celebrated his twentieth birthday. Elizabeth, at twenty-six, felt the weight of a generation between them.

Walker started questioning him on the drive back to the house. Did he have any problems getting across the border? Had he proper papers? What were his plans, now he was in Canada? The boy shrugged and stared at his knees, and Walker frowned into the rear view mirror.

When they got to the house, her husband drove the baby-sitter home, and Elizabeth introduced Brady to Sarah and Rosie, who stared up at him solemnly, then backed up the staircase until their eyes were level with his. He raised his right boot and wiggled it to make the sole flap up and down, and the girls giggled into their hands.

A worn canvas rucksack was his only luggage. Elizabeth led the way to Rosie's room and told him their youngest child would bunk in with her older sister while he was with them.

"I sure hate to put you folks out." Brady stood awkwardly in the centre of the room with its pink bunny wallpaper and stacks of blocks and Barbie furniture crowding the shelves.

"We're delighted you're here," Elizabeth's voice cracked with the effort of sounding enthusiastic. "Really. It's Sarah's seventh birthday today, and she thinks we've imported you just for her."

But dinner that night was awful. Sarah was too shy to open her gifts in front of a stranger and insisted on having her meal under the table. Rosie shot sly glances at Brady from under half-closed eyelids and kicked her foot out, causing bellows from beneath the tablecloth.

Walker left most of his dinner on his plate and strode to the kitchen, returning with a large glass of scotch and ice.

"There are a couple of organizations you might be interested in." He said as he sat back down. "The Community Action Committee helps draft dodgers find jobs. You might want to talk to them tomorrow."

"Okay. It's a bit confusing right now." The boy stirred his mashed potatoes, and a deep blush crept up his neck.

"There's another group that tries to put pressure on the U.S. government from here. I've been on their board for a couple of years." Walker began to fold and unfold his napkin.

"Well," Elizabeth broke in. "Maybe we could drive around tomorrow. Show Brady some of the sights." Her voice rose in an effort to sound cheerful.

Walker frowned at her and began again.

"Any idea what kind of work you'd like to apply for? I've got the forms in my office, but I need to know what you can do."

"I'm not fussy. Anything at all." Brady blurted the words out but kept his eyes on his plate. "I worked in a feed plant back home."

Walker sighed. "Well, that's fine, Brady, but I don't believe we have any farm co-ops in the city." He rolled the napkin into a tight cylinder then let it fall open again on the tablecloth. "Okay. Let me ask around. There might be similar work available. Anything else you'd like to try?"

But Brady only shrugged.

Elizabeth stood up. "Why don't we do this later." She began to gather up the debris from the birthday gifts and was glad to see Brady stacking dishes. Walker tossed his napkin on the table and carried his drink off to his study without another word.

Next morning, Brady came downstairs after Walker had left for work and Elizabeth had seen the girls off to school. He'd showered and changed into a clean shirt and jeans. Without the bandanna, his wet hair curled against his shoulders. His boots caught on the carpet, and he lurched into the banister. After he'd eaten, Elizabeth led him down to the basement to show him how to use the washer and dryer.

Brady watched while she went through the steps, then wandered around the open area, ducking his head to get under the beams.

"That toilet and shower were installed by the last owners." Elizabeth waved a hand into the gloom. "Otherwise, the basement is probably just the way it was when it was built in the twenties. We've talked about fixing it up but never got around to it."

Daylight filtered in through mud-spattered windows, highlighting dust motes and a badly pitted concrete floor.

"What would you think if I fixed it up and made a place for myself down here?" Brady put the sole of his good boot against the rubble-stone wall, and they both watched as sand and pebbles sifted to the floor.

"It's pretty dreary and damp."

"It'd be great. I could paint the walls and floor with sealant and put up a screen of some kind, maybe find a cot somewhere." His face had begun to lose its guarded look.

Elizabeth found crayons and tore some sheets of newsprint from the children's art easel, and they sat at the kitchen table working out a floor plan before driving to the hardware store. Together they chose three gallons of blue waterproof sealant, a couple of brushes and a long-handled roller. Brady tried to pay out of his small store of American dollars, but Elizabeth pushed his billfold away.

"I should be paying you for the labour. I'll be so glad to get the basement cleaned up." But by the time the bill was rung up, she had only a few dollars remaining from the grocery allowance Walker had handed her earlier in the week.

When they left the store, Brady stumbled on the curb, and Elizabeth grabbed his arm. "Are those boots the only shoes you brought?"

He nodded. "I didn't have much time to pack."

"Well, at least we can get them fixed," she said, steering him into the shoe repair shop.

Brady worked in the basement all that afternoon, and when the sun began to fade, Elizabeth carried a floor lamp down from the family room and set it up near the laundry tubs. Walker phoned to say he wouldn't be home for supper, so she made sandwiches and took them out to the picnic table in the garden.

Sarah and Rosie found turpentine and rags in the garage and helped Brady clean his hands. They laughed when they saw his boots, now spattered with blue paint.

"It's okay," he told them. "I'll finish painting them tomorrow, and then I can have waterproof shoes for rainy days." Their eyes shone with admiration.

Walker was furious when he got home about midnight and smelled the wet paint. "What the hell do you think you're doing? This is supposed to be a temporary arrangement, and you're encouraging him to fix up a place for himself down there."

"Taking in a draft dodger was your idea, not mine." Elizabeth turned up the TV, hoping to drown out their voices.

226

"I'm just trying to make him feel welcome while he's here."

In the morning, Walker went partway down the cellar steps and stood on the landing for a moment, but only sighed and shook his head when Elizabeth handed him his coffee.

Brady appeared with a small bag of furry green toast crusts in his hand. "I found this hidden behind a drawer in Rosie's bureau. I couldn't figure out why it wouldn't close all the way."

"She's our squirrel. Always hiding stuff. Who knows why." Elizabeth took the bag and dropped it in the garbage.

Brady stopped painting when the girls came home from school. They took turns running their hands over his shiny blue boots. He fetched a softball and mitt from his duffel bag and challenged them to a game in the backyard. Elizabeth found an old bat in the garage, and Brady taught the children how to throw the ball and when to swing. The bat was too heavy for Rosie, so he pulled a dead branch off the crabapple tree and carved a grip the diameter of her hand.

"What a beautiful penknife." Elizabeth watched as paper-thin slices curled away from the wood.

"It was my grandfather's. I never go anywhere without it." He passed the knife to her, handle first, and she ran her fingers over the deep grain on the bone handle.

For the rest of the week, while the children were at school and as soon as her housework was finished, Elizabeth perched on the cellar steps to watch Brady work. They talked a bit and listened to tapes on the portable cassette player. On the second day, he told her about the events that had led to his coming to Canada.

"I came home from work a couple of weeks ago, and there's my folks sitting in the parlour waiting for me." Brady poured more paint into the roller pan. "I could see the draft notice lying on the coffee table. They hadn't opened it, but they sure knew what it was." He worked the roller back and forth in the pan, until a thick layer of blue covered it. "My dad looked weird. Sort of frightened and proud at the same time."

He stood up straight, and his voice became so quiet that Elizabeth had to lean forward to hear. "We had one godawful fight. I said I couldn't see the point in going to Vietnam and killing people who never did us any harm, and my dad said some stuff about letting my country down. And then my mom starts crying. My little sister comes in from playing and pretty soon, she's crying too."

Elizabeth waited, saying nothing.

"My dad's a big cheese in the VFW. The Veterans of Foreign Wars. Fought in the South Pacific and never stops talking about it. Best days of his life, he says." He lowered himself onto an unopened gallon can. "So anyway, I went to my room and grabbed some stuff and took off. When I went past the parlour, they were all still where I'd left them. My mom crying and nobody else saying a goddamned thing." Brady drew in a deep breath. "When I was out on the sidewalk, my dad came out and told me I was through being a part of the family. If I deserted, that's what he called it. If I deserted, they never wanted to hear from me again."

Elizabeth sat still, a tight feeling in her chest.

He'd walked around town for a long time, he told her, eventually ending up at a bar on the outskirts where he found two other boys who were also being called up. They had some beer then around midnight, piled into a car and drove north. At some point, they pulled over and slept for a while, then crossed the border early the next morning, telling the customs officer they would be visiting friends for a couple of days. The others had the phone number of an organization in Toronto that directed them to a church, where they were given a meal and some Canadian money. His friends were billeted in

Toronto, and he'd been given a bus ticket to Ottawa and told that someone would meet him at the terminal.

"I think your husband was hoping for someone different, though. Someone with better reasons, maybe."

Perhaps that was the moment she could have told him it wasn't his fault—that few things measured up to Walker's expectations. But Elizabeth was only just starting to figure it out for herself, that the joy for Walker was in the anticipation, never the reality. Marriage, children, the law firm, none of it was quite what he'd hoped for. And now Brady, whom Walker had hoped would be his intellectual equal and planned to show off as proof of his own social awareness, had turned out to be just an ordinary, inarticulate boy.

Each afternoon that week, Sarah and Rosie would leap off the school bus and rush upstairs to change into play clothes. Elizabeth put Buffalo Springfield on the stereo, and Brady showed the girls how to ride their two-wheeler up and down the driveway and how to shoot a basketball.

"Draw us a hopscotch, Brady, please!" Rosie wheedled, her face pinched with longing. Brady took the chalk she handed him and drew a perfect series of squares and numbers on the driveway. The girls laughed when he threw a stone and then made exaggerated leaps from one square to the next.

"Wait till Daddy sees it. He'll murder him," squealed Sarah. "He never lets us put marks on the driveway."

On Thursday, Brady said he'd like to fix some things around the house. He changed the washers on the hot water taps and cut the frayed section of cord away from the toaster and replaced the plug.

"How about your husband. Doesn't he like to repair things?" he asked as he put the tools away.

Elizabeth laughed. "Are you kidding? He's a lawyer. Lawyers

would rather sue people than fix things."

Walker stayed late at work most of that week, but on Friday he came home early and invited Brady to walk up to the neighbourhood pub for a drink after dinner. Elizabeth put the children to bed and tidied the kitchen. She was in bed reading when she heard them return. When she asked Walker what they'd talked about, he yawned.

"Nothing much." He folded his trousers carefully over a hanger. "I told him if it was me, I'd rather fight this insanity on my own soil. Go back home where I stood a chance of making a difference." He slurred over the word "insanity."

On Saturday, Brady began building a partition in the basement, and Walker went out about noon, not returning until late that night.

Sunday dawned sunny and warm. Elizabeth caught Walker's elbow as he was heading into his study after breakfast. "This may be the last nice day of the year. Why don't I pack a lunch and we can go to the park? Just us and the kids." But Walker had to work on a case that was coming to court the next week. "Ask your boyfriend," he said, removing her hand from his arm. "I'm sure he'd like to go." He shut the study door behind him.

At the park, Brady said, "I think I better find somewhere else to live. Things feel a bit tense at the house." They had finished their picnic, and he and Elizabeth sat side by side on a park bench watching Sarah push Rosie on the swings.

"I'm sorry about Walker." She scratched at a bit of egg salad on the knee of her jeans. "He blundered into this draft dodger program for all the wrong reasons. His law firm is known for its stand on social justice issues. They do a lot of pro bono work for charities and left-wing causes, and poor Walker's never really fit in. I think he thought if he did this one thing, the others in the firm would admire him for it, see him as one of them."

"Only I don't fit the bill."

"It's not your fault. He's just a bit of a snob. It's the way his parents brought him up."

They sat quietly for a moment until the girls ran up and caught Brady's hands. "Come and play hide and seek with us. You're it."

Brady hunkered behind a huge maple tree whose leaves were beginning to turn a brilliant orange. He covered his face with his hands and began to count to one hundred in a deep baritone. The girls flew off to hide among the play structures.

Elizabeth felt tears prick her eyes. It hadn't occurred to the kids to ask her to play. When had she become so old in their eyes? How had she become so staid at twenty-six? She thought of girlfriends who were having the time of their lives teaching in the slums of Liverpool or backpacking across Europe and Asia. And here she was with two kids who thought she was ancient and a husband who at thirty was well on the way to becoming a lush.

Elizabeth sat watching the game and reliving the events of the last eight years. She squirmed as she remembered the weekend she'd gone up north on a ski trip with some girls from high school. Belinda's family owned a chalet, and the girls had expected to have the place to themselves, until Belinda's brother and some of his law school friends turned up on the Friday night. They'd brought booze and pot, and Elizabeth had gotten high and ended up in bed with Walker. It was the first time she'd slept with a boy, and she became pregnant. Walker had wanted to find someone to fix the problem, but her father had overheard a phone conversation, and before they knew what was happening the two families had frog-marched the pair down the aisle.

Monday was windy and overcast. Wet leaves piled up against the curbs, and the girls wore trousers and turtlenecks to school.

Elizabeth gave Brady the car keys, and he returned with boards to enclose the section of the basement that held the toilet and basin. On Tuesday, he landed a job at a local camera shop.

"It's only part-time right now. But when the Christmas rush starts, I'll get more hours."

Thursday morning, they awoke to rain. Elizabeth helped the children into their slickers and boots and kissed them goodbye at the door, but they reappeared in moments, their eyes welled up with tears.

"Daddy scrubbed away the hopscotch," Sarah said.

"He wouldn't do that. It must have been the rain." Elizabeth countered. But Rosie had dragged the push broom from the garage, and they both pointed accusing fingers at the wet chalk adhering to the bristles.

That evening, Brady worked late at the camera shop, and Walker came home early. During supper, he suggested the girls help him rake leaves in the back garden, but they protested, saying it was too dark and wet. Walker exploded in anger, throwing his plate to the floor. "You only want to do things with Brady. Is that it?" Spittle flew from his mouth, and the children cringed away from him. "Well, you know what? He's going to leave pretty soon, and then you're going to have to do as I say. You hear me? I'm your goddamned father!"

Elizabeth put both children into Sarah's bed and read to them until they slept.

The family had been invited to spend Saturday at a cottage in the Gatineau Hills owned by one of the partners in Walker's firm. Walker woke up that morning groggy and sick.

"You'll have to go without me," he said. "Give some excuse."

"You don't want me to tell them you're hung over?" She snapped at him, but he wouldn't meet her eyes.

The children argued that Brady should come, but Walker wouldn't discuss it. "Besides, he's got to finish the basement," he said while they were packing the car.

When Brady came up to say goodbye, the girls clung to him, saying they wanted to stay with him. "You go." He helped them into the car. "And I'll have a surprise for you when you get back."

For Elizabeth, it was a day fraught with tension. Wave after wave of thunderstorms kept them trapped in the cottage among people she hardly knew. The kids whined and clung to her. It was late when they finally got back to the city. She carried the children into bed and went directly to her room. There was no sign of Walker, and it was a relief to have the empty bed to herself for once. She was only vaguely aware of him getting home much later.

In the morning, they found a typewritten note from Brady on the kitchen table. He thanked them for everything they had done for him but said he realized if he was going to be serious about protesting the war in Vietnam, he should go back home to do it from there. The girls were devastated that he'd left, but they soon convinced themselves he'd be back in a day or two. They were certain he'd return when they found the surprise he'd promised them. On the driveway, he had painted a perfect hopscotch in blue sealant.

Walker went to the garage and returned almost immediately in a rage. "That cretin has stolen my car," he shouted.

Elizabeth watched mutely while Walker picked up the phone and reported the car stolen. Within days, they got word that it had been found abandoned near the Ivy Lea Bridge, at the border crossing.

Elizabeth waited throughout October and November for a letter or a phone call from Brady. She carried an ache of confusion and betrayal in her chest, and Walker began to drink more heavily than ever.

Halfway through December, the children began campaigning for Christmas lights on the house. "Brady promised he'd put them up," they cried together.

"I'll do it," Walker said after dinner one night. "I'm sick to death of hearing about all the things Brady can do." Sarah and Rosie fell silent, not used to being addressed directly by their father.

When the children were in bed, Walker put his drink down and pulled on boots and a parka.

"You hold the ladder," he told Elizabeth. "And keep it steady."

She urged him to wait until morning, but he brushed her away. "And keep this flashlight trained on the roof so I can see what I'm doing."

Together they lifted the extension ladder from the garage, and using the rope, hauled it up to its highest level so that Walker could reach the roofline above the attic. Elizabeth fetched the lights and untangled them while he fussed about finding twine, nails and a hammer and dumping everything in a pail that he could carry over his arm. He staggered a bit on the bottom rungs but managed to get to the top.

Elizabeth braced herself against the ladder and held the flashlight so it shone against Walker's hands as he pulled a bone-handled penknife from his pocket, opened it and cut a length of twine to tie around the eavestrough. He folded the knife and looked down at her.

"Hold the ladder steady," he shouted, but it had already begun to lurch from her grasp. He hardly made a sound as he thudded into the middle of the blue hopscotch court. The penknife skittered across the drive and landed in the grass at the side of the lawn.

*   *   *

Elizabeth roused herself and wiped her swollen eyes. She wondered briefly about calling Rosie to ask where she had found the contents of the shoebox and how she had kept it hidden all those years, but thought better of it. Both her daughters were married, with their own families now. They might not even remember Brady or the events of that fall of 1970. Their father's accident would have put most other things out of their minds.

But Elizabeth remembered. And she thought she knew what must have happened. She wondered if the blue hopscotch court had been the last straw for Walker. Or perhaps it was just an accumulation of jealous grievances that had tipped him over the edge that night while she and the children were driving home from the Gatineau Hills. He and Brady must have argued after the younger man was already in bed, or at least had removed his boots. Whatever happened would have been an accident, though. Walker was not a cold-blooded killer. He would have been drunk and in a rage, and Brady would not have wanted to put up a fight against his host. As soon as he realized he'd killed him, Walker must have come up with the plan to drive to a deserted section of the river close to the Ivy Lea Bridge, let the St. Lawrence River sweep the body away and then abandon the car. Such a respectable looking man would have had no trouble hitching a ride home.

He'd made a mistake with the typewritten note, though. That wasn't Brady's style at all. Brady would have used orange crayon on newsprint. But a worse mistake was not getting rid of Brady's penknife. The one he'd inherited from his grandfather. The one he never went anywhere without.

The actual death would have been accidental though, just as Walker's fall had been accidental. She had wanted to do as he asked that night in December. She had tried to hold the ladder steady and focus the flashlight on the eaves. But once she'd seen the penknife, the beam kept drifting to the rope hanging just in front of her. It was as though a hand belonging to someone else had reached around and tugged on that loop. She had been amazed that such a slight pull could cause the ladder to shift and Walker to begin his descent onto the driveway.

Elizabeth looked at her watch and realized she must get to her new apartment so the movers could finish their job. She placed the items back in the shoebox and carried it down to the driveway, where she dropped it into the garbage can, along with the other refuse from her move. She searched the grass at the edge of the lawn until she found a small, smooth stone to toss into the faint outlines of the old hopscotch court before climbing into her car and driving to her new home.

Sue Pike *has had stories in all of the Ladies' Killing Circle anthologies, and she co-edited the two previous books,* Fit to Die *and* Bone Dance. *Her stories have also appeared in* Ellery Queen Mystery Magazine, Storyteller, Cold Blood V *and Michael Connelly's* Murder in Vegas. *She won the Arthur Ellis award for Best Short Story in 1997.*

There was an Over-aged Hippie

There was an over-aged hippie from Clyde
Whose bigot neighbour committed suicide.
The tie on his neck was delicious,
But not his style, so suspicious.
One could say that he was…tie-dyed.

Joy Hewitt Mann

Seeing Strawberry Red

H. Mel Malton

How's the pickin' today?" It was the standard opening line at the basket-booth next to Plunkett's Pick-yer-Own Strawberry Paradise out on Highway 11, north of town. Joy and I had met in the parking lot at a quarter to ten on Wednesday morning. The fields open at ten on the dot—never before that, because they like the dew to burn off a bit and the owners like to pick a fair amount themselves for the take-out trade before they let the hordes in.

We'd been picking two days already, but it hadn't gone very well, so we were back for a third try.

"They're beautiful today," Shirley Plunkett, the owners' daughter said. She runs the booth in the summer to help pay for university down in the city. She's doing a law degree, so she can become an agricultural lawyer—whatever that is. The strawberry operation is only a small part of the family farm, and they're doing pretty well, I guess, if they can afford to send Shirley to school.

"It's a good day for it, at least," Joy said. "I'll take six of those empty baskets, dear."

Joy has this kind of strawberry obsession. Every year she picks seventeen six-quart baskets of berries and makes jam, which she gives out at Christmas. Her jam is famous around here. She's been winning blue ribbons at the Craddock Fall

Fair almost every year since we were in high school together, which was a good while ago. She learned to make it in Home Ec—the last year the course was offered—before the women's libbers forced the school board to axe it. Joy was the Queen of Home Ec. I don't think she ever got over Mrs. Beamish having to retire, and when they turned the Home Ec room into a computer lab, Joy actually picketed outside the door. That was back in the seventies, when demonstrating was the thing you did.

Joy is not a good name for my friend. I love her dearly, don't get me wrong, but she's never been a very joyful person. Her brother used to call her Misery. I wouldn't go that far— maybe Bitterness would be more like it, or Mission Control. Joy is a very active person, and she does a lot of good in the world, but she likes to get her way in things, and she hisses like a pressure cooker if you cross her.

We've been best friends forever. She lived down the street from me, and we met when we were about seven, the day my parents moved to Craddock from Toronto. I walked down the street with a bag of my Mom's peanut brittle, looking for friends, and in half a second Joy had taken official possession of the bag and was rationing pieces out to the neighbourhood kids and introducing me to everybody.

We've stuck together through both our weddings, my pregnancies and her miscarriage, her divorce, various accidents and personal disasters, and, of course, our triumphs, too. Hers have always been more public than mine. Joy's a big name in this town, in some circles. She's the president of the Community Womens' League, the Chair of the Meals-on-Wheels program, she started up an arts-and-crafts store (which she sold profitably a few years ago), she works on the organizing committee of the Craddock Fall Festival of Fun, and that's merely a sample of her activities. Now she's training to be a real estate agent. She's what you'd call goal-oriented, the strawberry-picking season is short and I've always been her sidekick, so it wasn't any big surprise that we were there together for the season opener at the Pick-Yer-Own.

You might have read about what happened in the papers. It got some pretty wide coverage, probably because nothing happens in the District of Kuskawa in the summer-time, so it got splashed in the local weekly, and the nationals picked it up. I know this kind of stuff because I write the community column for the *Craddock Chronicle,* so I'm a bit of a journalist, you might say.

The *Chronicle* originally headlined it as "Mysterious Deaths in Cottage Country." The headlines got more sensational after that, but that's how it started.

* * *

I should tell you about Monday and Tuesday, first—the picking days that didn't go very well. On Monday, we'd arrived ten minutes before opening, as usual. There was quite a crowd, and we were way back in the line, which made Joy all twitchy.

"The best berries'll be gone before we get a chance," she muttered, although the fields are huge, and it was the start of the season.

"Relax, Joy. There's plenty for everyone." I said. She shot me a look of pure contempt.

"That attitude is why you never win anything," she said. "The secret to my jam is, as you very well know, the fact that the fruit is hand-picked at the perfect moment. The perfect moment is now—and those people at the front of the line are going to trample the rows, take the best berries and leave us with the small, sour ones."

The Plunketts are pretty strict in the way they organize the pick-yer-owners. You can't just wander into the field and start anywhere. There are marshals who walk up and down the rows with baskets, in case you need extras, and they give you a row number that you're supposed to stick to. Flags mark off where you can and can't go. Most people obey the rules, but some don't. Some people row-hop, and it drives Joy crazy.

A certain part of the field will be designated for a certain day, and it's got to be stripped before the Plunketts open up the next section. If you come late, you sometimes get a second-hand row. But we were early enough that this wasn't going to happen to us. Still, Joy seemed to think it would, She was fuming already, and I had a sudden premonition of disaster.

*   *   *

The line on Monday moved swiftly, and we got our baskets and headed out, Joy at a trot, trying to overtake the family group in front of us—two hippie-looking people, man and woman, and four kids.

I'd been watching them in the lineup. They weren't your typical pickers for a weekday—usually it's older people, seniors and boomers like us—the people who are serious about picking and whose berries are destined for jars and bottles, careful labels and dates and entries into the Craddock Fall Fair homemade jam division. We'd already waved (at least, I had) to Joy's arch-rival, Selena Parrish, whose jam had once or twice stolen the blue ribbon out from under Joy's nose.

The hippie family didn't look like they were going to make jam. It looked like maybe they were going to sell their fruit at a roadside stand next to the trailer park. They had dozens of baskets, and the kids had that underfed, overly-serious look that you get from knowing you're never going to have a video-game player of your own. The man had a cigarette hanging out of the corner of his mouth, and his long hair was tied in a salt-and-pepper pony tail. The woman was huge, and I wondered how she would cope with all the bending down.

The kids aged in range from the mid-teens to a little fellow of about eight. As we passed them, the little guy was complaining already about the bugs.

"They're *biting* me," he shouted, like it was his mom's fault. The mosquitoes in June around here are fierce, no question. Joy and I were both slathered in Muskol, and I knew Joy had a bottle of it in her fanny-pack. I was going to suggest she lend the family a squirt, but she was already way ahead, scuttling along the path like a big strawberry beetle on a mission.

"The bugs ain't gonna kill you," the hippie Mom said to her child as I overtook them. "You won't notice 'em once you start picking, Dylan."

I hurried to catch up to Joy, who was standing with her baskets at the head of a row marked with a yellow flag. The marshal beside her was pointing to it, and it looked like she was giving him some grief already.

"Are you sure this hasn't been picked over already?" she was saying, like the marshal was trying to sell her a used Ford. "I don't see a lot of fruit." Which was nonsense, of course. Strawberry plants don't put their fruit out at the top like the flame on a candle—the best berries, the heavy ones, are near the ground, hiding under the leaves. Joy knew this as well as I did—she was just being ornery.

"It's a virgin row, guaranteed," the marshal said, trying to make her laugh. She didn't. She huffed at him, shot me a "hurry-up" look and got down to picking. I was assigned the row next to hers, and the hippie family, coming along right behind us, got the next couple of rows beside me.

Everything was fine at first. It was a glorious day—one of the kind they always use in Kuskawa tourism brochures. The sky was robin's egg blue, the early morning sun pouring over the fields like warm lemon sauce. I looked out along the rows at the pickers—colourful T-shirts and straw hats, the people nestled in the leafy greenery like berries themselves, or like multicoloured rabbits, hopping from plant to plant.

Joy and I worked in silence. Some people chatter while they pick, some laugh—it's a good time, out in the sun, no muzak, no traffic-noise, just the whisper of breeze from the lake in the distance, the occasional shriek of laughter drifting over the fields like the call of a blue jay. Joy's a fierce picker, two hands at once, like a machine, head down, utterly absorbed in the task. She never eats the berries—she has a self-control I've never been able to match. How could you not bite into a fresh-picked strawberry, plump and sun-warmed like a live thing, its scent making you dizzy? I bit into one and felt the juice dribbling down my chin, looked at the crimson flesh, the pale secret heart of it, and felt for a moment utterly happy. Next thing I knew, the family in the row next to me boiled over like a pot on the stove.

"Ma—Dylan's smushing them," one of the older girls called out.

"Quit it, Dylan. Goddamn it!" the woman shouted.

"I ain't doin' nothin'!" the boy yelled back. I risked a glance over. His mouth was smeared with strawberry juice, like he'd gone nuts with a lipstick.

"You better be doin' more than nothing," the man barked. He was still smoking, his eyes squinting to keep the smoke out of his eyes. "You fill that friggin' basket and stop eating every second one, boy, or I'll give a lickin' you'll never forget."

Joy looked over, too and made a little tssk sound. A few minutes later, the boy started row-hopping.

It wasn't as if each row didn't have more berries per foot than you could ever hope to harvest in one shot. The thing is, that not all of them are perfect. Some are small or have touched the ground and gone all soft, and some aren't ripe yet. You leave the unripe ones alone. Some people leave the small ones, too. But each plant, at least at Plunkett's, has at least three beauties—great big berries, perfectly ripe and succulent. I knew that Joy separated the beauties out when she got home—and it was the beauties that she used in her famous, prize-winning jam.

The boy Dylan was probably bored, or perhaps he had figured out that the beauties were the ones that filled up a basket the fastest. Anyway, he hopped over into my row and started poaching the big ones. I didn't mind all that much, to tell you the truth. My theory is, there's enough for everybody, and I felt a little sorry for the kid. Picking strawberries is fun, sure, but it's hard work, too. Joy didn't notice—she was still in combine-harvester-mode. Then Dylan hopped a row again and started poaching hers. I kept my head down, willing her not to look up. She didn't for a while, until she got to where he'd been.

I saw her stop and paw the leaves of the plants a bit, like she'd lost something. She made the tssk sound again and looked up. She honed in at once on Dylan, who was picking and eating his way through the beauties a little ahead of her in the next row over.

"Little boy, what are you doing?" she said, her voice like a bucket of ice-water down the back. He looked up, clearly startled by her tone.

"Nothin'," he said.

"You were picking in my row, weren't you?"

Dylan's parents looked up. There was an undercurrent of over-the-edge rage in Joy's voice, like a volcano rumbling before it blows.

"So?"

"So—that's not allowed. You're supposed to stick to the row you were given," she said.

"Fuck you," the little boy said, and gave her the finger. It sounded just awful coming out of such a little guy.

"How dare you speak to me like that?" Joy hissed and stood up.

"Dylan, come back here," the man said. It was clear that he had been eating a fair number of berries, too. His beard was stained red.

"I wasn't doing nothing," Dylan said, swearing again.

"You have some of my strawberries in your basket," Joy said.

"Excuse me?" Dylan's mom said. "*Your* strawberries?" She had a blob of strawberry juice on her chin.

"That's right, lady," Joy said. "Your brat has just poached the best fruit from my row."

"Oh, puhleeze," the woman said. "They're only strawberries, for God's sake. And don't you dare call my boy a brat." For Dylan's sake, I was glad she was defending him. But she wouldn't be any match for Joy in righteous-anger-mode.

"Make him give them back," Joy said and took a menacing step forward.

"Joy…" I said. She was acting like an eight-year-old herself. What had gotten into her?

"Give them back? You're crazy, lady."

"There's better ways to feed your family than letting them graze like cows and poach berries in a public strawberry patch," Joy said, viciously. That's when the hippie lady went for her, and it was pandemonium for a few minutes. By the end of it, both women were wearing most of what was in their baskets. They'd smushed strawberries in each other's hair and eyes, and both were breathing heavily, like they'd been mud-wrestling. The man and I had pulled them apart, so we got some on us, too. The kids just stood there with their mouths open, as if a circus act had erupted in the middle of a math class. The marshal came over.

"Just what the hell is going on here?" he said.

"Little disagreement," I said. "Turf war."

"I think you better leave," he said, meaning all of us. "We don't want trouble here at Plunkett's. We got a reputation to keep up. Come back when you've cooled down some." Joy was speechless with outrage. And she looked like she'd been pecked by a flock of killer chickens—strawberry blood all over her nice white shirt. Everyone from all over the field was staring. I could see Selena Parrish a couple of rows away, grinning like a maniac. "And you'll have to pay for the berries you, er, *spoiled,* as well," the marshal added.

The hippie family packed up and left quickly without argument. The look the big woman gave Joy before they left would have turned any normal person to stone. The man just looked sad, though the grip he had on Dylan's arm as he hauled the boy out of the field was hardly gentle. Joy was less acquiescent.

"They started it," Joy said. "I could press charges. I was assaulted." She spoke loudly enough for all the watchers to hear.

"Don't matter," the marshal said. "Just take your baskets and get out of here. We're open tomorrow. Come back then."

So we left, too. Joy paid for the three baskets she'd filled, plus the half-basket she'd wasted mashing into the hippie lady's face, and tossed the two unused baskets at Shirley, just daring her to say something. She didn't—wisely. Joy was getting strange looks from a couple of people lining up for baskets, but she stared them down. They looked away, hurriedly. Then she marched to her car, loaded the baskets up and glared at me.

"Tomorrow," she barked. "Same time, same place." And off she went.

* * *

I don't know if she made jam that night or not. She was certainly in a better mood on Tuesday morning, and we were closer to the front of the line, too, which was a blessing. Joy never bothered to look behind her to see the line forming—she just stood there, head held high, freshly laundered white shirt dazzling the eye, gazing at the fields as if every strawberry in there had her name on it. Her straw hat with the big sunflowers on it made her look like one of those fancy ladies at that English tennis thing. No—not the ladies—the Queen. She was back in top form, you might say. I was glad she didn't look behind her at the lineup, because about ten people back was the hippie family.

* * *

Things went okay for the first while, like the day before. The hippie family was far enough away that Joy didn't notice them, and they seemed to be working with purpose, no fighting, just picking hard. I wasn't staring or anything, but I did happen to notice that they were all eating just about as many as they picked. They'd all be coming down with a family case of the trots later in the day, I figured. But about forty minutes into it, that little Dylan started row-hopping again. His parents didn't seem to notice or care, and he was heading our way. Maybe he wanted to see another strawberry fight.

"Joy, how are you doing?" I asked, trying not to let panic show in my voice. "You want to take a break? Go get some lemonade?" She raised an eyebrow at me.

"Feeling your age this morning, are you?" she said. "We've hardly started. I've got three baskets filled already—how many do you have?"

"Just the one," I replied, humbly. I'd eaten a good few. Dylan picked that moment to hop into my row, about ten feet down from where I was picking. Joy caught the movement out of the corner of her eye and reacted like a pitbull who sees a chipmunk.

"Oh, for Chrissakes—get the hell out, you little bastard!" she yelled. He froze, then scampered back to his parents as if the devil himself was in pursuit. But it wasn't the devil, it was Joy, which was probably worse. She marched right on over there.

"Excuse me," she said in a loud voice. "Can you please keep your child under control? What kind of parents are you? If you keep on letting him break the rules, he's going to grow up into a little monster." The man stood up from where he was crouched over his basket.

"Lady," he said. "I can see you got some kinda mental problem, and that's too bad, but can you please keep *yourself* under control?"

You could see an internal struggle going on in Joy's mind. People were staring again, and there were a fair number who had been there the day before. The marshal was beginning to drift over, as well. She won her battle, I guess, because she just turned her back on the man and came back to where she'd left her baskets.

"I meant what I said, you know," she muttered to me through clenched teeth. "Kids like that turn into criminals. If that foul-mouthed brat comes near my row again, I'm going to murder him."

We picked for another hour or so, but Joy never really calmed down. She was shaking like a leaf—I could see her hands tremble, and she kept dropping berries, or squishing them by accident. Once, she gripped a berry so hard, it made an audible popping sound, splurting pulp and juice all over her pants. Even then, she didn't lick her fingers off. I wonder sometimes if she likes strawberries at all. Every once in a while, she said something under her breath, and I could see her darting sly glances in the direction of the family. Finally, she called it quits.

"It *is* hot," she said, standing and stretching her back. "I think that's enough for today, dear. Why don't we do the rest tomorrow?"

She had filled three baskets on Monday, before the fight, and on Tuesday she picked another five, so she still had nine to go to fill her personal quota. I had two from Monday and two from Tuesday. I freeze mine—I'm not a jam-person. I could never get it to set properly, and anyway, Joy usually gives me a jar or two of hers, so there's not much point. So, we agreed to meet on Wednesday—one more day of picking. Which brings me to where we started. Like the day before, we were up at the front of the line-up, and the hippie family had returned as well.

This time, Joy had brought a small cooler with her. I asked her about it, and she smiled sweetly, like she had a secret.

"Oh, just some treats, dear," she said. She left the cooler at the head of her row, and everything went on as before. She was quite calm and pleasant and even chattered a bit as we picked.

"I notice you're not eating as many today," she said.

"Well, you know how it is. They do kind of have an effect on you, eh?" I said. I confess I'd had some serious internal movement from all the berries I'd eaten while picking, but you probably don't want to know about that.

An hour or so later, Joy excused herself and went off to use the Johnny-on-the-spot. I'd just filled a basket and went back up to the top of the row to drop it off, and there was her cooler, unattended. I don't know what got into me, because I'm not normally a nosy person, but I couldn't help taking a peek inside. I was getting a little peckish, as I hadn't had any breakfast on account of my attack of berry-belly the night before. Joy is a fantastic cook, as you've probably already gathered, and when she says she's made treats, it usually means something spectacular. So, okay, I opened the lid.

There, nestled inside, were more than a dozen of the most beautiful strawberry tarts I've ever seen. Each one was perfect—a little bigger than bite-sized, made with Joy's patented butter-almond pastry—the kind that tastes like shortbread. Each tart had a single beauty-strawberry on top, and beneath was what I was sure was her *crème patissiere,* the kind of stuff that makes the best custard taste like library paste. Each tart was glazed and gorgeous, and when I lifted the lid, the smell of them wafted up and smacked me in the face so that I was powerless, I swear. There were, after all, plenty of them. And Joy wouldn't miss one little tart. I took a sneaky peek over at the Johnny, and she was still inside. She was wearing her button-up dungarees, which always gave her trouble, so I knew she'd be a while. Nobody seemed to be watching, and anyway, nobody but me knew that the cooler was Joy's and not mine.

I confess that I ate the tart sort of fast, feeling guilty. But sometimes, guilty pleasures are the very best. Just because I stuffed it into my mouth all at once doesn't mean it wasn't the most delicious thing I'd eaten in ages. I picked up an empty berry basket and floated back down the row, chewing. I wiped my mouth on my sleeve, in case there were any crumbs there, and went back to picking. Joy returned a moment or so later, and I knew she hadn't seen.

I had filled my new basket about halfway before I started to feel a bit funny.

"Joy," I said. "I have to disappear for a few minutes." I knew by the way my insides were working that I only had a small window of opportunity to get to the Johnny before I disgraced myself. She looked up, her eyes twinkling.

"All those berries from yesterday catching up to you?" she said. I nodded and ran for it.

*　　*　　*

I don't remember much of what happened after I got inside the latrine, except that what was inside my body made a rapid escape via whatever exits were available. I do remember lying on the floor at one point and finding that I could see outside, through a crack in the plastic wall. I was too weak to call for help, but I was still hoping that whatever had hit me—whatever kind of stomach flu-thing it was, would pass, and I'd be able to walk out of there. I had a perfect view of the field, and I could see the dazzling white of Joy's shirt, the sunflowers on her straw hat, and tried to send a kind of psychic message to her—*come get me and take me home.* She stood up, and I thought she'd actually received the message, but instead, she picked up the cooler, and started walking down the rows towards the hippie family. What was she doing? Surely she wasn't going to start another fight, was she?

I blacked out then, and woke up in Craddock General. I was there for a while, and it wasn't until a week or so later that I heard what had happened. Six people had died from pesticide poisoning, so the story went—a whole family, wiped out. They were found in their home at the Happy Hills Trailer Park, just north of town. Pretty gruesome, the reports said. They'd been picking strawberries at Plunkett's Pick-yer-own, so the pesticide was traced back to there, and the authorities figured that somehow, a few rows got some kind of lethal dose of the stuff. The hippie family had been eating as much as they were picking. They ended up shutting down the whole field for the rest of the season, and they put announcements in the *Craddock Chronicle*, warning pickers to wash their fruit in detergent, or better, just to throw the berries away.

After I recovered enough for visitors, Joy came to see me.

"I feel awfully guilty about what happened to you," she said.

"The doctors said I must have got a bad row, like those other people," I said, testing her.

"It wasn't the berries," Joy said.

"I know it wasn't, Joy. I ate one of your tarts."

"I guessed it must have been that," she said. "Serves you right for being greedy, dear. It's a blessing that you, er, purged the stuff before it shut you down for good."

"And the family?"

"Well, they were very pleased by my apology. I took them the treats and said I was so sorry for my rudeness, and I hoped they'd forgive me. Oh, they were suspicious at first, but one look at my tarts was all it took. And of course, they ate them right away. And on top of all the berries they'd been eating, it took a little longer for things to…well, happen."

"And you got away with it. I can't believe it."

"Well, they did some kind of analysis, but as soon as they found strawberries and pesticide, I guess whatever else they found wasn't important." She was utterly delighted with herself. I guess that, in her books, she'd just won another blue ribbon.

"Don't you feel any remorse at all?" She had been my best friend for over thirty years. What had I missed?

"Yes, absolutely," she said. "I'm furious, actually. The Fall Fair people have announced that, because of the tragedy, they're taking strawberry jam off the contest list this year. Can you imagine the nerve of them?"

I gazed into her eyes. I'd never noticed how cold they could get when she was angry. Or how empty. After she left, I started to write this down. I haven't quite decided what to do with it yet, but there's one thing I know for sure. My strawberry picking days are over.

H. Mel Malton *writes the Polly Deacon mystery series:* Down in the Dumps *(1998)—shortlisted for an Arthur Ellis First Novel Award,* Cue the Dead Guy *(1999),* Dead Cow in Aisle Three *(2001) and* One Large Coffin to Go *(2003)—all published by Rendezvous Press. Her first children's novel,* The Drowned Violin, *will be published by Napoleon in 2006. She lives in Muskoka, Ontario, with two dogs, Karma and Ego, and writes freelance to pay for kibble and smokes.*

Smoke Screen

Mary Jane Maffini

Cool. Buddy reached out and touched the first plant, ran a respectful finger around a leaf, traced each of the five points, felt the slight stickiness of resin. He sniffed. It wasn't everyone's idea of perfume, but that's what quality smelled like. This was his work. His plants, grown from carefully selected seeds started indoors, the seedlings protected under a jar until they were transplanted. Finally, it was paying off. For the first time in his fifty-five years, Buddy felt like some kind of god. He gazed around his small heaven in the far eastern edge of Mrs. Wilkins's corn field. Only fifteen plants. Buddy wasn't greedy. But what amazing plants they were: seven feet tall, buds bursting with THC, the best you could get from hot weather, careful watering, regular trimming with manicure scissors and plenty of 20-20-20. There was enough high-grade weed to keep Buddy and his small group of clients happy all winter.

Best of all, his crop was safe here.

Stan Fuhrman was renting the field from Mrs. Wilkins to grow corn. And for sure Stan had better things to do than tramp around corn fields looking for surprises. Buddy's crop was too small to attract the attention of the cops. Buddy wasn't stupid enough to plant near his cabin, especially because Mick LeMay, the sergeant at the local Sûreté du Québec detachment, had started dropping around unannounced. That's all he needed was the SQ stumbling on his babies.

Still, bikers were more of a worry, even with a few plants. The gangs were muscling in locally, intimidating farmers and squashing small producers. The only thing worse than bikers was teenagers. They'd clean out your patch in a night, leaving only a hill of crumpled McDonald's boxes as a useless clue. But after the first frost, Buddy would be able to harvest. Then he could stop worrying.

Today, he hadn't been able to resist a quick visit before he headed over to paint Mrs. Wilkins's kitchen trim. Keeping up Mrs. Wilkins's property was the only career Buddy'd ever had, if you didn't count his plants. Mrs. Wilkins needed Buddy's help, since her niece, Wanda, was too busy, and Wanda was Mrs. Wilkins' only relative. And Buddy had always had a soft spot for Mrs. Wilkins, ever since she had taught him in Grade Five, slipping him oatmeal cookies on the days his lunchbox was empty. Mrs. Wilkins was seventy-five now, with a happy heart and endless odd jobs. She and Buddy shared friendly chuckles and little jokes. Unlike Wanda, she didn't mock Buddy's long braid or spreading bald spot. She didn't sneer at his Grateful Dead T-shirt or the frayed jeans with the draggy hems. Buddy lived rent-free in the cabin at the western edge of her acreage. Kept the local youngsters from vandalizing it, she said.

Mrs. Wilkins was never in a hurry. Buddy appreciated that.

Buddy lit a joint to celebrate his achievement. Gradually, the field took on a magical appearance, the stalks shimmered. Beauty all around him, colours throbbing. Something glittered behind a row of corn near the edge of the field. Buddy smiled as he ambled over for a better look. He leaned in. His eyes popped. Wires. Two of them, no three, artfully placed, connected to—could it be? Yes, a shotgun, strapped to a stake. The wires were attached to the trigger. Buddy recoiled. To his left, he detected another glint. More wire. Another shotgun. As far as he could tell, the shotguns were pointed toward the end of the corn field near the old logging road.

"Bummer," Buddy said.

Must be bikers. They took over fields and set booby-traps for nosy strangers. Buddy might be proud of his plants, but he'd never shoot anybody to protect them. He tried to think clearly. Why here? Someone trying to get rid of him? But he always came down the hill from his cabin and backtracked from the river path. The guns seemed to be aimed at the logging road, but Buddy never used that way because he'd be in plain view. No one ever passed by, but why take a chance?

Buddy wasn't the best thinker in town, even when he wasn't stoned. Now he'd have to wait to figure things out. But he knew it sure didn't look good.

*   *   *

Buddy followed the aroma of freshly baked pastry from the end of the driveway. He was starving.

Mrs. Wilkins's bright blue eyes lit up as she opened the door. "Just in time, Buddy. Blueberry or apple today?" She twinkled at him as she headed for her big pine table.

Buddy followed, salivating. "Tough choice."

"Have both. Ice cream on that pie? It's French vanilla today."

The door slammed as someone stormed into the kitchen after them. Buddy jumped. The niece, Wanda, must have been coming down the driveway right after him. And Wanda was a world-class door slammer. Usually Buddy kept an eye open for her.

Wanda was the opposite of her aunt. She was loud, where Mrs. Wilkins had a soft, musical voice. Mrs. Wilkins was tiny, and getting smaller every year, like a bird with her tufts of white feathery hair and pointy little bones. Wanda was more like a walrus in pantyhose. Of course, even a walrus could be nice, and everyone agreed Wanda was mean as a snake.

Wanda leaned against the pine table and sneered, "Why do you let this grungy old hippie take advantage of you, Auntie?"

Buddy gasped. Take advantage? He would have done Mrs. Wilkins's odd jobs for free. He'd even pay rent if she'd accept it. Money wasn't important to Buddy, or he'd have a career where you'd make some. Instead he'd chosen a peaceful, happy life with plenty of primo weed and pie.

"He eats you out of house and home."

What was the matter with her? Wanda was ten years younger than Buddy, which made her forty-five. She wore a tight black leather mini-skirt and knee-high lace up boots. Her push-up bra was working hard. No surprise she hadn't made it big in real estate, which had been her last real job.

Anyway, she wasn't dressed like that at three in the afternoon to impress her husband. A few years back, Wanda Wilkins had married Mick LeMay, both on the rebound. But being an SQ officer's wife never restricted her social life. To put it mildly.

Everyone knew she spent a lot of time with Big Bob Beaulieu in his fancy new house overlooking the river. Or you could find her chugging Corona and lime at the Rusty Lock, Big Bob's bar. Big Bob made a bundle serving watered down drinks and otherwise hoodwinking his customers. He'd gone to school with Buddy and Mick. He'd even been in Mrs. Wilkins Grade Five class with them. Big Bob had been a sleazy wheeler dealer even then, stealing lunches, cheating at marbles. Maybe Wanda was impressed, but no one else was.

Another thing no one understood was what Mick LeMay had ever done to deserve Wanda. Mick was stubborn and hard-headed as they come, a good trait in the police, but not so useful in a husband perhaps.

Wanda was still bitching away at Buddy. "You're a real vulture, preying on this vulnerable old woman. She should have people looking after her, not be waiting on a creep like you." Wanda gave one last sneer before swaying her black leather butt toward the door.

Buddy's jaw dropped. That was pretty disrespectful, even for Wanda. Mrs. Wilkins wasn't vulnerable. She was smart and in charge, just like she'd always been.

Mrs. Wilkins said, "Don't mind Wanda, Buddy. She has a lot on her mind lately."

"Right on." Buddy dug into his pie. He knew he should be giving some thought to the shotgun problem. But later.

*　　*　　*

Buddy was on his way back to his cabin, carefully lugging a basket with what was left of the apple and blueberry pies, when Mick LeMay sneaked up behind him in his cruiser. Buddy was deep in thought about booby-traps, so he jumped when he heard Mick's voice.

Mick said, "Hold on, Buddy."

Buddy shuffled. He wasn't in the mood to chew the fat. He really wanted to get home and find a solution to those shotguns before someone got hurt. He could hardly tell Mick that.

"What's in the basket, Buddy?"

"Pie, man. From your wife's aunt."

"Oh, yeah? Mind if I look?"

"No problemo. These pies probably shouldn't be legal," Buddy chuckled.

Mick just lifted the lid on the basket.

Buddy felt a chill. Wanda was married to Mick, after all. What if she'd told Mick that Buddy was taking advantage of Mrs. Wilkins?

Mick said, "I've been hearing about you."

"Me?"

"Getting tips about your grow-op."

"I've been painting the trim in Mrs. Wilkins's kitchen all day. I chopped some wood for her too. Ask her."

Mick said, "A guy could paint trim and still look after a crop."

Buddy shrugged. No point in arguing. Mick never admitted mistakes.

"So, what's new?" Buddy said. He wasn't the type to hold a grudge, and he and Mick had grown up together. Mick was just doing his job, chasing people who sold weed, the same way Buddy was just doing his by growing it.

"Getting ready to retire," Mick said.

"You kidding me, man?"

"Full pension," Mick said. "Next month."

Buddy shook his head. "Time flies, man." He still hadn't found a career, and here was Mick LeMay retiring. He wasn't the only one. One minute you're hearing "Yellow Submarine" for the first time, and the next your friends are pensioners. Something else to think about. But first he had that shotgun thing hanging over his head.

"That's cool," Buddy said. "But I can't see you playing golf or nothing."

Mick said, "Don't plan to. Got an offer on the house, some savings, enough to buy a fishing lodge. Moving on to the next phase. Piece of paradise two hours north of here."

"No shit? Man, I can't see Wanda in a fishing lodge."

Mick's lips compressed. "She'll adjust."

"Hey, no sweat."

"Got that right."

"Peace, Mick." Buddy was still shaking his head when he got home. He used his time to worry about those shotguns instead of imagining Wanda Wilkins being miserable in a fishing lodge. What if Mrs. Wilkins stumbled over those wires? Buddy felt sick. Even if the shots missed, she could have a heart attack. She'd be alone, no one would hear, since nobody used the old logging track. Buddy couldn't really imagine life without Mrs. Wilkins. Not just the pies and the cabin and the steady supply of odd jobs. But having someone who cared about him. Someone to share a joke with. If something happened to Mrs. Wilkins, Buddy would lose it all. Wanda would get the house and the cabin and the property. Wanda sure wouldn't keep Buddy around.

He had to tell Mrs. Wilkins everything. As soon as he mellowed out a bit.

* * *

By early evening, a follow-up toke and both leftover pies hadn't been enough to calm him. Buddy ate a peanut butter sandwich. That didn't work either. Problem solving just wasn't Buddy's groove. He rolled another joint to help the process and shuffled outside to sit among the trees. The sunset and the leaves made for a beautiful moment. Buddy did his best to think hard, until all the colours got too intense.

The problem was bigger than Buddy. He had to tell Mrs. Wilkins for her own safety. She'd be disappointed in Buddy. She might not bake for him once she found out about his crop. Buddy contemplated a long, hungry winter, no weed, no feed. She'd probably tell Mick LeMay. He was her niece's husband, and she'd taught him in Grade Five too. Maybe Buddy could pretend the crop wasn't his. But then Buddy always told Mrs. Wilkins the truth, because it was like she could read his mind. She'd feel bad, but she'd do what she thought was right. Buddy had to respect that. Looked like he had no choice. Whoever booby-trapped the field didn't care if someone got killed. Even a really good someone like Mrs. Wilkins. Buddy struggled to his feet and decided. First thing tomorrow, he'd do it.

*   *   *

Buddy tossed and turned. In the middle of the night, he got a better idea. He sat up in bed. Why not take those shotguns down? Dismantle the wires and throw the guns in the river. He'd have to remember to wipe his fingerprints off first. That way he wouldn't have to lose his crop, disappoint Mrs. Wilkins and go to jail. No one would get hurt. Buddy grinned. He imagined the surprise on the face of whoever had set the booby-trap. The grin slipped. Whoever that was would just put them back up again. Or do something worse. Maybe Buddy wouldn't find the new thing on time. Bummer. Buddy got out of bed and lit another joint.

*   *   *

In the morning, he took the long way around to Mrs. Wilkins, circling the property and walking along the old dirt-track logging road, getting up his nerve to tell her. As he reached the point where the track passed close to his crop, he turned around, and his heart contracted. Mick LeMay's cruiser was bouncing after him. The cruiser stopped, and Mick got out, leaving the engine running. Mick set off striding briskly into the corn field.

Buddy's jaw dropped.

"Wait up, Mick," Buddy shouted.

Mick paid no attention. Kept moving, fast and confident, typical Mick.

"You don't want to do that!" Buddy loped after Mick.

Mick didn't break stride. He called over his shoulder. "Got you this time, Buddy."

Buddy pushed aside rows of corn and stumbled after.

"Mick!"

But Mick wasn't in a waiting mood. "Got another tip about you. The law's the law. Something you don't seem too clear on."

"What about de-crim-in-a-lize-a-tion?" Buddy was out of breath from stumbling after Mick.

Mick must be awful close to those wires now. Buddy launched himself through the air and connected with the back of Mick's legs.

The force of landing, half on Mick and half on the rough ground of the corn field, knocked the rest of the breath out of Buddy. That was nothing compared to the shock of the gunshots. Dozens of them.

Buddy rolled off Mick, and flattened himself against the ground, whimpering. Mick wasn't much more dignified. He turned around and crawled like hell out of the field and toward the cruiser.

Buddy speed-crawled after him.

"Hey, we're not dead. That's cool, man." Buddy couldn't hear himself because the shots were still ringing in his ears.

Mick said something.

"What?"

"What the hell have you done now, you moron?" Mick said.

"Me?" Buddy said.

"Well, who else?"

"Bikers maybe."

"Bullshit. Whose pot patch is that?"

Buddy blinked. "Pot patch?"

"I guess the tipsters didn't know you'd rigged up a deathtrap."

Buddy struggled to his feet and brushed off his jeans. "Just pot man. Not worth killing over. Not that it's mine."

"Give me a break. I'd have to be dumb as a post not to know you supply your friends."

"The law's changing, Mick. Supreme Court, eh."

"Don't count on it. It's going to get worse for growers, Buddy. Up to fourteen years if you have more than four plants."

"Hey, man. I just want to live in harmony with nature. Anyways, who'd call in tips about me? There's major grow-ops all over these hills."

"Maybe you pissed off the competition."

"Jeez, Mick, I don't know. For fifteen plants? Not that they're mine."

Mick LeMay struggled to his feet and rubbed his hand on his temple. He didn't look quite as smart as he usually did, because he was covered with mud and straw, with a bit of blood trickling down over his eye where he must have hit a rock. His nose might have been broken too. Buddy probably didn't look so hot either, but he was used to that.

Mick said, "One month left until I retire, and I'm not wasting a minute arguing with you. I can charge you with attacking an officer, aggravated assault, assault with a weapon, growing a controlled substance. They'll throw the book at you."

"That's the pits, man."

"Into the cruiser, Buddy." Now a stream of blood ran down Mick's temple.

"Hey Mick, your head's bleeding in two places, three if you count your nose. You better go to the clinic."

Mick said, "Paperwork first."

"You're wobbling, man."

"Good try, Buddy." Mick smirked briefly before his eyes rolled back in his head and he pitched head first onto the dirt-track road.

Buddy said. "Bummer."

Call 911. That's what you were supposed to do. The nearest phone was Mrs. Wilkins's. Buddy didn't want to run through the corn field and set off another shotgun. He could hardly leave Mick lying in the dirt. What if a biker came along? Buddy was in another tight spot.

It wasn't easy getting Mick into the back of the idling cruiser. Mick was breathing funny. Buddy got behind the wheel. First time he'd been in the front seat of a cop car. He couldn't help sweating. He flicked switches and pressed buttons in the hope he'd get the siren and the roof lights going. Then he burned rubber to Mrs. Wilkins's place.

Maybe it was a delayed reaction to the shock of the gunshots. Or the blow to his head when he knocked Mick to the ground. Or all that blood. Even stress from borrowing a cop car. For whatever reason, Buddy had a crystal-clear analytical moment. In that second, everything that happened made sense. But who'd believe what he'd just figured out?

*   *   *

An ambulance wailed in the distance as Buddy hurried Mrs. Wilkins toward the cruiser. He'd ended up parked in the bed of day lilies on the front lawn. The roof lights on the cruiser were still flashing. Buddy was a bundle of nerves.

Mrs. Wilkins carried a wool blanket. She wrapped it around Mick and spoke to him softly, firmly and kindly. Like he was still in her Grade Five class. "You just hold on, Mick."

Buddy's voice wobbled. "I couldn't leave him there, eh. Too risky."

"You did the right thing, Buddy." Mrs. Wilkins was pale as fog. For the first time ever, she hadn't offered Buddy anything to eat when he pounded on her door with the news. Buddy was so freaked out by the whole situation with Mick that he barely noticed her special chocolate hazelnut torte on the big pine table. Buddy felt too sick to eat anyway.

"I figured out what's going on," Buddy said. "If they wanted to kill me, they'd have set up the shotguns at my end."

Mrs. Wilkins said, "Start at the beginning, Buddy."

"Okay, they probably weren't trying to get anyone coming on foot from your house, because the shotguns were aimed the other way."

Mrs. Wilkins said. "Take a deep breath. Start at the very very beginning."

Buddy started. Mrs. Wilkins didn't interrupt once. Not even when he got to his idea.

"I think someone was trying to get Mick. That's why they were calling him up and telling him about my, um, you know… They knew he'd go and check out that field. He'd have to drive up that old logging track, because that's the only way he could get in with his cruiser. You know what Mick's like. Stubborn, eh. He'd go right through that field looking straight ahead. And he'd get shot full of holes."

"What a terrible thing."

"Yeah. And then it would be the perfect crime, because they'd say I set up that booby trap to protect my um… I'd get locked up forever for killing a cop. Especially a guy like Mick, that everyone likes and feels sorry for."

"We'd both have a problem, Buddy. Who would look after me if you were incarcerated? I'd lose my helper and my friend. Who would appreciate my baking? Who would laugh at my little jokes? I'd end up in some institution, with my home and property sold off to a developer."

Buddy sat right down on the grass in stunned silence.

"That's how it goes, Buddy. Nice place like this, view of the hills and the river. Fifty acres can handle a lot of fancy condos, a golf course and a crowd of city people. You think I don't know what it's worth?"

Buddy bleated, "What can we do?"

"We'll have to fix it."

"But like how? Mick is still alive. These guys could try again. Maybe the next time we won't be there. Anyway, the cops will never believe me. Mick didn't, and he's known me all my life."

"I will deal with the police," Mrs. Wilkins said.

At that moment, Mick opened his good eye. "Why don't you leave it to me?" Mick said before he passed out again, and the paramedics loaded him onto a stretcher.

*   *   *

Three hours later at the Rusty Lock, Wanda spilt her gin martini on the table. She stared at Mrs. Wilkins and Buddy. Then she let out a long high wail. "No, not my Mick. Is he…?"

"Well," Buddy said.

Wanda fished a wad of tissue out of her cleavage and honked her nose. "Tell me he didn't suffer much."

"Actually…" Buddy said.

"My god, I'm way too young to be a widow." Wanda took a sideways glance at herself in the mirror.

Mrs. Wilkins said, "If a policeman dies in the line of duty, the widow gets a pension, Wanda. That could provide some comfort."

Wanda wiped her eyes and stared at her aunt. "What's a pension without my husband? Now look what's happened. How many times did I tell you not to let this useless stoner hang around all the time?" Then she pointed an accusing red fingernail toward Buddy.

Mrs. Wilkins said. "What does Buddy have to do with it?"

"It's obvious, isn't it? Mick was planning to catch Buddy red-handed. A nice grow-op bust just before he retired. Something to be proud of. But Buddy killed Mick in cold blood to keep out of jail."

Big Bob came around the bar and laid a meaty hand on Wanda's bare shoulder. "That Buddy's an animal. A shotgun can make a real mess of a guy," he said.

"Poor Mick," Wanda moaned.

Buddy protested, "Hey man, I wouldn't kill Mick, even to stay out of jail, if I needed to, which I don't."

Mrs. Wilkins said, "Who said anything about shotguns?"

Big Bob sputtered. "What else would there be up there in that corn field?"

"And what corn field would that be, Robert?" Mrs. Wilkins said in her best teacher's voice.

Wanda whacked Big Bob with the back of her hand. "Shut up, you doorknob."

Big Bob looked hurt, "Well what other kind of booby-trap would there be in Buddy's crop? Shotguns is what everyone uses."

"I am not sure what you're talking about, Robert. Shotguns? Booby-trap? Mick just has a headache. He'll be fine."

Wanda whirled. "A headache?"

"All's well that ends well," Mrs. Wilkins said. "Wouldn't you say, Wanda?"

Big Bob frowned. "You mean he's still alive?"

Wanda blurted, "But you said…"

Mrs. Wilkins said, "I told you something terrible had happened to Mick. I was talking about betrayal."

"Don't worry about me," Mick said from the doorway. He might have looked funny with the splint on his nose, the patch on his left eye and the gauze on his temple, but he sure wasn't laughing.

Real tears welled up in Wanda's eyes.

Mick said, "If you didn't want to come north with me, Wanda, all you had to do was say so. You'd get half of everything. But half wasn't enough, was it? You wanted it all."

Wanda said, "What are you talking about, 'it all'? You're a cop, not Donald friggin' Trump."

Mick let that slide, "I mean the pension, the RRSPS, the proceeds from the house, the savings to buy the fishing lodge."

"You're so full of it," Wanda said.

"So you and Big Bob decided rig up a bunch of guns, make some anonymous tips so I'd head to the field where Buddy's got his little crop. I'm out of the way, Buddy takes the rap, you're a merry widow and you and Scumbag Bob here laugh all the way to the bank."

"Come on, eh," Big Bob said.

"Buddy and I had a really close call because of you two."

"That's such crap," Wanda huffed.

"Crap yes, but true crap," Mick said. "Plus the shock of my murder in Mrs. Wilkins's corn field and finding out that Buddy's got this grow-op on her property would probably kill her."

"Kill Mrs. Wilkins!" Buddy gasped. "That's awful."

Mick said, "Sure is. Then Wanda would get everything and sell it to some developer. Maybe Big Blob here."

"These are serious charges, Mick," Mrs. Wilkins said. Buddy

noticed she had a certain familiar look on her face. The one she used to use when she was dealing with her Grade Five boys. The look that meant she'd had enough funny business.

Mick didn't seem to have noticed that look. "Yes, ma'am. Attempted murder of a peace officer is very serious. So is running a grow-op."

Buddy's eyes widened. Wait a minute. Hadn't they agreed to cooperate before they arranged to trick Wanda and Big Bob? Had Mrs. Wilkins forgotten how stubborn Mick LeMay could be? Even if he did have a good reason to be stubborn this time.

Mrs. Wilkins said, "True enough, Mick. I imagine such a serious matter will mean a long and complex trial."

"Sure will," Mick said.

"We want a lawyer," Wanda said.

Big Bob said, "Listen, Wanda, you said nothing could go wrong."

Wanda said, "Make that two lawyers."

Mrs. Wilkins said, "Are you sure you want a trial, Mick? Give some thought to it."

"What's to think about?" Mick said. But he glanced at Mrs. Wilkins in a way that made Buddy think Mick had picked up on the look.

Mrs. Wilkins said, "How about this? With appeals and everything, I imagine Wanda's and Big Bob's case could take years in court."

Mick frowned. "That's good, isn't it?"

"Wanda's still your wife, Mick. She's entitled to half your assets. That would put her way over the limit for legal aid, I'm sure."

Buddy said, "Wow, yeah, it would, eh?"

Wanda said, "Damn right I'm entitled."

Mrs. Wilkins said, "I imagine the legal fees for a long case will eat up your savings and the profit from your house. That would be a shame, so close your retirement, Mick."

Mick didn't say anything. Buddy could see that he was thinking it though.

Mrs. Wilkins said, "I imagine there'd be nothing left even before an appeal."

Wanda said, "You'd help me, Auntie."

"Why certainly, Wanda. You are my niece. I'll help by proposing that if Mick wants to retire up north next month, he'll need his assets intact to do that. In other words, he won't be charging you or Big Bob with attempted anything."

Wanda's mean and snake-like smile emerged. "Hear that, Mick? You won't be charging us."

Mrs. Wilkins wasn't finished. "In order to achieve that, Wanda, naturally you would have to agree to forego your share in the matrimonial home and other joint assets such as Mick's pension. In writing, it goes without saying."

The snake-like smile vanished. "But I'm family, Auntie."

Mrs. Wilkins continued, "Indeed you are, and as such you may be surprised to learn that if anything were to happen to me, even such an ordinary event as a heart attack or a stroke, you will not be inheriting any part of my estate. I've left it to Buddy in trust for his lifetime. After that, the trust will pass to the Village Nature Fund. If you think about contesting my will, remember this: I already have a lawyer, and she's very good. At any rate, I'm sure you would not want your role in the unfortunate matter of the shotguns and Mick's injuries to come to light. Therefore, I think it's a good thing you have Big Bob to look after you."

Big Bob said, "What?"

Mrs. Wilkins turned to Mick. "I'm sorry you fell and broke your nose. I am glad your brush with that rock didn't cost you your eye. I hope the other fellows don't tease you too much at your retirement party."

"My nose is none of anybody's business," Mick said.

"I feel exactly the same way about my corn field," Mrs. Wilkins said, her bright blue eyes back to their usual level of twinkliness.

"Point taken," Mick said.

Mrs. Wilkins said, "And Buddy feels that way about his gardening venture. Now, are we all clear on that?"

Mick and Big Bob nodded. Wanda pouted. Buddy looked from one face to the other. Wow. Just like Grade Five.

"I'm glad we're all agreed. Now we can all get back to normal," Mrs. Wilkins said.

Buddy was impressed. It looked like Mick would get to retire to his fishing lodge, free of Wanda. Wanda and Big Bob would get to stay together and out of jail. Buddy would get to keep his crop, and no one would get killed. Mrs. Wilkins hadn't lost her touch. Buddy wasn't a hundred per cent sure what in trust meant, but it sounded impressive too.

"Time for us to go, Buddy," Mrs. Wilkins said.

Buddy grinned. Best of all, there was still that chocolate hazelnut torte back on the pine table waiting for him and Mrs. Wilkins.

Cool.

Mary Jane Maffini is the author of the Ottawa-based Camilla MacPhee mysteries and Lament for a Lounge Lizard, *the first in a comic series set in West Quebec. Her short stories have appeared in six Ladies' Killing Circle anthologies,* Ellery Queen's Mystery Magazine, Storyteller *and* Death Dines In. *A former librarian and mystery bookseller, she holds two Crime Writers of Canada Arthur Ellis Awards for short stories. She's not nearly as dangerous as she looks.*

Dear Tabby

Vicky Cameron

Dear Tabby,
   I don't know who to turn to, I feel so bad. I decided
you would be able to help, because I read you in the paper
every day, because you know so much, and because I can be
anonymous with you. So I can tell you the truth.

   And the truth is I am totally and completely fed up with
"Brian", my husband of thirty years. Everything was fine until
he retired from the factory. Then his Ward Cleaver became
Archie Bunker. I don't think I can stand his whining,
complaining, fault-finding ways for one more minute. He
wants a beer. The beer isn't cold enough. The beer is the wrong
brand. He wants lunch. He wants to eat on time, and why was
I running out to the beer store when it was almost noon?
Twenty years I've been teaching children to play the piano,
and he made me quit because he didn't want to listen to
fractured versions of "Twinkle Twinkle Little Star" every
afternoon. He never lifts a finger to help me. He says he's done
his time, and now he doesn't have to do anything. He says
that's my job, handling the house.

   I feel like I'm doing time. My June Cleaver has become
Princess Leia chained to Jabba the Hutt. I was feeling edgy,
with him slouched in front of the television like a greasy lump

of Hutt, and me vacuuming, chained to the wall with an electrical cord, and I thought, what's wrong with this picture? Some blonde woman on the television was going on about the hot new home décor colours, so I thought, why not? Off to the hardware store, back with a gallon of tangerine paint for the bedroom wall. He says there's nothing wrong with the pink that's been there since we bought the house in the Seventies, left from some stodgy homeowner who decorated it in the Fifties. He says walls only need one coat of paint, ever, to keep the dust in. If I insist upon change, he'd rather see it beige, but does he offer to go to the hardware store and exchange it? No. Does he offer to help with the painting? No. Does he at least help move the furniture and carry in the ladder? No. But by now I'm dying for fresh paint on the walls. It's become a Holy Grail. If I can't have this, I don't want anything in this house or this marriage. The blonde woman said colours can influence your actions. Like soft blues and greens slow you down, and reds and oranges speed you up. So I do all the hefting myself, and he watches me paint from his lounge chair, complains that I'm not going to serve his lunch on time, and says I'm painting myself into a corner.

I feel like I am cornered. Princess Leia didn't stand for this kind of treatment. She strangled that slug-monster with her chain. I'd like to climb down off this ladder and smack my Jabba's head open with the paint can. I'd like to push his pudgy face into the paint tray and hold him under until he drowns. I'd like to paint him into that chair so he's stuck there forever when it dries. Someday I'd like to start all over again, ride off into the sunset and never come back.

Please help me, Tabby. I feel so bad.

Had It in Halifax

Dear Had It,

You go, girl! Someday is not a day of the week. Seize the day. Life is too short. Wise up. It's not too late to turn your life around. Don't let him take the wind out of your sails; take your sails out of his wind. Today is the first day of the rest of your life. Don't get mad, get even. Be happy. Write to me again. I care.

Dear Tabby,

You were so right! I knew you could help me. I guess advising people on their problems every single day gives you an edge, a gift for seeing through the junk right to the heart of the problem. I'm not doing time for him. I walked out that door with a loaded suitcase, got in the car and started driving. Thank you for convincing me to change my life. I owe you. I'm a new woman, with a dotted yellow line ahead of me and tangerine paint under my nails.

Fleeing in Fredericton

Dear Fleeing,

You go, girl! You have to turn your own life around. Nobody else will do it for you. Turn your back on your troubles and never look back. Ride the horse in the direction it's going. This is where the rubber hits the road. Write to me again. I care.

Dear Tabby,

By the time I got to Woodstock, I wasn't feeling quite so strong. Where's the fun in liberation? Where's the adventure of the open road?

I missed all the adventure when I was young and innocent. Everyone told me the white picket fence and the two-car garage was the ultimate goal for a woman. I missed all the rock concerts, and then the folk festivals, because I was planting marigolds around my picket fence. I raised my allotted 2.3 children, but they're long gone, to their own lives in other cities, their own families, their own two-car garages.

I've got nothing left. It's just me, and my purse on the passenger seat, hurtling along this ribbon of highway. My life is as empty as Edmundston at three in the morning.

Funny, isn't it, how you can trade one kind of hell for another? Living with "Brian" was bad, but maybe this is worse. I'm sitting here at a truck stop near Blind River. I'm so tired. Sure, when I started I had a real adrenaline surge. But I've been driving and driving, with no end in sight. I've been napping in the car and eating donuts and French fries. Did I make a mistake? Should I have kept on painting that wall, making lunch, buying beer? I should feel free, liberated, buoyant with the energy of a new lease on life. But I'm a wreck. And I'm nearly broke. I don't know what to do.

Baffled in Blind River

Dear Baffled,

You go, girl! Don't use your can opener to open a can of worms. You need to take charge of your life. There's no one looking out for you but you. Get with the program. There's nothing wrong with you that fresh makeup won't cure. Get a square meal and a good night's sleep. Recharge your batteries. Remember, you're never broke if you own a charge card. They are designed to help you buy things when you need them, not when you can afford them. Indulge yourself. Pamper yourself. Feed your soul; feed your body. Write to me again. I care.

Dear Tabby,

You were so right. I checked into a fancy hotel in Winnipeg. I enjoyed an expensive dinner with a glass of wine and slept in a bed bigger than my kitchen at home. The next day I stopped at a spa and luxuriated in a massage and a facial. I feel rejuvenated. I look radiant. I deserve this, after all those years. I earned my day in the sun. I'm in the driver's seat again, pedal to the metal, born to be wild. Only this time I'll pace myself. It's not like there's anyone chasing me.

Winning in Winnipeg

Dear Winning,

You go, girl! Success is a journey, not a destination. It shows what a woman can do when she puts her mind to it. Rise above the crowd. Let the wind fill your sails. Be like a postage stamp and stick to one thing until you get there. Write to me again. I care.

Dear Tabby,

This freedom is just another word for nothing left to lose. I'm an invisible person. I have no home, no daily routine, no identity. I feel like a poor lost soul wandering around with four cents in my pocket. I hate eating alone in restaurants. I hate living out of a suitcase. I'm just another dowdy grey-haired woman who looks like her mother, moving from Holiday Inn to Best Western in a shabby sedan. Is this all there is? Help me, Tabby.

Morose in Moosejaw

Dear Morose,

You go, girl! When you come to a fork in the road, take it. Give yourself a makeover. Go see a hairdresser. Put a little life in your hair with a new colour, a new cut. Go back to school.

Buy a new house. Buy a new car. A little attitude makes a big difference. Write to me again. I care.

Dear Tabby,

I knew you were smart when I first wrote to you. I did what you said. I took that fork in the road. I never thought I'd see this giant mall. It's fantastic. I traded in my grey blunt cut for a soft brown pixie cut, and the hairdresser said she could hardly recognize me as the same person who walked in her door an hour earlier. I hardly recognize myself in the mirror. The department store across the mall delivered a rainbow of co-ordinates to complete my new look. I tossed all my old stuff in the dumpster. I withdrew a huge cash advance on Brian's charge card and filled my new purse with money. I'm going to chop the card up and throw it away, so I don't have to see Brian's name glaring up at me every time I use it, or feel his reproach, reaching across time and space. I'm my own woman. Now I just have to find my way out of here to the parking lot. This place is huge.

Ecstatic in Edmonton

Dear Ecstatic,

You go, girl! Dress for success. Clean out clutter. Shoot for the stars. When you're green, you grow; when you're ripe, you rot. It's nice to be important, but more important to be nice. Take time to smell the roses. Write to me again. I care.

Dear Tabby,

Have you ever seen the Rockies? They're even bigger than that mall. I've been driving toward them, and I don't think I can drive through them. There's snow up there, and I'm wearing a sundress.

There's nothing like a huge immovable object to make you face your situation bluntly. I'm tired of life on the road, eating in roadside diners. I want to arrive. I want to settle down. I want to read the same newspaper every day, sign up for yoga classes, get a library card.

Hold on. There are some men whispering at the next table and drawing little maps on the table napkins. One of them is squawking, something about a car. Be nice, that's what you said.

Well, that's better. I'm finishing this letter on a plane flying over the caps of those mountains, and they're not so scary from up here. Those men in the restaurant? I walked over to their table and asked if they wanted to buy a car, cash, no questions asked. Turned out that's exactly what they needed. They were kind enough to carry in my suitcase before they left. There was a shuttle bus to the airport. I'm headed for the coast.

Jittery near Jasper

Dear Jittery,

You go, girl! Climb every mountain. Don't try to nail jelly to the wall. Everybody can be partly right some of the time. Start fresh, with a new you. The sisterhood of women is on your side. Write to me again. I care.

Dear Tabby,

I can't believe how beautiful this city is. But so many old people. There seems to be a funeral entourage coming out of the church beside my motel every day. Yesterday's service had hardly any mourners, so I joined them, to show some support for the lonely dear departed. She was a woman slightly older than me, single, no relatives, and few friends. Frankly, the guests kept looking at their watches like they'd rather be on the golf course. I pretended she was near and dear to me, shed a few tears, and a nice gentleman insisted on driving me to the gravesite. He said I must be Janice's sister, we look so much alike, and he hadn't realized, after all these years, she still had family back east. Her name was Janice Hart. Miss Hart. Isn't that a beautiful name? I searched the phonebook for her address. Her house is a little bungalow on a quiet street with the key under the doormat. She has photos of herself on the mantel, and that man was right, she looked a lot like the new me. Her clothes fit me, too, even the yoga outfit. I found her library card in a book about the habits of successful people. And I love her decorating taste. The bedroom is burnt orange.

Victorious in Victoria

Dear Victorious,

You go, girl! Carve out a space for yourself in life. Seize the day. Today is the first day of the rest of your life. It isn't over until it's over. We're all in this alone. Write to me again. I care.

The Halifax Courier-Sentinel
POLICE SEARCH FOR MISSING WOMAN

Halifax police are asking the public's assistance in locating a 56-year-old woman who has been missing from her home in Halifax for several weeks. Police say Margaret Lucy Sanderson was last seen in the local hardware store purchasing home decorating supplies.

A search of the area by the canine unit and helicopter was called off after it was learned Mr. Sanderson's credit cards had been used at three gas stations in Ontario, a hotel in Winnipeg, and several establishments in the West Edmonton Mall. The Sanderson family car was found abandoned in a nightclub parking lot in Banff. Police in that city are conducting a search.

Anyone with information on Mrs. Sanderson's whereabouts

is asked to contact local police. Halifax police wish to contact Mrs. Sanderson regarding an urgent family matter.

The National Examiner
MAN PAINTED TO DEATH
Police in Halifax are close-mouthed about a man found painted into a lounge chair at his suburban home. Neighbours say he'd had his head split open. His body and the chair were completely coated with tangerine satin finish latex.
See page six for full colour photos.

Vicki Cameron *is the author of* Clue Mysteries *and* More Clue Mysteries, *each fifteen short stories based on the board game* Clue. *Her stories appear in the Ladies' Killing Circle anthology series and* Storyteller *Magazine. Her young adult novel,* That Kind of Money, *was nominated for an Edgar and an Arthur Ellis. She edits Sisters in Crime's* Books in Print.

A River in Egypt

Jenifer McVaugh

T he special care wing in the fancy nursing home called Hambleton Hall cost $350 a day and was furnished à la French Provincial to look as little like a nursing home as possible. Judge Livermore was paying to get the best, but he didn't give a rat's rump about the decor. He grimaced and cursed as he shifted position. I stood by, holding the old fashioned urinal that he had insisted on my bringing from home. I was dead on my feet. I had been travelling for two days and still hadn't caught up on my shaving, let alone my sleep.

"You're doing fine, Dad. You can relax now."

"Don't bug me!"

Judge Livermore had fallen and broken his tailbone. He was here for rehab; his doctor wanted to get him walking. At eighty-plus, a man can be sidelined for good if he isn't careful. I had flown into town to help him move into the complex, and to shut up his house for a month or two. The house was full of stuff I recognized, maybe valuable, I don't know. I left home when I finished high school and never came back. I have very few memories of growing up.

A round-faced woman in a print smock popped her head around the door, then came in. In an accent from the Islands, she said, "How are we doin' in here?"

"I don't know how *we're* doing," the Judge snapped. "*I'm* all right, if nobody starts bugging me. Tell them to bring me tea, they promised tea."

"Sounds like you're still upset from your movin'," said the aide. She tried to catch my father's eye, but he looked away. "The tea trolley come around at four, but your son can fetch you a mug from the lounge whenever you like. Your name is down for a single as soon as we have one. Let me know if you need anythin' at all."

"What are you talking about?" the judge demanded. "Who are you? Leave me alone."

The aide turned her smile to me. "Judge Livermore is upset. It sometimes happen when they move in. Don't you take it personally."

She pulled the curtain shut around the bed as she went to answer a bell across the room. There was banter from the other bed.

"What kind of noise is that?" My father struggled to lift his head. "Where am I anyway? What are you doing here?"

"They called me to come down, Dad. You're at Hambleton Hall. That's your roommate talking to the nurse."

"The hell with that, I need a single. Don't be so stingy. It's not your money yet!" His rude voice got louder. "What are you doing standing there holding a piss pot?"

I put the urinal down.

"Good boy. That was always you, my good boy. I'd say jump, and you'd say how high!" The old man had lost a lot of weight. His cheeks were sunken, and his skin looked pasty and irritated. "Jump! How high?" His lips hardly stirred in his still face. This move, or the pain of it all, had exhausted him. I was surprised he could be so changed and still so much himself. My dad.

He laced his fingers across his chest, and his eyes fluttered shut. His lips fell into a loose smile. "You won't remember, but you've got me to thank for that. You used to cry at first. Every time you cried, I'd pick you up and shake you until your teeth rattled. I'd say, 'No! no! Bad boy!' Like with a puppy. Finally, your head would droop, and you'd stop crying. Nowadays I suppose that wouldn't be politically correct."

I wondered if this punch to the gut was one of those things I shouldn't take personally. "I don't remember it happening," I said. "Thank you for telling me."

"Why, what did I say?" the old man's eyelids struggled open. "Stop mumbling."

"I'll go get your tea, Dad," I said. I walked out into the wide corridors to collect myself. My first thought was to find a drink, my second was to phone my wife to talk me through it. My third thought was to pay attention before it vanished into the denial which is for me, as my wife is fond of reminding me, much more than a river in Egypt.

"Rotten, stinking, destructive, child-abusing bastard," I ventured to myself, under my breath. Then I said it again. A wild-haired old woman gave me a frightened look.

I went into the lounge to make tea. As the kettle boiled, I did some neck stretches. I tried not to let myself imagine how a baby would feel being shaken.

When I got back to my father's room, the curtain in front of his bed was closed, and his roommate was wheeling out of the bathroom in a cloud of fresh aftershave. He squawked politely to get my attention. "You think you could help me back into bed, young man, so's I don't have to call Martha?"

I put down the insulated mug of tea. "I can try."

"I don't have the muscle to get in and out of the chair any more," said the old man. "Somebody has to help me. I'm virtually bedridden. Oop-la, thanks very much."

"Stroke," he confided, leaning back against the pillow, "but I beat it. I can do anything. I've been a cattle rancher, a millionaire, a chess grand master, I've sailed the seven seas, and I've been on TV a lot of times. But now I've lost my mobility, I'm virtually bedridden. Other than that, there's nothing wrong with me, except for talking too much." The man was small and birdlike, missing most of his hair and teeth. He did look very healthy, I was glad to see. He gave me a wistful glance.

"Your dad is out for the count. Why not sit down here with me. I hardly ever get visitors with all their marbles."

The wing-backed chair looked strong and comfortable, part of what you get for $350 a day. An insolent snore and a smear of gutturals came from behind the curtain around my father's bed. I sat down and introduced myself as Douglas Livermore, and told him that his new neighbour was Thomas Livermore.

"Old 'Twenty-to-life-Livermore'! I've heard of Judge Livermore. A wingnut! Screwed a friend of mine. I heard what he was saying to you earlier, too, nasty old asphalt! Forget it, he's probably making it up, their minds wander and they'll say anything. Still, holy cheese fried, what a bastard, you a defenceless baby and him gloating over it like that! A mental case! *Just like my ugly old, hairy old father, the brutal bully.*" A wave of purple rage flooded up the old face, then subsided.

"Brutal bully," he repeated, remembering. "I soon got rid of him. Heeh!" The old fellow had a bark of a laugh, accompanied by a cock-headed outlaw smile. "Killed him dead, not to put too fine a point on it. Oh, did you bring me tea? Very thoughtful."

I was too surprised to protest the hijacking. Anyway, "Twenty-to-life" Livermore was still snoring. I watched the roommate wrap shaky hands around the sides of the mug.

"How I did it—you'll be interested in this," he nodded. "I've had an interesting life—I invited him to a meal at the restaurant where I worked. I was a top chef at the Four Seasons restaurant. Brought arsenic in this very ring, it opens up, it belonged to a Borgia." He indicated a ring with a crest. "I sprinkled the arsenic into an omelette, and I ate half of it to put him off the scent. But unbeknownst to him, I had built myself up an immunity. I was studying chemistry."

Right, I thought. And writing Dorothy Sayers' mysteries in your spare time.

I said, "You better be careful who you confess to, you could get in trouble."

"What are they going to do to me? Lock me up? Besides, they've got to prove things nowadays, one of my lawyers could get me off like that." He attempted unsuccessfully to snap his fingers. "I keep a lawyer on retainer. You know, ninety-nine out of a hundred poisoners are never caught. Not that it matters any more when any foreigner can walk into a 7-Eleven and *mother of nuts and bolts, somebody tie a knot in that elephant's flabby old trunk!*"

The Judge's snores really were a piece of work. A mounting series of painful, halting intakes, as if he were getting more and more excited, and then a long whinny. A pause, just long enough to make you think he might have quit, then the tentative painful intake again. "Weest...... weeest...." It produced the horrible sensation of being jerked awake, time after time, without the comfort of sleep in between.

The roommate cackled and stuck out a wobbly hand. "My name is Culbertson, but you better call me Cubby, Cubby Culbertson. And I'm kidding about the lawyer on retainer, those days are long gone, and I was never actually a millionaire, although I did pretty good, well, some years." The hand bobbed around until I grabbed it out of mid air and pumped it. Cubby had a surprisingly strong grip.

"Sorry about the snoring," I said. Behind the curtain, a bubbling snarl degenerated into a series of loose-lipped mouth farts. I imagined shaking him until he shut up, but I didn't want to touch him.

"Worse things happen at sea." Culbertson shook his head. "I haven't heard anyone saw wood that bad since the Navy, I was on an aircraft carrier in the Pacific, our Sarge snored so loud none of us could get any sleep, and he'd put you on report if you complained. Heeh!" His shoulders began to heave up and down. "Sarge used to always have a jar of bromo beside his bunk, one day somebody switched it for Drano and the sarge woke up dead. The brass tried to hang it on somebody, but they had no evidence. Everybody in the barracks slept through it. Nobody heard a thing. Checkmate!"

"Cubby," I said, "could I ask you to go easy with the murder stories? First, I don't really believe them and second, I'm not in the mood. It's been a long couple days."

"Damned dog!" came my father's voice. Then he growled, then mumbled, then snored again, softer this time, with a nasty slurp.

"Like the one about my dad, hey?" Culbertson peered at me. "No, you're right, I was only kidding about killing my dad, I got that story out of a book. And I wasn't the head chef, although I should have been. I was in the Navy, though, four long years, and I've got my papers to prove it. Arsenic? Heeh! I don't even know where you'd get such a thing. I don't even know if they make such a thing any more."

His voice cut through the heavy static being broadcast from behind my father's curtain. "Household products is the way to go. That and the medicine chest. Now you take that valium *by the sweet suffering sassafras would you shut the heck up!*"

"Take him away," my father snarled. "He's bothering me." The snoring subsided to a murmur.

"Or Mother Nature," said Culbertson, in a lower tone. "We had a neighbour, not to speak ill of the dead, he was a lying son-of-a-bitch who tried to steal ten feet from my property line, excuse my French. You don't want me to talk about such things, but he ate a poisonous plant and died of it, and I'll tell you why. He was a long-haired hippie, and somebody told him nightshade would get you high! Checkmate! But you don't want to hear that."

"I'm not in the mood for fiction." I was becoming aware of the fur inside my mouth. "I've got trouble enough handling reality at the moment."

"But it's true, every word! I've had a very interesting life. Well, I forget the odd detail, but yes, I've been every *holy cognoggers, the horny catfish, if I could get a word in edgewise for once!*" The Judge's snores, which had sunk to a gentle idle, had built up again to a series of backfires. At Culbertson's shouts, they stopped.

"You were asking about my wife, and I don't mind telling you," continued Culbertson, raising a shaky hand to find a scab on his knobbly bald head and scratch it, "I used to take the valium to relax my muscles, I was injured on the job, at least my truck rolled on the way to work, not exactly on the way, but it was the company truck. Anyway, my nagging snitch of a wife—oh, she made your father look like an angel! She'd never let anything go, the sour old *hag!* She got into my prescription and she took a fatal dose of valium washed down with alcohol, that's what the coroner said. Checkmate!" He brought his hand down and looked with interest to see what he had caught under his nails. "I guess the police wondered if it wasn't me did her, but you don't want to hear about that. Suffice it to say they never charged me *in the name of mercy could you not keep it down, for crying out the window!*"

My father's snoring was getting louder again.

"Somebody enjoyin' a good snooze!" The aide's sunny voice was pitched for elderly ears. She was waiting at the door to be invited in. She had a tray in her hand. "I'm bringin' you a mug of tea, Judge Livermore! I leave it on your tray table!" When my father grunted, she pulled the curtain aside. Then she pressed a button to raise the back and the sides of the bed. My father opened his eyes.

"My God, you're as black as the ace of spades!" he said.

"Black is beautiful, Judge Livermore!" She turned her smile to me and lowered her voice to normal levels. "Mr. Livermore, when you have a minute, the social worker is in her office now."

"Excuse me," I said, nodding to Culbertson, who was unashamedly eavesdropping, and to my father, who was ignoring me. "Maybe it's about a single."

The young social worker's desk was tidy and furnished with flowers. She radiated health and sanity and competence. I wondered if I looked and smelled as bad as I felt. I wondered if she had even heard of the days of corporal punishment, or if she would consider shaking a child unconscious a fairy tale on a par with an arsenic omelette.

I told her that the Judge was distressed, and in a lot of pain. It was all pretty hard on him, and it would help a lot if he could be by himself. He was happy to pay any extra charges. I thought his roommate might also prefer it.

She let me talk it all out, then nodded and smiled her warm understanding. "Naturally you and I can't discuss Mr. Culbertson's situation. I can tell you that we're doing our very best for your dad. His well-being is our number one priority. He's a fighter, and that's a big plus for his recovery." She spoke with convincing authority.

When I got back to the Judge's room, his curtain was closed again, and I smelled fresh aftershave. "He closed it to take a leak, and he dozed off," Culbertson said. He leaned forward and pounded his chest. When he had caught his breath, he smiled wickedly. "That's what we'll tell them. But the fact of the matter is, I killed him for you, the old walrus. He deserved it after what he did to you. Admit it, you're glad."

"Grunt-*onk Onk!*"

"I guess I must have been kidding about knocking him off," Culbertson said.

"It's not that funny." I sank back into the chair, extended my legs and closed my eyes, hoping Culbertson would take the hint and shut up.

"I kid around a lot. But the confounded noise he's making it might be what they call the death rattle, no offence. Anything can happen, I've seen it myself, I've had a very interesting life, but enough about me, what do you do, Douglas? I know you live an interesting life. You'd probably rather not talk, you look washed up."

I kept my eyes closed. "I haven't slept much. I started out from northern British Columbia at four o'clock yesterday morning."

"Way out West! No wonder. What took you out there? My last roommate came from out west, well, west of the city, pretending to be so friendly, filthy rich, always with the clean pyjamas, reading his book, hey, are you awake?"

I opened my eyes.

"I didn't want to wake you, but I was pretty sure you couldn't be sleeping through *Beethoven's last movement, if you could turn down the arfing decibels!*"

The orchestra of my father's snores broke off mid-phrase. I thought of a child crying then suddenly stopping. A nasal duet for piccolo and snare drum began to whimper from behind the curtain, but at a lower volume. Satisfied, Cubby reached for the still untasted mug of tea.

"Then *bam!* Trouble in paradise. He starts sneaking out to the sun porch for cigarettes, coughing his guts out all night, how they expected me to put up with that I don't know. His heart failed, that's what the coroner said. Checkmate! But you don't want to hear about that *hey you old farthingale why don't you wake up and drink your nice tea!*"

How crazy was this roommate, I wondered. Could he really…but no, he was virtually bedridden.

"A call of nature! I tell you, old age is not for sissies!" The skinny fellow pushed himself upright and then used both hands to shove the table to the foot of the bed. He gave a button on the console a wobbly poke, and the bed lowered itself. Then he took a deep breath and slid his skinny legs over the side.

"I thought you needed help," I said.

"Why, that's right, so I do." He smiled up at me, large head shaking from side to side. "I sometimes forget. Ever since I had my pneumonia, I can't get in and out of the chair without help. I'm virtually bedridden. If you weren't here, I couldn't possibly get out of bed. Oop-la! That's good. Don't worry about the john itself, it's got a gadget that shifts me." He motored away into the bathroom and closed the wide door. I heard an electrical whine and another "Oop-la."

As soon as Culbertson was behind the bathroom door, I pulled back my father's curtain. He was sleeping peacefully, his mouth open, his cheeks vibrating with his snores. I tried to picture the face fifty-five years younger and swollen with rage. I couldn't see it at all.

Culbertson was clearly a crazy old man. But who knows what separates the ones that are crazy enough to be dangerous? Or feeble enough to be harmless? Or bad enough to deserve what they get? My father's mug of tea and Culbertson's looked identical. I sniffed, but all I could smell was the ambient aftershave. I felt myself sway. I was so tired, it literally hurt to think.

When I replaced the mug beside my father, he lifted his head and glared.

"What?" he said. "What now?"

"Your tea is here," I said. "I'm leaving the curtain open." Now that I was on my feet and the curtain was open, the room seemed smaller.

"Daddy, please look at me." I tried to smile and speak clearly. "What you were talking about before, when I was a baby—that isn't just out of style, that was a bad thing you did to me." My father's eyes lost focus, and his gaze shifted to the wall. "To me," I said. "Not a puppy."

"What are you talking about?" He waved at me as if I were smoke. "What kind of nonsense is this to bug an old man? If I want tea, I'll damn well drink tea." He reached for the mug and winced.

"You didn't hear me coming, did you?"

I jumped at Cubby's voice behind me. He had scooted to the side of his own bed and was waiting with his shoulders slumped, looking at the hands shaking in his lap. "I know how to move silently. It's because I'm part Indian, or at least I've spent quite a lot of time with them." He leaned towards me as I lifted him into the bed. Small as he was, my back still protested. "Oop-la!" He settled back and summoned his tray table. "At least reading about them, they taught their children to sleep silently not like a *hibernating bear!*"

"Watch yourself, Charlie," my father barked. "I'm a superior court judge, and you're Charlie-nobody. When I say jump, you say how high!"

"Just you wait, Your Honour!" Cubby gave me a wink and took a trial sip at the straw of his beverage cup. "Ah, that's the stuff," he smacked his lips and sucked deeply. He spoke in a stage-whisper so that my father wouldn't hear. "All I had to work with, you see, was my knowledge of human nature. So I doctored my own cup and got you to switch them." His voice went back to normal. "Heeh! You still don't know when I'm kidding, do you? Don't worry, I can alibi you, we can alibi each other. I hope you wore gloves."

"Tea," grunted my father. "About time." He raised the mouthpiece to his lips to suckle greedily, then he spat. "This tastes like plumbing!" He extended his tongue and drew back his lips.

"Oh dear," Culbertson shoulders shook with excitement, "your father doesn't seem to be enjoying his tea. Or should I say *my* tea? Hear that old man, *your son poisoned you, you abusive nutso freak bustard, you've just guzzled poison!*"

I saw a big red button and pushed it. A bell rang and a light came on.

"*I emptied my ring in my own cup,*" Culbertson shouted over the bell. "*I started dropping hints, lies, some of them. I made him think the poison was in your cup. I gambled, and I won. Checkmate!*"

"Silence I say, you're out of order."

"You're dead, so shut up! You're poisoned, and you're dead."

"I didn't switch the cups, Cubby," I said. "I thought about it, you're right. Then I remembered you were a chess player, so I switched them back. Then I realized I didn't want to poison you either, and there was more tea down the hall. Dad's a chess player, too, I wanted to tell you that before I left. You guys should have a game, have some fun together. I never got the hang of all the feints and gambits."

"Damned draft dodger, you're getting on my nerves," roared my father, his eyes screwed shut.

"Was I wanted?" the aide popped her round face around the door. "Sorry it took me a minute, we were all busy. Must be a full moon!"

"Mr. Culbertson tried to poison my dad. The cups he used are by the sink. I don't know the right response to this, but I'm sure you do." I gathered my jacket and my flight bag. "I have to go phone my wife, I'm out of my depth."

She picked up the two cups and wrinkled her nose. "Mr. Culbertson, what did we agree about you poisoning people? Don't worry, Judge Livermore," she raised her voice, "Mr. Culbertson's bark is worse than his bite. In the first place, he's bedridden. Best thing is just ignore him, then he stop. You have your new room soon."

Cubby looked stubborn. "Won't do any good, I'm resourceful, I'll track him down, and I swear *I'll get him, we've got a score to settle, the old chicken strangler.*"

"You're not leaving me with this homicidal maniac," said my father glaring at the ceiling in alarm. "He's making death threats."

"Mr. Culbertson is no threat, Judge Livermore," said Martha, folding her arms in a no-nonsense gesture. "No way he can get out of bed. You going to be fine."

"You think you won't die like the last one did?"

"Make him stop bugging me," demanded my father. His voice rose in pitch. "I order you to shut him up!"

"Take it easy, Dad," I reached over to pat his knee, but I could feel him cringing from the touch. "Don't panic, it makes things worse."

"Yeah, don't get paranoid, Livermore. Relax and enjoy it."

"No!" shouted my father, "You're bothering me." His face was stupid with fear and frustration. His hands clutched blindly at the railings beside his bed, and he shook them as if to shake some sense into them. "No! No!"

The aide pulled the door shut behind us. "You put it out of your mind, Mr. Livermore, it's just the anger and the depression talkin'," she said. She pushed the elevator button for me, flashed a conspiratorial smile. "It's hard for them to adjust. You know what they say; denial is more than that river in Egypt, and a lot more live in it than crocodiles." She hurried off down the wide French Provincial corridor. I pulled out my scribbler to make notes, never mind making sense of it, just the details so I won't forget.

Jenifer McVaugh *studied philosophy and literature at the University of Michigan, where she won a Hopwood Award. She divides her time between the Ottawa Valley, where she owns the Bookstore in Golden Lake, and the Sierra Madre Mountains of western Mexico. Her novel* The Love of Women *is available through Borealis Press.* Alfred Hitchcock *and* Antigonish Review *have published her short fiction. Her most recent publication, the long poem "First," appeared in* Oyster Boy Review.

The Top Ten

Cruisin' on a Friday night
Listenin' to A.M.
Been lovin' that Top 40
Since I was close to ten.

Listenin' to Bobby Darin
Singin' Mack the Knife
Dreamin' that Paul Anka
Would never take a wife.

Wishin' I could be like
Little Brenda Lee
And hopin' that Del Shannon
Would Runaway to me.

I thought, He's A Rebel
At least a Duke of Earl
You were my Johnny Angel
I was Blue Velvet girl.

Now I'm...

Bruisin' on a Friday night
Listenin' to you shout
Easier Said Than Done
To try to throw you out.

Listenin' to your rantin'
Thinkin' of a knife
Dreamin' where I'd stick it
If I just weren't your wife.

Wishin' you were nicer
When you talked to me
Oh Where Did Our Love Go?
Do Wah Diddy Diddy Dee.

Joy Hewitt Mann

RendezVous Crime

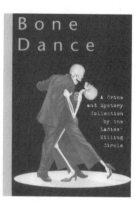

BONE DANCE

Music may soothe the savage breast, but in this collection from the Ladies' Killing Circle, music provides the background for tales of murder and mayhem. Stories and poems take their inspiration from titles as varied as the upbeat "Wake Up Little Suzie" through the romantic "Summertime" and musicals such as "There's No Business Like Show Business". You'll never listen to your favourite songs again without wondering what nefarious deeds they may have inspired.

ISBN 1-894917-05-7, 272 pages,
5 1/8" x 7 1/2", $12.95 U.S., $14.95 CDN

FIT TO DIE

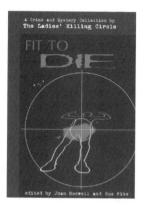

Sport, fitness, games and murder are the main themes of this collection of muscular crime fiction and poetry. From the gym to the golf course to the supposedly peaceful practice of tai chi, murder, rage and revenge refuse to respect the human quest for immortality through fitness and can victimize the most tanned and toned bodies as easily as those of couch potatoes and gourmands. Excessive good health can lead to an early demise in this energetic anthology.

ISBN 0-929141-87-3, 288 pages,
5 1/8" x 7 1/2", $12.95 U.S., $14.95 CDN

www.rendezvouspress.com